COURTING GRACE

Mark led her to the barn, hidden out of sight from her haus, set the lantern on a tree stump, and put his arms around her.

Her heart raced and her knees weakened. Not sure what to do, she placed her hands on Mark's shoulders.

Gently, he raised her chin and leaned close to her face. He rested his forehead on hers and hugged her closer. "My heart is about to jump out of my chest."

"I can hardly speak," she said. "I don't want our time together tonight to end."

He'd said what she wanted to hear, and she had no doubt he meant it. Words she hadn't expected to hear from a man. Not with her ugly birthmark marring her face. But Mark had looked past her flaw and taken the time to find out what was on the inside. . . .

Books by Molly Jebber

CHANGE OF HEART

GRACE'S FORGIVENESS

Published by Kensington Publishing Corporation

Grace's Forgiveness

MOLLY JEBBER

ZEBRA BOOKS
KENSINGTON PUBLISHING CORP.
http://www.kensingtonbooks.com

ZEBRA BOOKS are published by

Kensington Publishing Corp.
119 West 40th Street
New York, NY 10018

All Kensington titles, imprints, and distributed lines are available at special quantity discounts for bulk purchases for sales promotion, premiums, fund-raising, educational, or institutional use.

Special book excerpts or customized printings can also be created to fit specific needs. For details, write or phone the office of the Kensington Sales Manager: Attn.: Sales Department. Kensington Publishing Corp., 119 West 40th Street, New York, NY 10018. Phone: 1-800-221-2647.

Zebra and the Z logo Reg. U.S. Pat. & TM Off.

First Printing: February 2016
ISBN-13: 978-1-4201-3763-7
ISBN-10: 1-4201-3763-8

eISBN-13: 978-1-4201-3764-4
eISBN-10: 1-4201-3764-6

10 9 8 7 6 5 4 3 2 1

Printed in the United States of America

To Ed,
my soulmate,
loving husband,
and partner.
My friends call you "Mr. Wonderful,"
and I agree!
Thank you for your unwavering love and support.

To Misty,
my precious and beautiful daughter.
I'm so thankful for you and love you so much.
You continue to bless my life and amaze me with what
you're doing with yours.

Acknowledgments
and Thank You to

Dawn Dowdle, agent, and John Scognamiglio, editor-in-chief, and Jane Nutter, publicist, for their kindness and support. To my elegant and wonderful mother, Sue Morris; Mitchell Morris, brother and trusted and close friend; and Jebbers and Melnicks for their love and encouragement.

Lee Granza, Debbie Bugezia, Elaine Saltsgaver, Patty Campbell, Diana Welker, Melanie Fogel, Donna Snyder, Southwest Florida Romance Writers, Southbridge, church, and Florida and Ohio friends—you know who you are and how much you mean to me.

Chapter One

Berlin, Ohio, 1900

Grace Blauch pushed the door open to Grace and Sarah's Dry Goods Shop on Wednesday morning and shut it against the August heat behind her. Who was the attractive Amish man laughing with Sarah? *No beard. He's unwed.* He towered over her friend and partner's petite frame. She dropped her birthing supply bag on the hardwood floor. "I'm sorry I'm late. If Mamm hadn't dropped a pan in the kitchen and woke me, I'd have been even later."

Sarah Helmuth waved her over. "Don't apologize. I'm pleased you're here. Meet Mark King." She hooked her arm through Grace's and grinned. "This is my friend and partner, Grace Blauch."

Smiling, hat in hand, he bowed slightly. "It's a pleasure to meet you."

Her heart raced. Most strangers turned away from her face the first time she met them, but Mark gazed into her eyes. He didn't stare at the red apple-sized birthmark on her left cheek. What a refreshing change. "Wilkom to Berlin."

He had a small thin jagged line under his right eye. The scar added character to his handsome face. What was the story behind it? She liked his thick, dark wavy hair, straight white teeth, structured jawline, and broad shoulders. He held his tall black hat, without a speck of dust on it, by his side. Dressed in a crisp white shirt, black pants, and suspenders, he had a neat appearance. "If you'll pass me your hat, I'll hang it up for you." She hung his hat on the knotty maple rack.

Sarah pushed a stray curly blond hair into her white kapp. "Mark moved to Berlin from Lancaster, Pennsylvania, on Monday. Levi went over briefly and introduced himself to Mark." She separated from Grace and leaned against the counter. "The Stoltzfuses sold him their place not far from us. Mr. Stoltzfus wrote and asked Levi to plant his hay and garden in May. Levi asked some of his friends to help him, and they have been taking care of it."

Sarah tossed a loose thread on the counter in the trash bin. "Mr. Stoltzfus didn't write in his letter to Levi whether he planned to return to Berlin or sell his property. He'd gone to Lancaster to help his bruder, who was ill back in February. He sold off his livestock before he left. We were surprised to learn from Mark that Mr. Stoltzfus and his fraa died just days before Mark left to kumme here."

Grace pressed a hand to her mouth. "I'm sorry to hear this. I had met them, but I didn't know them well."

"It's understandable. Their time in Berlin was short."

Mark gazed into her eyes. "Mr. Stoltzfus's bruder died and left his haus to them. They had planned on moving back to Berlin, but they had grown to like Lancaster better."

Sarah retied her loose apron strings. "Mark visited Levi

and me before supper last night. He invited us to his haus and showed us Mr. Stoltzfus's, now his, workshop on his property, where he handcrafts his things." She bounced on her toes. "Levi liked the oak shelves Mark built. My husband wasted no time offering to buy them for here, but Mark insisted on giving them to us."

Grace pointed to overstacked quilts on a table. "That's wonderful. We need them."

"Mark has offered to hang them, and I accepted. No telling when Levi would ever have built them for us. No doubt he means well, but he puts work such as this off."

Mark King will be hanging the shelves in our shop. She'd get to speak to him again. *What good news.* "We appreciate your help."

"If you don't mind, I'd like to hang the shelves tomorrow."

"Grace opens early most days, and I kumme in a little later. She doesn't have a husband to cook breakfast for yet. Today we switched to give her a break. You can schedule a time with her to start work." Sarah winked at Grace.

Grace's cheeks heated. Sarah's attempt to play matchmaker was far too obvious. She glimpsed at Mark. His face had reddened, but his grin remained. His reaction couldn't have been any better.

He coughed and covered his mouth. "Miss Blauch, what time would you like me to start working tomorrow?"

"Please call me Grace. Is eight all right?"

"Eight is good." He met her eyes. "Please call me Mark." He retrieved his hat. "Have a nice day." He grinned at her then departed.

Her heart pounded. His smile, the sparkle in his eyes, and his strong but kind voice lingered in her mind. She couldn't wait to learn more about him if Sarah hadn't scared him away with her obvious matchmaking. Grace lowered her chin and crossed her arms. "You embarrassed me when you said I didn't have a husband."

Sarah gently tapped Grace's nose. "I didn't exist after you walked in the room. Mark King is smitten with you." She chuckled. "I'll not apologize. His face brightened when I told him. You're glad I blurted it out. Admit it."

Grace's face softened. "He met my eyes while talking to me instead of staring at my cheek like most people I meet. His reaction was refreshing."

"Since he'll be working in the shop, you'll have a chance to learn more about him."

"What have you found out about him?"

"Two years ago, a stagecoach hit his parents' buggy and they didn't survive." She leaned against the maple table. "I asked if he had siblings, and he said not anymore. You came in before I could find out what he meant."

Grace moved to the small wood-burning stove in the corner, opened the door, and found logs inside. She added crumbled paper and a small amount of kindling, lit a match, grasped the poker, and coaxed the fire to take hold. "Maybe his bruder or schweschder died and the subject is too painful to discuss. You said he visited you and Levi. What did Levi have to say about him?"

"Levi likes him. They talked about carpentry, farming, and fishing for over an hour."

Two Englischers entered. The tall elegant woman wore a fitted red and blue dress, showing off her long, slender legs. The short round woman with full cheeks had on a too-tight yellow dress. She scurried to catch up with her long-legged friend.

Grace faced them. "Wilkom. How may I help you today?"

The two women narrowed their eyes, frowned, and grimaced. "We came in to browse."

She held a hand to her face. Would she ever remain unaffected by strangers' stares? "Take your time. I'll help you with whatever you need."

The taller woman raised her eyebrows and leaned close to her friend. "Did you notice the poor girl's birthmark?"

"Yes. The discoloration is hard to miss. What a pity."

The women should have kept their voices down. Her birthmark hadn't damaged her ability to hear. Grace hurried to the back room but kept the door open to view the patrons.

Sarah followed. "Don't let those customers' comments upset you."

Her friend meant well, but Sarah had flawless skin. She had no idea what it was like to have strangers wince and stare at her. "I am working on it, but it's difficult."

Sarah put her hands on Grace's shoulders. "God gave you pretty brown hair, deep brown eyes, a petite nose, and a tall thin frame. I'm certain many women would love to have any one of those features. You possess them all."

She shouldn't complain. God had blessed her with a healthy body. She straightened her shoulders and smoothed her white apron. "I agree. I shouldn't let their remarks bother me." She threw back her shoulders. "I'll assist the women while you check our supplies."

The tall woman fingered the green and brown friendship quilt hanging on the wall. She patted the pocket. "What's this for?"

"You write a heartfelt letter to the person you're giving the quilt to and tuck it inside the pocket. We call them keepsake pocket quilts."

The short woman with curly brown hair held a white eyelet one. "I want this one for my daughter. Who came up with this wonderful idea?"

"Becca Carrington and her schweschder, Ruth Kelly, sell

them in their shop in Massillon, Ohio. The schweschders suggested we and several women in our community stitch the keepsake pocket quilts and sell them here."

The taller woman beamed. "I love the idea. I must tell my friends to shop here when they visit Berlin."

Sliding back the curtain under the pinewood table used for checking out customers, Grace removed the dented gray metal cashbox hidden underneath the counter.

Both women unclasped their reticules and paid Grace for their selections.

"Danki." She dropped the coins in their proper spots, closed the box, and recorded the sale in the journal. She and Sarah would have extra money to pay Mark for building the shelves, without taking it out of the money they'd planned to use for buying new fabric. "I hope you'll have a chance to visit us again. Have a safe trip." She stowed the cashbox underneath the counter. She'd never tire of recording a sale.

Grace joined Sarah in the supply room at the back of the store. "With the two quilts off the walls, we have the perfect spot for Mark to build the shelves." She yanked a sheet and white blanket from the top of an old oak chest and put them on a cot. "The shelves will allow us to display more of our products, and we won't have to store as much of them back here."

Sarah sighed. "I appreciate you managing the shop with me in addition to helping women birth their bopplin. I wouldn't want to manage this place alone. I could never be a midwife. I can't stand the sight of blood." Sarah frowned and crossed her arms. "Something you said earlier bothered me."

Grace paused and raised her eyebrows. "What did I say to upset you?"

"You shouldn't tell our patrons Becca and her schwescder gave you the idea to sell the quilts in our shop. We have no need to communicate with her. If Bishop Weaver finds out, we'll be chastised. You are to shun Becca and Ruth for joining the church then leaving our Amish community." She heaved a big sigh. "Enough said on the matter. We don't need to discuss it any further."

Grace opened her mouth to speak but shut it. Becca was her dear friend. She missed her. Shunning Becca hurt her worse than customers making rude comments about her birthmark. Her friend had no problem adhering to Amish law when it came to Becca. Sarah hadn't experienced losing a best friend to the outside world.

"I understand your concern. I won't mention to patrons again that Becca and Ruth gave us the idea to sell the keepsake pocket quilts."

"Like I said, we can put this behind us." Sarah nudged Grace's arm. "I'm more interested in talking about Mark. Are you excited he'll be working here?"

Grace clasped her hands. Of course she was, but she didn't want to dwell on him. New in town, it wouldn't be long before other available women would find him handsome too. "I am, but I don't want to get my hopes up." Grace moved to the stove. She touched the small pan on top and withdrew her hand back. The coffee was hot. Mark came in. She turned in surprise.

He strode over to her and removed his hat. "Did I leave a paper marked with shelf measurements here?"

She searched behind the desk, bent, and snatched a note from the floor and held it up. He had a striking, suntanned face. "Is this what you're looking for?" She passed the note to him.

He scanned it. "Danki. Now I don't have to measure the walls again."

Sarah grabbed her small, plain reticule. "Mark, I apologize for not offering you anything to drink earlier this morning. Please stay and have a cup of hot coffee with Grace. I'm going to the General Store. I'll be back in a few minutes."

"No need to apologize."

"I appreciate your understanding, but really, don't rush off. Customers may kumme in and interrupt, but I'd like for you and Grace to get better acquainted." She winked at Grace, tied her kapp strings, and departed.

Grace loved her friend, but she could be too direct at times. Putting the embarrassing moment out of her mind, she shrugged her shoulder to the small pan. "Would you like coffee? I brought some from home and it's on the stove and ready to drink."

"Jah, danki."

This man affected her like no other. She couldn't explain it. Grace poured the coffee and passed a mug to him.

The mug slipped through his hands. *Bang. Splat.* Pieces of glass slid across the floor. He blushed. "I'm as clumsy as an oaf. I'm sorry about the mess." Mark bent to pick up a shard of glass and cut his hand. "Ouch!" He jerked his hand back. Blood dripped onto his shoe. "You'll never invite me again if I keep dropping things and bleeding all over your floor."

She waved a dismissive hand. "You're wilkom here anytime. Accidents happen. Are you all right?" She grabbed a clean towel and threw it to him. "Wrap your hand. I'll be back in a minute." She ran to a porcelain pitcher filled with water in the back, wet a towel, grabbed two dry ones, and picked up her medical supply bag by the front door. Next to him, she stooped, threw open her bag, and dug out what she needed and tended to his hand. *I like his large, strong, calloused hands. He must be a hard worker.* "You don't need stitches and the bleeding has stopped. You may take the bandage off in a day or so."

"Are you a nurse and a shop owner?"

"I'm a midwife. My daed and Sarah's husband, Levi, bought the shop and gave it to her and me to manage. It adds extra income to both our families to tide us over, especially in the winter months."

Grace grabbed the soiled cloths, stuffed them in an empty flour sack from under the shelf, and dropped them out of sight behind the counter. "I'll pour you another mug of coffee."

"I'd like another one. Danki." He grabbed a broom and dustpan propped against the wall behind the counter, swept up the broken pieces, and threw them in the trash bin. He returned the broom and dustpan to their original spot then snatched towels to wipe up the remaining liquid and added the soiled cloths the bag Grace had dropped rags in.

Grace poured steaming coffee in Mark's mug. She then scanned the floor where the glass had been. "You didn't have to clean up the mess, but I appreciate it."

"Glad to do it. My mamm taught me well." He pointed to her middle door. "We'll be neighbors. I bought the empty space next door after I left your shop this morning. We'll have a connecting door between our shops, making it easier for us to visit. I didn't tell Levi or Sarah. I didn't want to say anything about it to anyone until I was certain the previous owner and I could agree on a price. I'll open my store a week from Saturday."

What wonderful news. This day kept getting better. "Congratulations." She slid her hands in her white apron pockets. "Did you have a store in Lancaster?"

"No. I built homes. In the evenings I constructed tables, chairs, and bread and potato boxes out of oak and maple. I carved miniature toy bears and other animals out of pine. I wanted to have a sampling of different items to sell before I opened my shop. I had hired a man to manage my farm so I'd have more time to construct my things. I'm thankful my worker found another job before I left."

"Why did you choose Berlin to start a new life?"

"My haus caught on fire and burnt to the ground. I had gotten acquainted with Mr. Stoltzfus, and he offered to sell me his property here."

Grace sighed. "What caused it?"

"Someone I knew accidentally knocked over a lit lantern in my barn. The fire spread and destroyed it and my haus. I stayed with my other neighbor until after the Stoltzfuses' funeral and then came to Berlin."

Mark had endured a lot of pain in his life, losing his parents and his haus. It must be hard to move to a new place where he wasn't familiar with anyone. She couldn't imagine doing the same. "It must've been disheartening for you to lose your barn, your haus, your parents, and the Stoltzfuses."

"It was a shock. As far as the fire goes, I'm relieved my handcrafted furniture and such in the workshop weren't harmed. It would take a long time to replace them."

"I'm surprised you bought Mr. Stoltzfus's haus sight unseen."

He laughed. "We had become fast friends. I trusted him." He shrugged his shoulders. "I needed somewhere to live, and the man asked a fair price I could afford. If anything had been wrong with the haus, I knew I could repair it." Pausing, he walked over to a quilt. "This caught my eye while we were talking. Did you make this one?"

"I did. The Jacob's ladder pattern is one of my favorite ones."

He put his mug on the counter. "This would be perfect to drape over the back of my settee." He studied the pinned price note. "I'll buy it."

Mark helped her unhook his purchase off three wooden pegs, folded the material, unpinned the small white paper, and paid her. She patted the pocket. "You could write a letter, tuck it inside, and give the quilt to someone special for a keepsake."

"Maybe I will someday."

His rough-skinned fingers grazed hers, and she warmed. Mark King had left his friends and church and everything familiar behind. How intriguing. Did he have other reasons why he left Lancaster to begin a new life in Berlin? "Won't you miss your friends?"

"Jah, but I'll write to them." He tucked his quilt under his arm and then glimpsed at the small wooden pine clock on the counter. "I should go. I bought livestock, a rooster, and hens from an Englischer I met at the General Store. His name's Jed Post. He told the storeowner he's moving and selling his livestock. He asked if the storeowner knew anyone who'd be interested in buying them. I introduced myself, and Mr. Post sold them to me for a good price. He's bringing them to me around ten."

"The man's timing and yours couldn't have been better. Have a nice day. I'll meet you here tomorrow morning."

"See you then, Grace." He closed the door behind him.

Sarah returned several minutes later. "Did you have a chance to get better acquainted with Mark?"

Grace traced the top of his empty mug. "Yes, and he bought the store next to us this morning."

"I'm surprised he didn't tell Levi about it. We assumed he was going to sell his things out of his workshop beside his barn. Having a store in town will give him better access to walk-in customers."

"He didn't want to tell anyone until he'd settled on a price with the owner. He'll open it to patrons in a week from Saturday."

"Oh, Grace, I'm so excited! He'll be right next door. It'll give you an even better chance to talk to him."

Grace glanced at the clock. Eight in the morning couldn't kumme soon enough.

Mark stepped onto the boardwalk, shielded his eyes from the bright sun, and headed for the livery. The morning had flown. It was 9:40. He should've left Grace's earlier, but wild horses couldn't have pulled him away from her. She'd captivated his interest with those deep brown eyes. He walked faster. Mr. Post might already be at his haus.

He dodged horses and buggies while crossing the road. Townsfolk filled the streets, and stores buzzed with activity. He passed Amish and Englischer patrons exiting and entering Berlin's General Store and post office. He glanced at the blacksmith hammering a horseshoe. The aroma of fresh baked bread filled the air in front of the bakery. He ducked in the store and bought a loaf for supper.

His purchase in hand, he sidestepped past the hunched-over peddler selling carved oak canes to a patron. Threatening gray clouds rolled in and covered the sun. The weather wouldn't dampen his mood today. Not after meeting Grace. Her choice of work forced her to deal with patrons face-to-face. Her birthmark hadn't stopped her from being a midwife and store manager. *Impressive.* She had a melodious voice, big brown eyes, and a cheerful attitude. Kind and sweet described her best.

He hadn't known whether to mention his bruder or not when Sarah asked if he had siblings. Amish law stated he should shun anyone who joined the church then left the Amish order, as if they were dead. His bruder might ask friends in Lancaster where he had moved to. If Abel came to his haus or shop and asked for help, what would he do? He pushed the anguish out of his mind.

Mark approached the liveryman, paid his fee, and retrieved his horse and buckboard. On his way home, the soft wind blew the dark clouds away, allowing the sun to shine. He'd open the windows to invite the fresh air inside when he arrived home.

He climbed out of the buckboard and tied the horse's reins to the white hitching post. Jed Post stood on his porch. He motioned to a young man who sat in a spring wagon loaded with crates of hens and a rooster. Three other young men managed the livestock.

"I hope I haven't kept you waiting long."

"No, we arrived a few minutes ago. We'll follow you to the barn and help you secure the animals." Mr. Post introduced Mark to his sons. "Call me Jed."

"Danki, and call me Mark." He unhitched his horse from his buckboard and stowed him in a stall.

The men guided and secured the plow horse, sow, hogs, cows, hens, and rooster inside the barn.

Mark indicated the haus. "I'll go inside and get the money I owe you. You're wilkom to kumme inside and rest. Would any of you like something to eat or drink?"

"Danki, but we can't stay long. We're getting ready to move and have a lot of work to do before the sun sets. I'll wait here."

Mark went inside, retrieved coins from his money jar, and joined Jed. He pressed the coins in his hand. "Danki." He chatted with his visitors for about ten minutes.

Jed gestured to his sons. "It's been a pleasure doing business with you, Mark. We should be on our way. My bruder is expecting us. He's much older than I am and not in good health. We're going to move into his big place and take over his farm in Lancaster. He's got more livestock than I need. I'm pleased you bought mine."

"I'm sorry your bruder is ill. I hope all goes well as you travel there." Mark bid them farewell and checked the livestock again. The animals appeared healthy and were what he needed.

Several minutes later, a horse's neigh caught his attention. He peeked outside. Who was coming toward his haus? This day had been busy. It was a good thing he'd finished a lot of his chores at six this morning. A short, round Amish man got out of his buggy and held his horse's reins. Wire-framed spectacles sat low on the man's nose. "I'm Bishop Weaver."

"I'm Mark King. Would you like to kumme in?"

"Jah, may I call you Mark?"

"Of course, but before we go inside, I'll give your horse food and water."

"Don't bother. I mean to stay only a short time." Bishop Weaver secured his horse to the hitching post and patted the animal's head. "There you go, boy." He then followed Mark inside.

Bishop Weaver removed his hat and hung it on a sturdy new maple rack displaying thick hooks Mark had nailed to the wall next to the front door.

Mark should've prepared answers for questions Bishop Weaver and others might ask about his family. "Have a seat." He opened the windows and breathed in. "It looks like the clouds have departed." He approached his guest. "Would you like anything to eat or drink? It's close to eleven thirty. I have stew I can heat."

"Nothing for me, danki." Bishop Weaver placed his hat on his lap. "Levi Helmuth told me about your parents' and the Stoltzfuses' accidents and the fire. The Stoltzfuses were good friends of mine. I was surprised to hear they are with God in Heaven. You're a young man to have suffered such tragedy and hardship."

Mark frowned and folded his hands in his lap. "I miss my parents and the Stoltzfuses. The haus and barn were replaceable." He heaved a deep breath. "With God's help, I was able to move on with my life."

The bishop leaned back against the feather-filled black cushions and drummed his fingers on the oak armrest. "Levi told me you're a talented carpenter." He pointed. "Your oak desk and matching spindle chair sitting in the corner are exquisite. I now realize those pieces match the furniture you and I are occupying. You do fine work."

"Danki. I bought and am opening a furniture store next to Grace and Sarah's Dry Goods Shop a week from Saturday. I'll sell similar chairs, settees, desks, and tables, along with potato bins, cashboxes, toys, and household items. You're wilkom to stop in and browse."

The bishop moved to the door. "I will, and I'll also spread the word we have a new furniture store in town."

The man's offer was generous. Mark appreciated his kindness. "I would be grateful if you would."

The bishop stopped. "I hope you'll like living in Berlin. We're a close community. The townsfolk help those in need of clothes, money, food, and care. We keep to ourselves. I ask you to do the same. Englischers visit and buy our goods, but otherwise leave us alone. We don't want any trouble from the outside world." He withdrew a booklet from his jacket pocket and passed it to Mark. "Please read our Ordnung. You have been born and raised in the Amish faith, but each community has its own set of rules.

You'll be expected to follow ours if, by chance, they differ from the ones you're accustomed to."

Mark accepted the Ordnung. "I understand." *He* wouldn't cause any trouble. He couldn't help it if trouble followed him. He hadn't been sure how to answer Grace when she'd asked him how his barn caught on fire.

It hadn't been long ago when Abel, his drunken bruder, had shown up at his haus in Lancaster. He'd asked for money, knocked over a lantern, and set fire to Mark's barn when leaving. Before help arrived, high winds and grass fed the flames and the fire burned out of control and spread, destroying everything he owned, except his workshop. Thankful he'd hidden his money in his workshop and not in his haus, he was able to buy what he needed to move to Berlin.

His bruder hadn't meant to do it, but for his bruder to still have the nerve to ask for money had disappointed him. He had begged him to turn his life around, to no avail.

His neighbors in Lancaster knew his new location. If his bruder found out where he lived and came to his haus, the bishop and community wouldn't approve. He loved his bruder, in spite of his bad judgment. He'd continue to pray for Abel to turn back to God and his Amish life.

"I'll expect you to attend our church service a week from Sunday. Our services are held every two weeks. Mr. Ropp donated land to the church to build a separate barn and stable on his property for the purpose of holding services. He's on South Street. You'll find the barn and a sign out front not far from here. The ladies bring a simple but delicious meal for us to enjoy after I finish delivering my sermon. Do you have any questions?"

"No. Danki for the directions."

"Get acquainted with the people in our community.

I'll introduce you to our members on a Sunday of my choosing and ask you to acknowledge your agreement to follow our Ordnung. Then I'll ask the members to accept you into our Amish order."

"I understand, and I'm looking forward to it."

The bishop shook Mark's hand. "It's been a pleasure to meet you."

Mark followed the bishop outside, retrieved the man's horse, and bid him farewell. He waited until the bishop had reached the end of the long dirt road before heading inside. The bishop had spoken in a gruff voice and been direct with his points. He'd been kind and wilkoming too. Mark respected him. The bishop seemed to have a genuine concern for the people in the community. Mark liked him.

They had talked for longer than Mark had thought. *Two o'clock already.* Hunger pangs rumbled in his stomach. What should he fix for dinner? The first thing he'd do was start a good fire.

Mark went into the sitting room and headed for the fireplace. He added small pieces of kindling to the two logs, lit a match, and waited a few seconds. He swung out the pole hook and removed the black cast iron pot before it became too hot. He reached for the old bellows and used it to encourage the flames.

His daed had taught both him and his bruder how to build and maintain a good fire. Even though he had a small stove, he still liked using the pot for his stew. It reminded him of his daed building a fire and his mamm cooking food this way.

He snatched the pot, carried it to the kitchen, and set it near the old icebox. The leftover vegetable and venison mixture would satisfy his hankering for a hot meal. After dumping it into the kettle, he carried it back to the pole hook, slipped it on, and placed it on the low-burning fire.

Beautiful Grace popped in his mind. No other woman had stirred him like she had. Except for her birthmark, her skin was flawless. Her smile lit up the room. Had she experienced the same spark he had when they talked? Her gaze held his before he left, and she beamed when he told her he'd be working next door.

The venison stew was nice and warm. He breathed in the scent of the meat, carrots, green beans, onions, and tomatoes. *Good choice.* He snatched two thick towels and removed the pot from the fireplace and returned it to the kitchen. From the cupboard he removed a bowl then ladled the hot mixture into it, set it on the kitchen table, bowed his head, and gave danki to God for his food and meeting Grace. He'd had a wonderful day. Minutes later, he'd finished his dinner and put his dishes in the sink.

Crash!

Horses neighed.

Slam!

Mark dashed outside to his large gray barn, noticed the doors open, and darted inside. Hens flapped their wings and squawked, hogs grunted, and the horses nickered with nervousness. His ladder lay on top of a metal tub. Not in its proper place. He would've never left it there. The ladder must've fallen and created the noise.

He moved to the haystacks. They'd been moved. Had his handcrafted furniture in the workshop been disturbed? He rushed there. He threw open the door and studied the shelves and hooks on the walls. Tools hung in place and his things were right where he'd left them. If any of his furniture and such had been destroyed or harmed, these things would've been impossible to replace in time to open his shop.

He returned to the barn and circled behind a pile of tall haystacks and found half-eaten butter cookies, an empty can of beans, and a jar of water. Ashes lay on gathered logs. Mark rubbed his chin. The intruder had picked a good spot to conceal his things where Mark wouldn't have a reason to look earlier.

A chill marched down his spine. *Abel.* Why would his bruder hide in his barn? He hadn't hesitated to barge into his haus in Lancaster the last time he needed money. He had no idea what decisions Abel would make these days. Nonetheless, whoever the person was who had kumme here had put his barn at risk of catching fire. He picked up a used match. He hadn't seen anyone. The intruder must've kumme and gone when he was sleeping last night. Had the stranger returned for something, but what? Why didn't the intruder wait until dark? He couldn't have gone far, but there were plenty of places for the intruder to hide in the woods behind his haus.

Mark strode outside and surveyed the grounds. The quiet, dense woods showed no movement, but it would be easy to hunker down among the trees and thick brush. Birds chirped and the wind whistled. A red squirrel scampered up an old oak tree. He walked the grounds again. Whoever had been in his barn was long gone. Shaking his head, he went back inside the haus.

He lifted the shotgun off metal hooks above the door and opened it. A bullet was chambered inside. This shotgun had kumme in handy. Coyotes and foxes had threatened to have his chickens for supper too often.

Levi told him to fire two warning shots at the sky if he ever had an emergency. Neighbors would recognize the signal to kumme running to his aid. He'd keep it near. To shoot a man had never entered his mind. Something he hoped never to do. The Amish law to avoid violence at all costs was clear. A law he had practiced all his life.

Later, a knock sounded. He placed the shotgun against the wall and opened the door. "Levi, kumme in."

"I won't keep you long, but I need a few minutes of your time. I've got some disturbing news."

Mark frowned. "What's wrong?"

"Someone came in our haus while we were out yesterday. Sarah had baked oatmeal cookies, and they were gone when we returned. Matches and loose change are missing from the jar we leave in the cupboard."

Oh no. He hoped the one stealing wasn't Abel. It was hard to believe his bruder would hide in his barn and steal from him and his neighbors. He couldn't imagine Abel resorting to this type of bad behavior, but again, he wasn't certain what to think at this point. The intruder could be anyone.

Mark gestured to a chair. "Have a seat." He rubbed the knot in his neck. "A short time ago, loud noises came from my barn. By the time I ran outside, the man had left." He recounted to Levi what he found. "I'm angry the intruder started a fire to keep warm and heat his beans. I'm bothered he'll return and do this again. He might burn it to the ground if he's not careful."

Levi crossed his arms. "I'm concerned for our community's safety. Townsfolk in Berlin don't lock their doors. We haven't had a reason to. The women in our community are comfortable walking alone to visit each other. Sarah and Grace drive their wagons to work by themselves."

Mark raked a hand through his hair. "I would assume the thief who stole your things is the same man who hid in my barn. This stranger must be in trouble with the law or up to no good. Otherwise, he'd ask us for help. The women shouldn't walk or drive alone until we catch this thief. This man could be dangerous. I'll stay awake as long as I can tonight. Maybe he will show up again and I'll capture him."

Levi rose and patted Mark's shoulder. "Stay alert. Fire shots in the air tonight if you need any help."

"I'll be fine. You watch over Sarah."

"Sarah told me you're opening a store in town a week from Saturday. Congratulations. We need a store like yours."

"Danki. You're welcome to visit here or my store anytime. Take care, and enjoy the rest of your night."

Levi waved and departed.

Mark went to his workshop and finished cutting and sanding wood for two chairs. The sky darkened, and he lit a lantern to walk back to the haus. It was time for supper. A bacon and tomato sandwich would hit the spot and satisfy his hunger. He gathered what he needed, set the items on the table, and then reached for a plate. He'd use his small wood-burning stove for the bacon.

He tossed in a couple of sticks and corn cobs in the stove, poured a bit of kerosene over the kindling, and lit the fire. Flames flickered and he replaced the plate and waited until the fire burned hot.

He set a cast-iron skillet on top and dropped six slices of bacon in it. Moments later, the pleasant scent of the smoked hog meat he bought yesterday from the General Store sizzled and filled the air. He sliced two pieces of the fresh bakery bread and then cut a slice of tomato. *I'm thirsty.* He poured a glass of water and sipped it then layered his sandwich.

Positioning his chair in front of the window, he had a perfect view of the barn while he enjoyed his meal. Eyes heavy, he put his plate on the floor beside his chair and blinked his eyes to stay awake. Darkness fell, and he sat without light but left the lantern at his feet. Eyes on the structure, he settled back in the chair.

The early morning sun shone through the window on Thursday and heated his face. Mark opened his eyes and glanced at the clock. *Four in the morning.* He'd fallen fast asleep. Bolting to the barn, he scanned the area on the way there. No sign of anyone.

He would have to warn Grace not to travel alone until this thief left town or was caught. His heart quickened. He didn't want her or anyone else getting hurt.

Chapter Two

Grace woke and dressed earlier than usual. Then she went to the kitchen and poured coffee into a container, darted outside, secured her horse to the wagon, and went to town. She stopped at the livery and handed her horse's reins to the liveryman. The townsfolk filled the board-walk this glorious, bright, sunshiny Thursday morning. Dodging in between the men and women entering and exiting shops, she breathed in the apple scent as she passed the bakery. They must be preparing tarts. *Yummy.* The familiar peddler's loud voice coaxing passersby to buy his hand-carved canes rang in her ears.

She gritted her teeth at the squeaky spring of the wagon's wheels ahead of her. Hurrying past them, the smooth rhythm of the horse's hooves clippity clopping next to her was a pleasant change. The aroma of beef wafted out the window as she passed the Berlin Restaurant. She closed her eyes for a brief moment and breathed it in. She'd swallowed a gulp of water and had three bites of a buttered biscuit in a hurry at home. Mark was coming to her shop, and she planned to arrive early.

Butterflies in her stomach danced with excitement.

Mark would be in the store most of the day. What would she discover about him? She paused and her breath caught.

Mark stood at the front door. "Good morning, Grace."

Oh no. He had arrived before her. Shelves and a crate of supplies were already stacked outside the door. He'd been busy. She left home forty-five minutes earlier than her usual time in order to get to work to have coffee ready for him before he arrived. It didn't matter. The more time they had to visit before customers came in, the better. "Good morning, Mark. Please kumme in. I'll heat coffee." She reached into her pocket, pulled out the worn brass key, and opened the front door for him.

Smiling, he entered with her and held a straight wooden handle attached to his open toolbox. "I'll set this down and then bring in the rest of the wood and supplies. I'd love a cup of coffee before I start work. I came early hoping we'd have a chance to visit."

She stepped back and opened the door for him to exit. He had kumme early to visit with her. Maybe this would be the start of something wonderful. She bit her lip, a nervous habit she'd tried to break. *Don't jump to conclusions.* She hardly knew the man. "The corner would be fine."

Moving to the back of the room, she threw kindling in the small woodstove and lit a fire to heat the coffee. Each time he walked in and out of the shop, her heart fluttered.

He brought two shelves in at a time and stacked them on the floor. He then carried in the rest of his things. "Do I smell coffee?"

Her heart fluttered again at the sound of his voice. "Yes." She handed him a mug.

"Did you kumme to town by yourself this morning?"

"Yes, I always do. Why?"

"Someone broke into my barn yesterday. Blankets

piled on straw lead me to believe he sought shelter there. He hasn't returned, but he may be hiding in the woods. You and Sarah shouldn't travel alone until we're certain he's gone or caught."

His face showed concern. Should she be worried? The stranger might be harmless and in need of a warm place to lay his head. Maybe he was shy and afraid to ask for help. "I would be upset about this news if our community had experienced trouble from Englischers, but we haven't had reason to lock our doors for years. If the stranger meant to harm anyone, he would have done so. He probably needed a place to sleep and necessities to help him survive."

"Levi visited me. He told me things are missing from his haus. I suspect the same intruder robbed him and slept in my barn. Please don't go anywhere alone."

"I'm not afraid. He hasn't harmed anyone. I doubt he will."

"Grace, I understand you want to find the good in people, but you must be careful. I don't want any harm to kumme to you."

He's frowning. I've upset him. He had her best interest at heart. Was their meeting the start of something special? She shouldn't be difficult. "I'll heed your advice."

Grace and Mark talked about the exact placement of the shelves. At eight o'clock, customers entered and interrupted their conversation. Grace greeted the women. They requested she unfold one coverlet after another. She explained the patterns on each.

Mark set his coffee on a small table then removed his carpenter's apron and tools from his scuffed and weathered toolbox. He tied on his apron, hammered, braced, and nailed ten long shelves on the longest wall on the right side of the shop throughout the morning.

Grace fretted patrons would complain about the noise, but she overheard customers comment on the excellence of his work and on the beauty of the wood grain in the shelves. She liked a man who could fix and build things.

Every chance she got, she stole glimpses at him. She caught him looking over his shoulder at her several times. Would they have time to talk today? Maybe he'd stay for dinner. She had prepared an extra thick ham and bacon sandwich for him before she left home this morning, hoping he'd stay for the noon meal. Maybe they could eat early.

Sarah entered and dropped her plain reticule under the counter. "Hello to you both." She kissed Grace on the cheek and stroked the last board Mark had hung. "This shelf is far more striking than any I'd anticipated we'd have for our shop. You're a fine craftsman, Mark. The finely sanded oak you used to make the shelves is exquisite. Grace told me about your furniture store. I told Levi, and he's thrilled for you. He and his friends are going to help you manage your farm until you have a chance to hire someone." She stepped back and admired his work. "They are sturdy and will hold a lot of quilts, blankets, and other textiles."

"Danki, Sarah. I'll appreciate their help."

Grace joined them. "The shelves are gorgeous. Our space will look less cluttered, and customers will have more choices." She poured more coffee in his now half-empty mug. He gripped the cup with such force, she expected it to break. No doubt he wanted to ensure he wouldn't drop it again. Poor man had a time holding on to things. He'd dropped his hammer a couple of times.

"Danki. I'm pleased you like them. They will fill up the wall quite nicely." He held up his mug. "Danki for the coffee. I better get back to work."

The bell clanged. "Grace, is my pocket quilt ready?"

"Yes. I have it right here." She crossed the room, ducked behind the wooden counter, and passed Mrs. Paulson a gray and white circle of love keepsake pocket quilt.

The gray-haired Amish woman removed the exact amount of money from her black reticule with her bony fingers and paid for her purchase. "Someone robbed Samuel and Irma's haus last night, while they were visiting her parents." Mrs. Paulson shook her head in dismay.

Sarah startled, tripped on her dark blue dress, caught the table edge, and straightened. "What did they find missing?"

"The bandit stole a tin can full of loose change they keep by their bread box. If a man or woman needs help, why wouldn't they knock on the door and ask? I'm afraid he's running from the law. Please keep a watchful eye."

Berlin hadn't had trouble from outlaws for a long time. Older kinner got into mischief now and then, but nothing serious. She hoped this wasn't the start of trouble for her community. She and Sarah reassured their friend they'd heed her advice as Mrs. Paulson exited the store.

Sarah lowered her voice. "Levi is up in arms about this thief helping himself to our things. I told him he shouldn't overreact. The intruder who came into our haus while we were gone didn't steal anything we couldn't replace." Her brow lifted. "Maybe Levi's right. We don't know what this man is up to. After listening to Mrs. Paulson's news, I'll be more cautious walking or driving my wagon alone. You should too."

Grace whispered in Sarah's ear. "Yes. Mark is worried and asked we be aware of our surroundings."

Two customers entered, and Sarah left Grace's side to help them.

Grace studied Mark as he pounded a brace in the wall.
His long, lean arms stretched high. She couldn't help from
swooning over him. His strong arms, tall legs, manners,
kind eyes, and pleasant voice were some of the reasons,
she supposed. She joined him. "Is there anything I can
get you?"

"No. You have enough to do managing your store. I
don't want to interrupt your work. I overheard your customer say an intruder had stolen things from another
haus."

"Yes. I'm surprised. Sarah and I will be on alert from
now on."

"Good. I apologize for all the noise. I'll be done around
eleven."

She didn't mind the noise. She liked watching him
work. After he opened his store, she hoped he'd use the
connecting door between their shops. If he didn't, she
would. She and Sarah waited on a steady stream of customers. The store emptied and Grace stretched and
yawned.

He packed his tools and supplies then joined her. "I'm
finished."

"I brought sandwiches. I wouldn't want you to leave
hungry. It wouldn't be right after all the work you've done
for us."

His handsome face lit with a smile. "I appreciate the
offer. I'd like to join you."

Her cheeks heated. Mark was a gentleman and generous. Two more reasons to add to her list as to why she
liked him. If she were writing his wonderful traits on
paper, she'd need another sheet. She washed her hands,
served the sandwiches, then removed three jars of water
from an icebox. She tilted her head to a small table and
chairs off to the side of the room. "We can sit here."

He patted his stomach. "Danki. This is kind of you, Grace."

Sarah joined them. "I didn't have much breakfast. I'm glad we're eating earlier than usual."

"I'll say a prayer of danki for our food." Mark bowed his head. "Dear Heavenly Father, forgive us for our sins and danki for the food we are about to eat. Danki for your love and mercy. Amen."

Grace raised her head. "Danki, Mark."

"The air is warm, the birds fill the trees, and wild-flowers fill the meadows. It's difficult to stay inside on a day like this." Sarah sipped her water.

This was the perfect place for her, sunny or not. Grace liked watching Mark work. She looked at his plate. He'd devoured half his sandwich before she had taken two bites out of hers. He must like ham and bacon. She chatted about the weather with Sarah and Mark in between bites.

The three of them finished with their food. Grace wiped the plates with a rag and put them in the basket to take home and wash later as she carried on her conversation with Sarah and Mark about Mamm's new recipe for corn pudding.

A woman rushed into the shop.

Grace wiped her mouth and stood. "How can we help you?"

The woman paled. "Is there a midwife here? I asked the postmaster where I could find one, and he sent me here. He said to ask for Grace Blauch."

"I'm Grace Blauch. How can I help you?"

"My friend, Annabelle Watson, is in my buggy outside. She's ready to give birth. Please help us."

Sarah addressed the woman. "Madam, you stay with

me. We don't want to get in Grace and Mark's way when they bring Mrs. Watson to our back room."

Grace dashed out after Mark and stood behind him.

"Madam, my name is Mark King. I would like to help you inside. Grace Blauch is behind me. She's a midwife."

The distressed woman held her arms out to him. "I'm Annabelle Watson. Yes, please help me."

He reached inside and lifted the Englischer out of the open doorway of the buggy and carried her inside. "Where should I take her?"

"Lay her on the cot in the back room." Grace darted ahead and opened the entry door, and then she led him across the shop, where the small room's door was already open for him. She smiled at the woman's friend. "Make yourself comfortable. I'll fetch you after the boppli is born."

Mark lowered Mrs. Watson on the cot and backed out of the room. He closed the door behind him.

The distressed woman groaned and pressed her hands against her swollen belly. Her eyes rolled with fear.

Grace brushed sweat-dampened hair off the woman's cheek and tucked a pillow under her head. "Take a deep breath and relax." Grace washed and dried her hands then untied her medical bag. On a small table close to the bed, she arranged clean towels, a stethoscope, a syringe bulb, scissors, a needle and thread, and saline solution.

Mark knocked on the door. "May I do anything for you?"

"If Sarah is busy, please warm two pots of water on the stove. I'd appreciate it."

Grace positioned herself at the end of the cot. "How are you doing?"

The woman trembled. She held a hand to her stomach. "Ack! My baby is coming."

Grace pushed Mrs. Watson's dress to her chest and removed the woman's undergarments. She eyed the boppli's head. "I'm going to count to three. On three, push hard. One, two, and three."

Mrs. Watson grunted and pushed. "Ack!"

Grace caught the slippery tiny maedel. "You have a dochder."

The newborn wailed.

After cutting and tying off the umbilical cord, Grace suctioned the newborn's nose and mouth. She grabbed her stethoscope and stuck the tips in her ears with one hand and checked the boppli's heartbeat. She wiped the infant with a dry cloth. "She didn't waste any time coming into this world." Grace placed the infant on Mrs. Watson's chest. She washed her hands again. "You rest while I clean your dochder. I'll remove your afterbirth and wash you in a few minutes." She placed a lightweight blanket over the mamm's legs and took the newborn.

Sarah cracked the door open and peeked in. "Mark warmed water. Do you need it?"

"Yes. I would appreciate it." She accepted the water. "Boppli and Mamm are doing fine."

"I'm Sarah Helmuth, and I understand from your friend, Mrs. Opal Fox, you are Annabelle Watson. In addition to being a midwife, Grace is also my business partner. We manage this shop together." Sarah joined Grace and put her finger in the newborn's hand. "She's so tiny." She glanced over her shoulder. "What did you name her?"

"Her name is Julia Watson."

"Grace, I'll fetch anything you need. I'll be out front. Mark left for a bit, but he's back. I suspect he was uncomfortable. He's filled another pot of water and put it on the stove to warm while I assisted a patron. He'll knock on the door when it's ready." Sarah nodded at the mamm and dashed out of the room.

Grace suspected Sarah wanted to escape the blood-stained sheets. Her friend couldn't stand the sight of blood. She washed the infant and checked her from head to toe. The wrinkled red-skinned maedel kicked her long legs, fisted her hands, and cried. Grace found no visible signs of anything abnormal. What a beauty. She had coal black fuzzy hair, a button nose, and fat cheeks.

A soft knock on the door caught her attention. "Yes?"

Mark's voice startled her. "I have more warm water. Would you like me to leave it by the door?"

"Yes. Danki."

Sarah returned with a pot of warm water and set it on the floor next to Grace. "Here's the water Mark heated for you." She beheld the little maedel. "She's so pretty." She grinned at the mamm and motioned to Grace. "Again, if you need me, give me a shout." She rushed to leave.

Grace yanked a small pink blanket from a shelf and swaddled the infant in it and then delivered Julia to Mrs. Watson. "How are you holding up?"

Tears stained the new mamm's cheeks. "I'm tired, but happy. The baby blanket is beautiful."

Grace retrieved the two pots of warm water and set them on the table next to the exhausted woman. "We sell these smaller blankets in our store. You may have this one as our gift." She scooped Julia into her arms and laid her in a wooden box on top of a soft blanket. *This little one is so precious.*

After washing her hands again, she massaged the woman's stomach and worked to remove the afterbirth and then cleaned her. "You don't need stitches. I have an extra plain dress for this reason. You can have it."

Reaching for the dress, she stole a glance at the newborn. Helping bring a new life into the world never grew tiring.

She cleaned her hands and escorted Mrs. Watson to a chair next to the bed. "Can you raise your arms for me?" The woman upstretched her arms and shivered as Grace removed her dirty clothing and shrugged the new dress on her. Pulling clean sheets off the shelf, Grace changed the sheets on the cot and assisted Mrs. Watson back onto it. She covered her with a clean blanket and passed Julia to her.

"I was scared, but you calmed me. Thank you for helping me and my daughter."

"It was my pleasure. Mrs. Fox must be worried about you. Would you like me to ask her to kumme in?"

"Yes, if you wouldn't mind."

Grace opened the door, poked her head out, and gestured to Mrs. Fox. "Would you like to join your friend and her new boppli?"

Sarah didn't seem to notice her. Two customers stood with her friend asking questions. Grace would join her in a few minutes. No sign of Mark. Where was he? She stepped back inside with the new mamm, friend, and infant.

Mrs. Fox sat in a chair near the bed. "How are you feeling? I was worried."

"I'm weak and sore. After I rest for an hour or so, I'll go home. Do you mind?"

"No, I don't mind at all." Mrs. Fox reached for the newborn and rocked the boppli in her arms. She paused and peeled back the blanket. "You have a girl. She's so pretty." The friend peered at the infant. "She's perfect in every way."

Grace bundled up the woman's soiled clothing and

placed it in a bag for her. She placed it on the floor at the end of the bed.

"I named her Julia."

Mrs. Fox's eyes glistened with tears. "I'm thrilled you'd choose to name her after my daughter. It means so much to me." She gave Julia to her mamm.

Mrs. Fox faced Grace. "Annabelle and I met as children and have been friends for a long time. A year ago, my daughter, Julia, died five months after her birth."

Grace put a hand to her heart. "I'm touched by your story. There's nothing like the comfort and support of a best friend."

"Annabelle's husband is in Canton helping his father build a workshop. He'll be home in a few days. We came to shop. We were certain she had another month before Julia would make her grand entrance. Her pains surprised us. We appreciate all you've done for us." She turned to Mrs. Watson. "Mr. King delivered our buggy to the livery. Why don't you close your eyes, and I'll sit with you until you're ready to go home."

"My eyelids are heavy. I'll feed Julia then rest for a few hours."

Again, Mark had not hesitated to jump in and help. Grace brought the new mamm and her friend two jars of cold water. "Take all the time you need. Sarah and I will be out front if you need anything."

Sarah met Grace halfway across the shop. "Earlier when you were helping Mrs. Watson birth Julia, we had a full store of women for about a half hour, and you couldn't hear a thing out here amidst all the chatter. When two women were left in the store, they asked why a woman was moaning in the back room. I explained you are a midwife and that you were birthing a boppli. Each patron asked me to pass on their best wishes to the new mamm."

"They're going to rest for a little while before they leave. We've had an exciting morning." She darted her eyes around the store. "Where did Mark go?"

"He's in his store waiting until the women are ready to leave to fetch their buggy from the livery."

Mark opened the connecting door inside their shops and peered in. "I'm next door sweeping and mopping the floor if you need anything. How are the new mamm and boppli doing?"

"The new mamm needs rest before she heads home. Julia is adorable."

Sarah hugged herself. "I wanted to stay and ogle the newborn, but I got woozy seeing the soiled sheets and had to dart out of there."

"I understand." Grace yawned and covered her mouth. "I'm sorry. I'm weary from all the activity today."

Mark waved off her remark. "Don't apologize. You amaze me, Grace Blauch. Not many Amish women are midwives and manage a shop. I'm certain you also help your parents with chores at home. I'm impressed."

"I will have to close my eyes when I give birth. The ordeal scares me." Sarah rested her hand on Grace's shoulder. "Injuries or births, no matter how messy, don't make Grace pale, she handles whatever the task is with ease. I wish I had half her bravery."

"You two stop. You're embarrassing me, but danki. I'd wanted to learn midwifery since I witnessed Hester deliver our neighbor's boppli. She offered to teach me how to assist in births. I loved learning midwifery from her." She grinned at him.

He had voiced his appreciation of her talent and taken care of her needs without her having to ask him to do a thing.

"It's good you enjoy your work." He glimpsed at the

connecting door to his shop. "Is there anything I can do for you before I go back to my store and wait until the women need their buggy?"

Sarah smoothed her apron. "You've been a big help to us today. Danki." She stepped away to greet a customer.

Grace put her hands in her apron pockets. "Danki for everything you've done." She tilted her head. "I can't wait for you to bring in your furniture. I imagine your things are all exquisite, if they're anything like the shelves you installed for Sarah and me."

His face reddened. "On Saturday, you'll have to visit and I'll show you what I've crafted to sell."

"I look forward to being your first patron."

"Not more than I, Grace Blauch." He threw her a sideways glance. "Call me when the women need their wagon." He returned to his store.

She beamed. It wasn't her imagination. He was interested in her. The rest of the afternoon, Grace pictured Mark's brown eyes and soothing voice as she and Sarah assisted customers.

Grace slipped away and peeked in on the mamm, Julia, and Mrs. Fox. The mamm stood with Julia in her arms, and Mrs. Fox had her arm circled around her.

"May I get you anything?"

"No, thank you. I slept and am stronger. I'm ready to go home."

"I'll ask Mark to bring your buggy to the front of the shop."

Grace sauntered to the connecting door, swung it open, and spotted Mark. "The women are ready to go home."

Mark propped his broom against the wall. "I'll bring their buggy out front."

Grace and Sarah took turns holding Julia until Mark

arrived. They escorted the women and Julia to their buggy, bid them and Mark farewell, and walked back inside the shop.

"I'll tidy the store while you clean up the back room. My dinner will struggle to stay in my stomach if I help you clean up your mess." Sarah chuckled.

"Good idea." Grace moved to the back room, opened the rear door, and threw out the dirty water from the pots onto the grass. She unhooked a clean pot from its wooden peg, went out back and pumped water into it, and put it on the stove to heat. She checked the fire. It was sufficient. This had been a challenging and rewarding day.

She dropped the soiled rags in a flour sack to take home to wash later. Her body was tired from all the activity; her arms ached as she changed the cot's sheets and blankets. Julia Watson was the nineteenth boppli she'd helped bring into the world on this cot. The women in her community knew, from word of mouth, they were welcome to kumme to the shop if they needed birthing assistance. If she wasn't there, Sarah was always aware of her whereabouts and could direct them to her.

She retrieved the new pot of hot water from the stove and poured half into another basin. She cleaned her rubber syringe and scissors in steaming hot water then used the other pot of water to clean the tables. She finished then stowed her things and joined Sarah in the front room.

Sarah untied her kapp strings and closed her eyes for a moment. "I'm done for the day. It's five o'clock, and I turned our sign to read closed." She plopped in the spindle chair. "You've not had a minute to yourself. Mark proved helpful. He may be the man for you. I've been praying and asking God to introduce you to a hardworking and loving Amish man."

The life of a spinster was what Grace had resigned herself to for the rest of her days on earth even though she was only twenty-one. Available Amish men had shown no interest in her thus far. She would love to get married one day, but she'd given up on meeting a man looking past her birthmark. Mark's interest gave her hope. Would she learn anything about him she couldn't accept? She blew out a breath. She wouldn't worry yet. She had plenty of time to find out more about him. She'd pray for God's guidance. "I hope so. Time will tell."

She waited on the boardwalk and watched Sarah lock the door. Together, they went to the livery, collected their wagons, and headed to their respective homes. On the way home, she played the delightful day with Mark over in her mind.

The scent and sizzle of fried chicken caught her attention as she walked in the haus. "Mamm, my nose tells me we're having one of my favorites for supper."

"Your daed requested fried chicken, and I didn't expect I'd get any complaints from you." Mamm patted Grace's cheek. "Your eyes are half open and your face is pale. Are you sick?" She placed a hand on Grace's forehead. "You're not warm."

"I helped birth a boppli today. She was adorable with tiny fingers and toes. Mamm and little maedel are doing fine. I, on the other hand, am not so fine. I'm not ill, but I'm exhausted."

"You are my strong and talented dochder. You wear yourself out helping others. Sit down and rest. Your daed should join us any minute. He's in the barn. After supper, you rest. I'll wash the dishes."

Grace told her about the stranger stealing things from

Levi and Sarah's and evidence Mark found in his barn this intruder might be hiding there.

Daed entered and Mamm told him Grace's news.

He raised his eyebrows and sat. "We should be careful and keep a watchful eye. He didn't harm anyone or steal any animals. I would guess he got what he wanted and has left."

Mamm nodded. "I hope so." Mamm served Daed and Grace fried chicken and potatoes.

Grace didn't want to talk about the stranger anymore. She agreed with Daed. The intruder must've needed shelter, food, and supplies and had moved on. She told them about Julia's features and how much she loved holding her. She waited until Daed finished his meal and left before telling Mamm about Mark King and what she knew about him so far.

"Are you interested in him?"

"Yes. He doesn't stare at my birthmark. He's kind, a gentleman, and handsome. His store is next to Sarah's and mine."

"I'd like to meet him. Pray for God's guidance. Maybe Mark is in God's plan for your life."

Pressing a hand to her heart, she leaned in. "Oh, Mamm, I hope so."

"I hope so too, dear dochder."

She finished her meal, carried her dishes to the sink, and offered to wash them.

Mamm protested and sent her to her room.

She plopped in the chair by her window and gazed out at the green grassy meadow. What did the future hold for her and Mark? She'd been teased by boys in school. She'd given up on men not shying away from her, until she met Mark. He met her eyes and seemed to hang on her every word. Mark was the only man who'd ever made her feel pretty besides her daed. To have her interest in a man reciprocated was a wonderful and new experience. She'd envied her friends getting married and starting families. For the first time in her life, she felt like it might be a possibility for her someday.

Chapter Three

Thump. Startled, Grace shot up in bed in time to find a sparrow falling from her window Saturday morning. The poor bird wasn't the first to wake her up this way during her lifetime. Rubbing her eyes, she slid her legs over the bed and stood. Her heart soared at the thought of Mark. She had hoped their paths would cross this past week. She'd missed him. The shelves he'd crafted and hung for them were sanded and painted to perfection. She couldn't wait to visit his store today and run her hand along his furniture.

She gobbled down her breakfast of fried eggs and white bread and butter. She had to hurry if she wanted to arrive at the shop before Mark. She rushed through her chores and changed into her shop clothes. She bid farewell to her parents and grabbed her medical bag, coffee container, and dinner box Mamm packed for her.

She threw her supplies in the wagon and prepared to leave. The sun warmed her face and the grass appeared greener. The cows grazing in the pasture and ducks swimming in the pond off to the left of the the weathered white barn painted a charming picture as she drove down the lane and headed for town.

Mark added excitement in her life. No doubt Mamm would tell Daed about her mention of Mark, and they'd want to meet him soon. Tomorrow, Mark would be at church. Maybe church would be a perfect place for her to introduce him to her parents.

Arriving at the livery, she passed her horse's reins to the liveryman.

"I'll take care of your horse, Grace."

"Danki." She climbed out of the wagon. She passed townsfolk on the way to the shop. Englischers wore the prettiest clothes. Big floppy hats decorated with flowers and colorful printed dresses showing their ankles. She could never be comfortable in a dress fitted to her body. She liked her loose-fitting plain light blue dress and white apron.

Pins instead of buttons didn't bother her. Her friend Becca Carrington loved buttons and must like wearing fancy clothes since she abandoned Amish life to marry a doctor. In her heart, she was happy for Becca, but she missed her.

The desire to write and tell Becca about Mark had overwhelmed her the past several days, but she wouldn't chance it. In her last letter, she'd told Becca it would be her last letter she'd send to her. The commitment she'd made not to correspond with her friend any longer had been the right decision.

She'd been fortunate to not have been caught thus far. If the bishop found out about her transgression, she and her parents would suffer. She'd been selfish to put her mamm and daed in such a position.

Pausing in front of Mark's shop, she scanned the words above the door. KING'S FURNITURE. *I like it.* The bold letters were cut thick and dark against the light wood behind them. It stood out as the best crafted sign on the boardwalk. Customers would find the beautiful masthead hard to miss. She opened the door to the dry goods shop and found Mark with a cup of coffee in his hand talking to Sarah.

Her heart raced as she dropped her bag behind the counter. "Good morning."

Sarah hugged her. "Good morning."

"Mark, I'm surprised we didn't bump into you last week." Grace straightened her kapp blown to the kumming in the door.

"I brought in a couple loads to my shop on Tuesday and Thursday after the stores were closed. I didn't want to deliver my things during the day when there were customers shopping. I was afraid they'd stop me and want to peruse my things before I had a chance to get them out of the wagon."

"I understand. How will you manage a store and your farm?"

"Levi and his friends have been helping me manage my property and animals until I hire someone. It's been a pleasure to be better acquainted with Levi and his friends. They're very supportive of me opening my store."

Waving a dismissive hand, Sarah grinned. "Levi and his friends are always helping each other out. They'd rather work together than alone."

Smiling, Grace poured herself a cup of coffee. "Are you ready to open your doors to customers?"

He sipped his coffee. "Jah. I hung my sign and arranged my stock on the floor and shelves. First, I wanted to invite you to kumme over."

Sarah plucked a hair off Grace's sleeve. "I peeked at his store. His furniture and household items are the prettiest I have ever laid my eyes on. You must let him show you around. I'll manage our shop."

Grace put her hands in her apron pockets. "I admired your masthead above your door before I came inside. It stands out on the boardwalk. It's plain in big letters and easy to read."

"Danki. It will be a reflection of my work to customers, so I'm relieved to hear you say you like it." He gestured. "Kumme on in."

She followed him to the connecting door but stopped. She recognized the woman coming into her and Sarah's shop. Why couldn't she remember this woman's name?

The Englischer held her chin up and scanned the room. "What a lovely shop you have." She clicked her shoes across the wooden floor to a multicolored pinwheel quilt hanging on the wall and fingered the corner of the note pinned to mark it sold. "I must buy this quilt. How much is it?"

Grace set down her coffee cup and joined her. Sarah stood behind the counter.

"This quilt has been sold. The woman who bought it is picking it up later this afternoon." Grace picked up another similar patterned quilt. "Do you like this one?"

"No, I do not. I will pay you double what your customer has paid. What do you say?"

Sarah moved next to Grace.

Grace flexed her hands by her sides. "We won't sell you a quilt already promised to someone else. We would be willing to stitch you a similar quilt. You may choose the fabric and pattern. The quilt would be ready in about a week."

The woman frowned and narrowed her eyes at Grace. "You look familiar to me. You're a friend of my daughter-in-law, Becca Carrington. Am I right?"

Grace swallowed hard. How could she have forgotten meeting Becca's mamm-in-law? The woman had her nose in the air when meeting her at the wedding. Her tone was direct and cold. She was intimidating. The stories Becca had told her about Mrs. Carrington before her friend and Dr. Matt Carrington had wed weren't pleasant. She understood why. Her pinched face and stern demeanor showed the woman's prejudice toward her and Sarah.

She hadn't told Sarah she'd attended Becca's and Ruth's weddings. Mrs. Carrington hadn't attended Ruth's wedding, but she might mention Becca's. It would be best if she admitted to it before Mrs. Carrington did. "I'm sorry, Mrs. Carrington. I should've remembered you from the wedding. Yes, Becca and I are close friends."

"Becca has taken to high society life quite well, after having been raised in your simple and sheltered lifestyle. Of course, I have taught her how to dress, speak, and conduct herself among our friends." She cocked her head and patted the quilt. "Are you certain you will not reconsider selling me this quilt? It is my friend's favorite color."

Grace darted her eyes to Mark. He stood and studied a black and white patchwork quilt. He could hear every word of this conversation. How should she handle this woman? She was certain Sarah wouldn't approve of her attending Becca's wedding. Neither would Mark. She had put herself and her parents at great risk. She and her parents would be shamed if the bishop found out. Mrs. Carrington's blatant rude behavior about the quilt added to her headache. "No, I'm sorry. Are you positive there isn't another quilt in the shop you'd like? As I said earlier, we could have a quilt like the one you want ready for you in about a week."

"My husband and I are passing through town on our way to visit friends. I must purchase a birthday gift for my friend. I need it today, and I want this one. Please do not be stubborn."

This woman was merciless. Grace had never met anyone quite like her. "Mrs. Carrington, I won't change my mind. Please choose another quilt, and we'll lower the price for your inconvenience."

Mrs. Carrington glared at Grace and slid on her gloves. She opened her mouth but shut it, swung open the door, and slammed it shut behind her.

Mark winked. "You treated her with kindness. I couldn't keep a straight face. The woman was determined to badger you until you agreed to her demand. You stood your ground and didn't compromise your principles, which is very commendable. Good for you."

His words echoed and warmed her heart. Grace pressed a hand to her neck. "Poor Becca. She's told me stories about how ruthless Mrs. Carrington's actions were to separate her from Dr. Matt Carrington before they married. Becca claims she treats her like a dochder now, but she said Mrs. Carrington's rudeness to folk not in her high society circle of friends embarrasses her when they're out together. She obviously doesn't hold us in high regard. Nonetheless, I didn't like having to disappoint her."

Sarah waved a dismissive hand. "Don't give her another thought."

Grace rolled her shoulders back. "You're both correct. Danki for your support."

"Go visit Mark's shop, and then we need to talk later." Sarah gave her a stern look.

"I won't be long." She stepped inside his store.

Dreading her conversation about Becca with Sarah, she wondered if Mark would also want to speak to her about Becca. Maybe she should approach the subject first after perusing his store. She didn't want any awkwardness to linger between them.

Mark viewed the wall clock. "It's time to open my store." He slipped to the front door, turned the key, and flipped a neatly lettered wooden sign to OPEN and rejoined her.

The finely crafted oak headboards and bed frames stacked along the wall caught her attention. The light-colored desk and spindle chair in the corner gleamed in the sunlight in front of the window. She studied the rocking horses, bread and potato boxes, cedar chests, and kitchen furniture. "Your work is exquisite. You're quite talented."

The maple potato and bread boxes and pine carved trains, dogs, cats, rabbits, and *X*'s and *O*'s for tic-tac-toe were all arranged neatly in the store. She reached for a rabbit he'd carved and sat it upright in the palm of her hand. "I'm amazed at the detail you were able to create in the bunny's big eyes, ears, little nose, and mouth. The Englischers' kinner will love them. Everything you have is stunning."

"You're too kind, Grace." He reached for a carved doll the size of her hand, without a face, and pressed it in her palm. "This doll is for you."

Her breath caught. His slender fingers and the calloused skin on his hands warmed hers. "Danki, I love it." No man, other than her daed, had ever given her a present. She would treasure the doll. The toy would remind her of him every time she beheld it.

He slid his hand off hers. "I'm pleased you like the gift."

A tingle rose from her head to her toes. She liked him a lot.

The door opened. Mark stepped back and greeted a customer. "May I help you?"

The Englischer stroked the ornate oak headboard. "If you don't mind, I'd like to browse on my own."

"Please take your time." The woman moved to the far end of the store.

Grace studied the second shelf. "Your ideas for wooden trains with moving side doors are smart. Little boys will like them. I believe your store will be empty in no time. Customers will want to buy everything."

"I would be happy if they did, but I doubt they'll be half as excited about my things as you. Danki for your support. Your opinion means a lot to me."

She didn't want to put off discussing Becca with him any longer. Mark's customer was out of earshot.

She lowered her voice. "You must have overheard me say I attended Becca Carrington's wedding in Massillon. She's my Amish friend who joined the church but left our community to marry a doctor. Her parents invited me to go with them to visit her. We went to Massillon to buy supplies, but I also spent time with Becca. I attended her schweschder Ruth's wedding too."

"I could tell by Sarah's frown and tone, she disapproves of your actions. Has she lost anyone to the world?"

"No, and she and Becca weren't close."

"I'm not going to pass judgment on you. My bruder, Abel, joined the church then departed to live among the Englisch. I understand I'm to act as if he's dead, but I find this Amish law the most difficult. It pains me to not know if he's all right. I love my bruder. We were close. I miss him." He shook his head. "It's hard to separate ourselves from friends and family who leave this life."

"I agree. Where is he?"

He shrugged his shoulders. "I don't have the slightest idea."

A tall Englischer with a thick black mustache and tailored suit entered. Mark greeted the patron. "May I help you?"

Grace swallowed around the lump in her throat. She had struggled with obeying Amish law where Becca was concerned, but it must be harder for Mark to shun his flesh-and-blood bruder. She was glad he trusted her enough to share such an intimate detail about his life. His face read relief when a customer interrupted their conversation. She wouldn't question him about his sibling. This was his first day to open his new shop. She didn't want to ruin his excitement or run the risk of someone overhearing them talking about anyone who had left Amish life. They'd be punished.

The man studied a chestnut hope chest. "I'd like to buy this. Would you help me load it?"

"Of course. I'll be with you in a moment."

Grace whispered to him. "I'll leave and kumme back later. You're busy."

"Please wait. This won't take long."

Mark accepted the patron's money and helped him carry and load the chest in his cart.

She viewed him through the window. What strong arms he had. He'd delivered the heavy chest into the man's cart as if it was as light as a feather.

He returned. "What a nice way to start the day. I've spent time with you and collected money already." He held up his fistful of silver dollars.

"And the day's not over yet."

They both laughed.

Her face warmed. This Amish man had it all. Handsome features, a kind heart, and was talented.

"I should let you get to work. Kumme to our shop for dinner. I brought sandwiches again today."

"I will. Do you have butter cookies?"

"Yes, are those your favorite?"

"Jah, and oatmeal cookies."

Grace chuckled. "I'll bring oatmeal cookies another day."

The door between their shops opened. Sarah waved her over. "A wagon train is traveling through town. A crowd of women entered our shop, and I need help."

Grace bid Mark farewell and scurried behind Sarah. The women huddled around her and asked questions about the quilt patterns. Beads of sweat formed on her lip, and her body heated. Sarah stood behind the counter. A line of women clutched quilts to their chests, had coins in their hands, and were ready to pay for their purchases. Other patrons were perusing their selection of textiles. Grace answered customers' questions and, upon request, unfolded coverlets for them to view.

The last woman in the store departed. Grace fanned a hand inches from her face, plopped in a chair, and gestured for Sarah to join her. "I'm thankful we sold a lot of quilts, but I'm exhausted." She remembered the small miniature wooden doll in her pocket. "Mark gave me this toy today. Isn't it pretty?"

Sarah traced the outline of the doll. "It is pretty. He must like you a lot to give you a gift. I'm hoping he's the one for you. He's kind and a hard worker." She passed the toy back to Grace and dipped her chin. "I'm sorry to dampen your mood, but we must discuss you attending Becca's wedding. I'm upset with you for what you've done, Grace. You said you went with her parents several times to buy supplies in Massillon last year. You know better than to put yourself and your family at risk."

Grace chewed her lip. "I'm sorry. I did buy supplies, but I also went to Becca's and Ruth's weddings. I couldn't tell you and compromise you, too. Since Becca's parents have passed, I won't be visiting her again."

Sarah sighed. "I accept your apology, and I forgive you. Don't worry. I won't tell anyone what you've done. You're my friend, and I love you."

Grace wiped tears from her face. "It's hard for me to let her go. She means a lot to me. We've been close most of our lives."

"I sympathize, but Becca understood she'd be shunned by her family and the Amish community when she left the Amish life. You need to accept she can't be a part of your life anymore." She smoothed her apron. "Did you say anything to Mark about attending Becca's wedding? You might ruin his positive impression of you if he learns you're not abiding by Amish law and shunning her."

"I told him about her. He has a bruder who joined the Amish church then left to live among the Englisch. He understands my struggle to sever ties with Becca based on his own situation with his bruder."

Sarah covered her open mouth. "He shouldn't have mentioned him to you."

"He's not in communication with him."

She should've known better than to share this information with her friend. Sarah didn't have any compassion for anyone who left the Amish life. "A patron interrupted us. We didn't discuss his bruder any further."

"For your sake, I'm relieved he understood your situation with Becca, even though he should've scolded you for communicating with her. He's abiding by Amish law and staying away from his bruder, and so should you stay away from Becca. I don't want anything to change his mind about you. I have said enough on the matter." She sat in silence for a few moments then opened her mouth. "Something else is bothering me."

Grace sucked in her bottom lip. What else had she done to upset Sarah? Nothing came to mind. "What is it?"

"I wish I could have a boppli. What's wrong with me? It's been a year. I'm scared. What if I'm unable to have kinner?"

Breathing a sigh of relief, Grace slid her chair close to her friend. "God has a plan for your life. Be patient. You're young and have plenty of time for kinner. I believe you will have a boppli when you least expect it." She prayed Sarah would find herself with child soon.

Her friend longed for a child more than anything else in her life.

"I hope you're right." She rubbed her tummy. "Are you hungry?"

It's dinnertime. Her stomach grumbled. "I'll check with Mark and ask if he's hungry." The door swung inward before she could put her hand on the knob. She jumped back, waved her arms, and regained her balance.

Mark reached for her. "I should be more careful when opening this door. Are you all right?"

"Yes, I'm fine." She hugged herself. *No, I'm more than fine. Thanks to the joy dancing in my heart from your touch.* "Kumme in. Are you ready for dinner?"

Grace lifted the lid on the worn wicker picnic basket and pulled out beef sandwiches and butter cookies. "It's time to take a break."

Mark dragged three chairs and a small table together in a circle in the middle of the floor. "A flood of people filled my store all at once. I had a line outside waiting to get in. I collected a pretty good sum of money this morning. I'll have to carve more toys this week. My top shelf is almost bare."

Grace readied three plates of food. "You're off to a good start." She handed Mark a plate.

Sarah clasped the handle of the white china pitcher and filled three glasses. She set them on the table and sat.

Mark bit into his sandwich. "Grace, this beef sandwich is tasty."

"Mamm packed dinner for us today. I'll pass along your danki to her."

"Wait until you try her mamm's famous butter cookies. She wrote out the recipe for me, but she must've left out an ingredient. Mine aren't as sweet as hers."

"She does make the best butter cookies." Grace wiped her mouth with a napkin. "Mark, is there anything I can do to help you?"

"Not at the moment. It's nice to know you'll be next door if I need anything." He met her gaze.

Her skin tingled and her body warmed. No, it wasn't her imagination. He liked her, too. His eyes were like mirrors to his soul. She held a hand to her heart. Would Mark shun his bruder if he encountered him? Had Mark ever contemplated leaving the Amish life like his bruder? She swallowed hard and hoped not.

Mark added more toys to his shelves and contemplated meeting Grace's parents. She'd be at church with her parents tomorrow. Maybe she or Levi would introduce him to her parents. If they didn't, he would introduce himself. Would Mr. and Mrs. Blauch approve of him? Would they ask questions about his family? He told Grace about his bruder. Would she ask more questions about Abel? At least she understood since she was experiencing the same dilemma with her friend Becca.

The Ordnung came to mind. It clearly stated anyone

who left the Amish order shouldn't be mentioned and should be considered dead. He hung his head and scratched his chin. This law was the hardest for him to follow.

Mark reached for his razor and sharpened it on his leather strap Sunday morning. After he splashed his face with water, he lathered it with soap. Putting the razor to his neck, he shaved a small patch of yesterday's growth. Wanting to look his best for Grace, he'd be careful not to nick himself.

Mark dressed in a crisp white shirt, pants, and suspenders. Grabbing a clean cloth, he wiped the dirt off his plain black leather boots. That should do it. Ready to attend church, he put on his black hat and headed to the barn to fetch his buggy.

He steered his horse to the church. Heart pounding, he prayed. "Dear Heavenly Father, please give me words to say to Grace's parents. This I pray and ask in your name. Amen."

The big two-story white barn stood surrounded by buggies and wagons in the middle of a green grassy field. A stable stood next to it for the horses. He handed the reins to the young Amish stable hand, no doubt selected by the bishop to handle the horses, and thanked him. He spotted Levi outside the front door. "Can you show me where to sit?"

"Jah. Kumme and I'll introduce you to Mr. and Mrs. Blauch."

Mark's heart thudded against his ribs.

The hay stacked in the loft and on the sides provided his favorite fresh scent. Men dressed like him in all shapes and sizes filled the structure. Husbands sat with their fraas and kinner, and unmarried men sat apart from the unwed women.

Levi gestured to Mr. and Mrs. Blauch. "I'd like you to meet Mark King. He is the man who bought the Stoltzfuses' haus next to my place. You should visit his furniture store in town. He will have to tell you about it."

Mr. Blauch stood and accepted his hand. "Wilkom to Berlin."

Mrs. Blauch rose. "It's a pleasure to meet you. Grace told me what stunning shelves you built for her and Sarah's shop. It was generous of you to take the time to help them out." She pointed to Grace and Sarah. "They will be back in a minute. They are speaking with Jonah Keim, our neighbor's little boy."

Mark traced the brim of his hat with his fingers. "It's a pleasure to meet you both." He sat across from them with the other unwed men and studied Mr. Blauch, who had taken a seat next to Grace's mamm. The man was average height and build. His hands had raised thick blue veins on top. Very little hair remained on his head.

Mrs. Blauch had dimpled cheeks and spectacles sat halfway down her nose. A wisp of brown hair, like Grace's, had escaped her kapp. She was a round, short woman with bright brown eyes like her dochder's. He found them warm and welcoming.

He recognized Grace's voice. She and a little boy, he guessed about six years old, were laughing. The child had an angelic face, brown eyes, brown hair, and a small frame. He was jabbering away.

Grace and Sarah joined him, with the boy between them. "Good morning, Mark. I'd like you to meet my friend, Jonah Keim. Jonah, this is Mark King."

"It's a pleasure to meet you, and you can call me Mark."

Sarah kissed Jonah's head. "He's a sweetheart. I want a son like him."

Jonah pointed to his open mouth. "My tooth popped out when I jumped off the porch last night. I had a hard time bitin' into my apple this mornin'."

They all laughed.

Mark patted the boy's shoulder. "Don't worry. Each day you wake up, little by little your new tooth will appear." He eyed Grace talking to Sarah and returned his attention to Jonah.

"My grossdaadi lost five teeth." Jonah held up his hand. "He told me they won't grow back. I'm scared mine won't grow back either."

"No, your grossdaadi lost his boppli teeth then his big boy teeth grew in, and those are the ones he lost. You're losing your boppli teeth."

"That's good. I need 'em to bite and chew apples and hard candy."

He chuckled. "Grace and Sarah are right. You are a delightful little boy." He tousled the boy's hair.

Jonah swayed to and fro. "Can I sit with you?"

"Jah, if your parents approve of you sitting with me."

Jonah skipped to where his parents were seated.

"He's an adorable little boy." Grace blushed. "Have you met Mamm and Daed?"

"Jah. They're very kind."

She bit her bottom lip and folded her hands. "I'm glad you had a chance to get acquainted with them." She blushed. "Levi, Sarah, and I have told them about you. Now they'll have a face to put with your name." She lowered her chin. "Will you attend the after-church meal?"

Her shyness warmed him. Of course he'd stay for the meal. He wanted to spend time with her. If he wasn't with her, she filled his mind. "Jah, I am. Are you?"

"Yes. You can sit with me and my parents when we eat. I'm sure they'd like to learn more about you. Would you mind?"

"No. I appreciate the invitation."

"The bishop is walking to the front. I should go find my seat."

He waited until Grace sat with her parents and then followed Jonah to his seat with the men. Each time he encountered her, his heart beat a little faster and his mouth went dry. He hadn't experienced this with any other woman.

Jonah beamed and moved close to him. "Mamm and Daed said I could sit with you."

"I'm glad to have a new friend sit next to me. We should be quiet and listen to the bishop."

Jonah put a finger to lips. "I'll be real quiet."

"Please refer to your Ausbund and join me in singing this hymn."

Mark turned the page and shared his Ausbund with Jonah. He recited the song along with the members. Mark's voice and heart soared with the familiar words. This was music for the soul.

Glancing at Grace, he could envision spending many more Sundays with her. He paused. Her voice was faint, but the sweet and smooth sound of it warmed his heart.

Jonah stood obediently by his side and chanted the words he must've known from heart. He vocalized the song in rhythm with them and stared straight ahead at the bishop. The child was well-behaved and splendid company.

The bishop led them in several hymns and then asked them to bow their heads for prayer. He prayed then preached on obedience for the next two hours. At the end of the sermon, he closed his Bible. "Everyone must adhere to the Amish laws written in the Ordnung. These laws are meant to protect us from the outside world. Be fervent in your prayer life and diligent in obedience." The bishop prayed for the after-meeting meal and dismissed them.

Jonah tugged at his sleeve. "Danki for letting me sit with you."

"You can sit with me anytime, as long as your parents give their permission. You are an adorable little boy."

Jonah waved and scampered toward his parents.

Mark watched the child. His mind drifted back to the sermon. It was as if Bishop Weaver's message was directed at him. Would he wilkom Abel into his haus if he showed up on his porch? He needed prayers for himself and his bruder.

Grace interrupted his thoughts. "I'll find you after I help the women prepare the table."

"All right. I'll talk with your daed."

Searching for Mr. Blauch, he spotted him heading out the door. He caught up to him. "The bishop gave a good message."

"He's an excellent bishop. We're blessed to have him." He stopped under the shade of an old oak tree. "Levi told me your parents suffered a tragic accident. I'm sorry for your loss. I was saddened to learn the Stoltzfuses have died. We were mere acquaintances, due to their short time living here. I understand from Levi you had the opportunity to befriend them in Lancaster."

"Jah. They were a kind couple."

"You must be glad Mr. Stoltzfus had a workshop on his property. Levi tells me you handcraft items out of wood. What do you create and from what type of wood?"

Nerves had given him a slight headache, but Mr. Blauch had put him at ease. The pain diminished. "The workshop is perfect for me. When I resided in Lancaster,

I handcrafted wooden furniture, toys, and household items out of maple, pine, and oak. I sold half of my supply before I left and brought the rest to sell in my store. When you have time, kumme in. I'll show you around."

He crossed his arms. "I'll take you up on your offer and stop in sometime. Do you need advice on where to find livestock to buy?"

"No, danki." He recounted his story about meeting Mr. Post and how he bought the man's livestock for a reasonable price.

"You have set yourself up to provide a good living in a short time. Will you have time to manage a store and tend to his hay, and livestock?"

Mark understood he was new in town. It wasn't unusual for elder Amish men to ask the younger men these questions. Grace's daed didn't waste time getting to the point. Mark didn't mind and stifled his urge to chuckle. "I'm in need of a man to manage my place. Who would you suggest?"

"Let me introduce you to Noah Schwartz. He's eighteen and needs work. His mamm, Jane Schwartz, is a widow and works at the bakery in town. They scrape by and could use the money." He gestured for Mark to follow him.

Mr. Blauch approached a man with blond hair and deep blue eyes. The man stood.

"Noah, meet Mark King. He's recently moved here from Lancaster and needs help at his farm. Are you interested?"

Noah stretched out his hand. "It's a pleasure to meet you, Mr. King. I am interested. When can we discuss this?"

Mark shook Noah's hand. He liked Noah on sight. His long legs and muscular arms would kumme in handy lifting bales of hay and minding the animals and his farm.

Noah's enthusiasm impressed him. "We best not discuss this on Sunday. Kumme to my haus at six o'clock tomorrow morning. We'll speak about it then. And call me Mark."

"Danki. I'll be on time."

Mark followed Mr. Blauch to their seats.

Jonah approached him. "You met my friend, Noah. He brings me treats on Sundays." He dug in his pocket and pulled out a wrapped piece of hard candy. "It's red, my favorite." He plopped the sugary gift in his mouth. "I'm going to find Mamm. She helps me fill my plate for dinner." He skipped away.

Mark returned Jonah's wave. Noah's gesture of kindness toward Jonah impressed him. He looked forward to getting better acquainted with him. It would be a worry off his mind to have someone managing his farm.

He turned to Mr. Blauch. "Danki for introducing me to Noah. I'm relieved to find someone to possibly lighten my workload."

"Good." Mr. Blauch put his hand on Mark's shoulder. "Don't hesitate to ask for help if you get in a bind." He pointed at Grace. "And another thing, you're wilkom in our home anytime. It must be tough to live alone without family." He dropped his arm to his side. "The main table is full of food dishes. The women must have everything set out. People are filling their plates. Let's fill ours." Mr. Blauch's pleasant expression showed his approval. This had been a splendid conversation.

Mark swallowed around the lump in his throat. Mr. Blauch had taken an interest in him and treated him like family. The man's kind comments reverberated in his mind. It was a generous offer, considering Grace's daed had his property to manage. If he did need help, he would ask Grace's daed. Mr. Blauch's demeanor and tone seemed sincere.

Mark and Mr. Blauch set their heaping plates on the picnic table and sat.

He winked at Jonah. Did he have anything with him he could give to Jonah? "Mr. Blauch, I'll be back in a minute. I need to fetch something from my wagon."

Mr. Blauch, mouth full, nodded.

He strode to the stable and removed a miniature horse he'd carved from a bag he'd stuffed there to take to his shop tomorrow. He found Jonah with his parents. He exchanged pleasantries with Mr. and Mrs. Keim and then presented the horse to the little boy. "This is for you."

Jonah's mouth flew open. He set his spoon on his plate. "Danki. I'm going to name him Star."

Mark cocked his head. "Why?"

"You painted a white spot on his head. I'm going to pretend it's a star."

He laughed. "I like the name." He ruffled Jonah's curls. "Take care, Jonah."

The boy hugged Mark's legs then sat on the bench next to his daed.

Jonah's parents thanked him and wilkomed him to the community.

Mark returned to his seat and pulled his plate closer. "I'm anxious to sample everything on my plate." He picked up the soft white bread and slathered it with chicken spread, then separated his pickles, beets, and celery into sections. He placed two oatmeal cookies on the corner of his plate.

Mr. Blauch dipped his spoon in buttered peas. "Everything is scrumptious."

Grace passed them two jars. "Here's lemonade to drink. Do you need anything else?"

Mark smiled through full cheeks and shook his head.

Moments later, she returned with her plate arrayed with much smaller portions of vegetables. She sat next to him.

Mrs. Blauch joined them and held an apple. "Would you like this, Mark? I grabbed it for you. I noticed you don't have any fruit."

The act touched him. Mrs. Blauch's thoughtful gesture reminded him of his mamm. He missed her love and attention. A decent cook, he could almost taste his favorite foods of vegetable stew, bread pudding, and apple tarts. He accepted the apple. "Danki. I appreciate it."

They conversed about the warm day, the delectable food the women had prepared, and how blessed they were to have a bishop to deliver such a fine sermon.

Mark drew in a breath. The message was good, but the man's subject matter touched a little too close to home.

After they finished their meal, the women gathered baskets and loaded them in their wagons.

Ever since he met Grace, he sensed a spark between them. The more he talked to her, the more he liked her. They had skirted around their emotions with longing looks and kind words. She had captured his heart. He gestured her aside. "Your parents are delightful. Your daed offered me an open invitation to visit him at any time. You're blessed to have such gracious parents."

"Mamm and Daed have soft hearts. I'm pleased you're comfortable around them."

Levi and Sarah joined them, and they quieted. "We wanted to say farewell before we left. I'll see you both tomorrow." The couple sauntered off to retrieve their wagon.

"I should go home and check on my animals, but I don't want to leave you." Mark darted his eyes around. No one paid attention to them. He squeezed her hand for a moment. She didn't jerk it away. Her soft skin and dainty fingers warmed his heart. He released it before anyone noticed.

Her face pinked. "Join Sarah and me for dinner tomorrow."

"I look forward to it." He waited until she'd reached her parents then walked to the barn to retrieve his buggy. On the way home, he laughed at the deer frolicking in the meadow. He nodded to the stagecoach driver passing by.

He liked the direction his life was taking, and especially the prospect of having Grace as a potential fraa. He was twenty-two and didn't want to wait much longer to wed and start a family. Precious Grace might be the one. Jah, this had been a perfect day.

Arriving home, he secured his horse. Last night he'd searched for a larger kettle he remembered packing when he left Lancaster. Where had he put it? Maybe he'd find it in the old trunk he brought from home. In the corner of the barn, he peeked inside.

He gasped and lifted a flour sack. He hadn't packed this bag. Dropping it, he ran outside and scanned his property. Quiet, and no one in sight, he rushed to the trunk. Who put it in here? He reached for it and untied the bundle. A box of Blue Diamond matches and a jar of water lay inside. Had the same intruder who'd sought shelter in his barn left this here? *Abel?* He shook his head. Abel would ask him for help. The stranger must be hiding from the law or too proud to ask for food and shelter. Why had this stranger chosen his barn to stash his belongings? He didn't want any trouble. He stuffed it where he found it. Maybe the owner would kumme back and claim his stash, and he'd confront him. He'd keep a close eye out.

Chapter Four

Grace woke to the rooster's crow Monday morning. She blinked a few times and sat up in bed. Her life had taken a wilkom change meeting Mark. His face flashed in her mind before she went to bed and when she opened her eyes. She'd pictured herself living with her parents or in a small home alone for the rest of her life. Mark presented possibilities she hadn't allowed herself to dwell on. She hoped their interest grew and resulted in marriage. She was enjoying the hope she felt in her heart that she may experience being a fraa and mamm someday. She rose, dressed, and joined Mamm in the kitchen. "Bacon smells delightful."

Sliding the rest of the bacon from the skillet onto a plate, Mamm raised her eyebrows. "You're chipper this morning." She gave her a mischievous grin. "Does Mark King have anything to do with your cheery mood? You like him, don't you?"

She suspected her mamm worried her dochder would remain a spinster. Grace had wondered if God planned to have her remain unwed, since more than one man had rejected her daed's offer to arrange a marriage with her.

She remembered waiting for her daed to kumme home and the first time he'd left to ask a man to marry her. The man had met her in church. He'd stared at the ground, and she'd hoped he was just shy and not avoiding looking at her cheek. Hope rang in her heart until her daed told her the man had declined his offer. No matter how kind her daed was in delivering the hurtful news, the words *ugly, alone,* and *unwanted* flashed in her mind and filled her with dread.

Six months later, her daed begged her permission to arrange another marriage. She had relented and regretted it. The man came to the door, took one look at her, winced, and said he couldn't look at her face for the rest of his life and left. Her daed told her with tears in his eyes how sorry he was to have asked the man. He'd misjudged him. She felt ugly, alone, and unwanted all over again.

Grace never wanted to settle for an arranged marriage in the first place, but she thought it was the only way she'd ever have kinner. Her desire was to fall in love with the man she would wed, but she hadn't thought it might be possible until now. "I do like him. I've enjoyed learning about him these past weeks."

"At church yesterday, I noticed the gleam in his eye when he looked at you." Mamm patted her hand. "The good news is your daed likes him." Mamm joined her at the table.

It was important her parents approved of Mark, since she considered him a potential husband. "Maybe God sent Mark to Berlin for me."

Mamm spooned scrambled eggs onto Grace's plate and hers then sat. A smile lighted her face. "God sends us surprises when we least expect them. Maybe you're right."

Grace gulped her breakfast down in four bites, grabbed

her bag, the picnic basket, and crossed the grassy yard to the barn. She raised her chin, closed her eyes, and let the breeze spread across her face. Summer was delightful. She secured her horse and buckboard. On the way, she waved to friends passing her. She waited her turn at the busy stable then handed the liveryman her horse's reins. Strolling to the shop, she waved to friends opening their stores. The familiar rattle of wooden buggy wheels sounded on the dirt road in the middle of town. The peddler stood haggling with a man over one of his more elegant canes. An Englischer shook his fist at a driver kumming to close to him.

She turned her key in the lock and opened the door to their store. The connecting door opened. She jumped and brought her hand to her mouth. Mark's handsome face stared back at her.

"Good morning. I didn't mean to startle you."

She giggled. "I'm fine."

"I met with Noah Schwartz this morning, and he's agreed to work for me. Thanks to your daed, my life should be much easier from now on. Noah was determined to start work right away. He's working at my place as we speak."

"You'll not regret your decision. Noah's a hard worker and has a cheerful disposition. He's a pleasant person to have around. My daed has asked him for assistance a number of times. He liked Noah's work ethic and his bright outlook on life."

"Do you have any concerns about him?"

"He's curious about the world. Daed worries he's too inquisitive. He's eighteen and has joined the church, committing to the Amish life, but he seems restless at times.

Daed fears he'll visit the outside world and not kumme back."

"Maybe his choosing to work for me is a sign he's planning on staying. I'll do what I can to tamp down his interest in the outside world." Mark perused the shop. "You're not busy yet. Let me show you what I brought in today."

She stepped inside his shop. He'd added more rocking horses for small Englischer kinner. The wooden horses had carved manes and big eyes. Unlike the first rocking horses he brought in to the store, leather reins hung attached for small fingers to grasp. Amish maedels would like the faceless dolls. Full-length trains on the bottom shelf now had cabooses next to them. The same three-inch tic-tac-toe wooden *X*'s and *O*'s on gray and black squared boards filled the second shelf.

Sarah entered. "Good morning. I hoped I'd find you here."

Grace waved her over. "Cast your eyes on this hope chest. It's exquisite."

Mark blushed. "Jah, kumme in, Sarah."

Sarah scurried over. "This is the most gorgeous hope chest I have ever laid eyes on." She stroked the top. "It's smooth and the perfect size. I love it."

Grace opened the lid. "Mark, you outdid yourself on this piece." She bent over and inhaled the fragrant scent of the wood. "Cedar smells so fresh and clean."

Mark stuffed his hands in his pockets. "You're kind. I must admit, cedar chests are my favorite to make."

"I'll go back to the store. Grace, you stay for a while and visit." Sarah strode through the open door.

Mrs. Fisher and her dochder, Eve, entered. Both women ignored Grace but smiled at Mark. The woman paraded her dochder past Mark twice then paused. "I'm Mrs. Fisher." She gestured to the attractive young woman beside her. "I'd like you to meet my dochder, Eve. She baked you a sugar cream pie to wilkom you to the community. Are you free for supper this evening? She's not married and I understand you aren't either. The two of you should get acquainted. She's quite the cook. Wait until you taste her pie."

Grace stepped back and stiffened.

Eve blushed and stared at the floor as she handed the dessert to Mark.

Mark accepted the pie. "I'm sorry. I must decline your offer, but it's a pleasure to meet you both. I appreciate your invitation and the pie. Danki."

Grace grimaced. Could the woman have been more obvious? How awkward this must be for Mark. Mrs. Fisher spoke with a sharp tongue and direct tone and seldom smiled. The woman would be a difficult mamm-in-law for any man. Grace studied Eve. Available and two years younger than she, Eve had flawless skin, a sweetheart-shaped face, a petite frame, blond hair, and the biggest deep blue eyes. She had said nothing. Would Mark consider her for a potential fraa? Maybe Eve's mamm's forward behavior wouldn't bother him. She quaked at the troublesome thought.

Mrs. Fisher pinched her lips. "No. We'll be on our way. I must warn you, Eve won't be available for long." She winced at Grace's birthmark and paused. "And there aren't many marriageable *attractive* Amish women in our community at present."

Grace gasped and put a hand to her mouth. This woman had some nerve staring at her birthmark at the same time she emphasized the word *attractive*. She opened her mouth to speak but bit her tongue. No good would kumme from arguing with the abrasive woman.

Mark set the pie on the counter. "I understand, Mrs. Fisher. Have a nice day."

"Mark, I should join Sarah." Grace hurried to her shop before he had a chance to say a word.

Sarah gave her a sideways glance and peered out the window. "Were Eve and her mamm in Mark's store? They're getting into their buggy out front. You raced in here. Did Mrs. Fisher have anything to do with your hasty exit from Mark's store?"

"Yes. Eve and her mamm brought him a pie. Eve didn't speak a word. She might have if her mamm had given her a chance."

"Mrs. Fisher is overbearing and rude. A smile doesn't cross that woman's face unless she's in the presence of the bishop." She hung an apron on a maple wooden hook rack for display. "I was going to kumme and fetch you. I need help unhooking a pinwheel keepsake pocket quilt from the wall for Lydia Keim, Jonah's mamm. I told her I'd ask you to help me take it down while she goes to the bakery for a few minutes."

Together, they unhooked the quilt Sarah pointed out.

"Mrs. Fisher has her sights on Mark for Eve's husband. I'm afraid he'll want to rescue Eve from her mamm. She's also the prettiest Amish woman in our community."

Sarah scoffed. "Mrs. Fisher has remained a widow for a reason. In my opinion, she's the pushiest Amish woman in our community. She's ruined her dochder's chances of marrying any Amish man. They don't want to put up with her mamm."

Frowning, Grace lowered her voice. "Mark is a compassionate man. She's like a wounded bird who needs saving."

Sarah marched in front of Grace and placed her hands

on her friend's shoulders. "You mustn't dwell on Eve and Mark. He's smitten with you. His eyes sparkle when you walk into the room." She tapped Grace's nose. "The man hangs on your every word." She waved a dismissive hand. "Eve's mamm is too late. She'll have to find another man for her dochder to wed."

Grace circled her arm around Sarah's waist. "What would I do without you? You put my fears to rest when I doubt myself. Danki."

"You do the same for me. We're blessed to have each other."

Jonah's mamm entered. "Good morning, Grace and Sarah. You two look as fresh as daisies. Grace, I noticed you talking to Jonah's new friend, Mark, after the service Sunday. You two are the perfect picture of a happy couple." Lydia Keim fluttered her eyelashes. "Don't let him get away. Word has gotten around town Mark is available and a very ambitious young man to manage hay, garden, animals, and store. My neighbor, Mrs. Fisher, has her sights set on Mark for Eve's husband. She hasn't stopped talking about what a splendid match he would be for her dochder. You and he are a better match, in my opinion. Mark would find Mrs. Fisher a nuisance. Your mamm is a delightful woman."

Sarah blew a stray hair from her face. "I agree with you, Lydia." She removed the price note from the quilt and penciled the sale in the journal. "This star pattern is one of my favorite quilts. I hope you'll be pleased with it."

Grace held her tongue. She fought to not agree with Lydia. Her excitement about Mark was a private matter. Not one she wanted to discuss with anyone but her family and Sarah. Lydia meant well, but she had a wagging tongue. "Danki for your encouragement." She wanted to change to the subject. "How's Jonah?"

Lydia removed the reticule off her wrist, dug into it, and pulled out coins. She pressed the money in Sarah's palm. "Danki, Sarah." She beamed. "Jonah's fine. He carries the miniature wooden horse Mark gave him in his pocket. Last night, he put it on his bedside table." She picked up her quilt. "I must be on my way. It's been nice talking to you both."

Sarah opened a tin of pins. "I agree with Lydia. You and Mark do make the perfect picture couple, not Eve and Mark."

"We can speculate all we want, but we don't have any idea what Mark's thoughts are on Eve and her mamm. He is a man, nonetheless." The door opened. Hester Harris had kumme at the perfect time. Grace didn't want to talk about Mark and Eve anymore today.

"I've missed you. It's so good to see you."

Hester entered carrying a package. "I was in town and thought I'd stop in and pay you a visit." She pushed her long, dark braid over her shoulder and adjusted her spectacles. "My neighbor is friends with Mrs. Watson. She told me you delivered the woman's newborn and said the birth went without a hitch." Her eyes twinkled. "As your midwife teacher, I'm proud of you." She kissed her on the cheek.

Sarah pinned a price note to a quilt and put it on the shelf. "Mrs. Watson's dochder arrived earlier than she expected. She'd kumme to shop and spend time with her friend. I'm amazed every time she tells me about helping a mamm birth her boppli."

"Grace studied the books I lent her and did everything I requested. She was an excellent student." She beamed. "I visited Becca Carrington in Massillon last week. She loves working as a nurse for her husband, Dr. Carrington. We reminisced about the two of you learning midwifery together. She asked if I'd bring you this gift." She passed the package wrapped in a white cotton fabric held together with pink ribbon tied in a bow.

"I miss her." Grace untied the pink ribbon and peeled back the delicate material. Her mouth opened as she unfolded and held up the blue and white friendship patterned quilt. "She sewed a little heart in the two circles intertwined." She hugged the quilt to her chest. "She and I shared many happy memories together. I love it."

Hester fingered the material. "I like the feel of this cotton." She patted the pocket in the corner. "Becca sends her love along with it."

Grace tilted it to examine the pattern closer.

Sarah frowned and scrambled to catch the note fluttering to the floor. She drew her mouth in a grim line and offered it to Grace.

"Danki, Sarah. I'll read it later." Grace accepted the note and tucked it in her apron pocket. She loved Hester and Sarah, but Becca had been her true best friend. It hadn't been long since Sarah had scolded about communicating with Becca. She suspected Sarah would admonish her again about accepting Becca's gift and mentioning her friend's name. She'd discuss this with Sarah later.

Two patrons entered. Sarah went to help them. She furrowed her eyebrows. "Grace, you visit with Hester. I can help these women."

"Danki, Sarah."

Hester dragged a wooden chair over to the table and sat. "Becca delivered twins two days after I arrived. I wish you would've been there with us. As an outsider, I don't understand why the Amish refuse to maintain a friendship with their loved ones who have left the Amish life. I'm thankful it's acceptable for you and me to converse since we're both midwives."

Grace covered Hester's hand. Her friend had dark circles under her eyes and the lines had grown in number on her face. She loved her teacher and friend. She relished having an outsider to talk with about Becca. "Since you've never been Amish, I understand why you wouldn't agree with it. The law to shun those who joined the Amish church then left the Amish life is meant to protect us from world views. I struggle with it where Becca is concerned."

"It's easy for me to visit her since I've never been Amish, but I feel sorry for you. You're fortunate your parents turned a blind eye to your writing to her for as long as you did. Sarah didn't ask about Becca. Her stern face tells me she's upset about the mention of Becca's name. She obviously agrees with the law to shun Becca."

"She is angry about my contact with Becca. It's not a subject I care to discuss with her. Although, she's right. I would be horrified if the bishop found out."

"Please understand, I wouldn't mention you contacting Becca to anyone else. I thought Sarah would be the exception, since you two are close." Hester stared at her lap. "I'm sorry. I shouldn't have brought this gift here or discussed Becca in front of her. I've put you in a terrible position."

Grace gripped her apron. "She doesn't realize how hard this is for me."

"Should I apologize to Sarah for bringing up Becca?"

Grace patted her friend's hand. "No. Don't worry about it. She'll be fine."

Hester stood and hugged Grace. "Come visit me when you can. I must go. Thank your father for feeding my livestock while I've been away." She opened the door and departed.

Sarah handed change to the women who'd bought pink and white ruffled aprons and bid them farewell. Sarah joined Grace and pointed at the quilt. "You shouldn't have accepted this gift from Becca or talked about her with Hester. We've discussed you having anything to do with her a number of times." She scoffed. "I never understood your friendship with her. She complained about wearing pins on our clothes instead of buttons, and she talked openly about what it might be like to live in the world. It was wrong. I stayed away from her. You should have done the same." She rested her hands on her hips.

Grace wiped a tear. "My memories of spending time with Becca quilting, delivering bopplin, and sharing our hopes and dreams are precious. I care about her very much. She's a lovely person with a big heart. She's a mid-wife and a nurse who helps the sick and those in need. When she married Matt, she didn't abandon her good moral values or her strong faith in God." Grace covered Sarah's hand. "Please don't be angry with me. I thought we'd put this subject to bed."

Sarah's voice softened. She dropped her chin to her chest but kept eye contact. "I didn't mean to upset you. I apologize for my wagging tongue. You're my best friend." Her lips quivered. "Please forgive me. I must ask forgive-ness for my harsh words against Becca in my prayers tonight." She grasped Grace's hand. "Please tell Hester to deliver any gifts from her to you in private."

"I told Hester I was wrong to keep in touch with Becca. She understands. Hester offered to apologize to you for bringing up Becca's name and delivering the quilt to me here. I told her you wouldn't expect her to apologize. Am I right?"

Sarah fidgeted with her kapp ribbon. "Jah. Hester is innocent in this. She didn't mean any harm. The bishop finding out about your offense scares me. If we were ordered by the bishop to shun you, it would break my heart. I don't know if I could do it."

Grace blew out a sigh of relief. Thankful she and Sarah agreed on Hester's innocence in this matter. Sarah's warning sent shivers through her. She pictured neighbors and friends passing by them without a word, not socializing with them at church, picnics, or anywhere. It would be like they were invisible. "I'm not writing to her anymore."

Sarah stood. "I'm glad. Then I can stop worrying about you getting into trouble. It's for your own well-being."

Grace pulled out the sales journal and pretended to read it. Memories flashed through her mind of times spent laughing, sewing, and baking with Becca through the years before she departed for Massillon. She would love Becca until the day she died. The connecting door squeaked open.

Mark rubbed his forehead. "Is it time for dinner yet? I have sugar cream pie."

This had been a difficult day. First, her encounter with Mrs. Fisher and Mark's introduction to Eve, and then her spat with Sarah, and now Mark had mentioned Eve's dessert. She wanted to throw Eve's pie out the back door. She didn't want Mark to have anything to do with the young woman. Could this day get any worse? Oh yes, it could. He'd probably bite into the pie and find out Eve was a wonderful baker. "Kumme in. I'll set the table."

Grace removed her picnic basket from behind the counter and brought out ham sandwiches and jars of water. She couldn't get Eve's face out of her mind. Guilt pricked her heart. The woman had done nothing wrong. Grace's fear and jealousy were taking over again. She should rise above it, but the anger stewing wouldn't go away.

Mark slid their chairs in a circle, and Sarah joined them. "I'll pray." Mark bowed his head. "Dear Heavenly

Father, forgive us for our sins. Danki for the food we are about to eat. We praise You for your love, mercy, and protection. Amen." He brought the sandwich to his mouth then paused. "I found a flour sack in an old trunk in my barn. It doesn't belong to me. The man must've left it."

Sarah traced the rim of her jar. "Levi's convinced he's gone, since there's been no sign of him lately. He's asked around town and not one person has had anything stolen lately."

"The intruder could've stashed his bag in my trunk weeks ago. It's hard to tell when he put it there."

Grace gasped. "What did you do with the bag?"

"I put it back. Maybe he'll return for it and I'll catch him. I'd like to talk to him about why he's hiding and stealing things."

"I still believe he was in need of shelter and food." Grace sipped her water. She swallowed around the lump in her throat. More important things were on her mind, namely, Eve. She wasn't in a pleasant mood. She'd stay quiet. Maybe a long prayer of asking God's forgiveness for her jealousy and anger and a good night's sleep tonight would improve her demeanor tomorrow.

Mark finished his sandwich in minutes. He tugged the pie close and cut three pieces. He served a piece to each of them. He spooned some in his mouth. "This is the best sugar cream pie I've ever put into my mouth. Wait until you taste it."

She'd been correct about Mark liking Eve's pie. She wanted to scream and bit her tongue.

Mark paused. "Grace, is anything wrong?"

She wouldn't admit she was jealous of another woman. She pressed her hand on her birthmark. Could she blame him if he found Eve or any other available Amish woman attractive? The threat of other women being interested in

Mark hadn't entered her mind until Eve showed up. Grace had enjoyed their time together, and he treated her with respect, helped her when she needed it, listened to her worries, and delighted in her joyful times. But was it more than friendship to him? The way he gazed into her eyes, squeezed her hand the other day, and listened to her every word had convinced her she meant more to him than a friend. Had she misunderstood?

She closed her eyes a moment to hide her despair. "No, I'm fine."

Sarah covered her hand. "Your eyes are bloodshot and you haven't been your usual chipper self. Go home and get some rest. I can manage the store this afternoon."

"No, I want to stay."

A customer entered. Grace hurried to get away from Mark and greeted the woman. "May I help you?" She turned back to look at Mark.

Mark shrugged. "Danki for dinner."

She nodded then waited for the patron's response.

The woman fingered a star-patterned quilt in pink and yellow fabrics. "I'd like to purchase this beauty." Grace unhooked the quilt from the wall and carried it to the counter. She showed the woman the pocket and explained its intended use.

"What a brilliant idea. I must have it." The customer unpinned the price note. Digging in her reticule, the woman pulled out the money and paid Grace. She accepted the quilt. "This is a magnificent handcrafted quilt. I'm going to give it to my beloved aunt."

The patron departed, and Grace joined Sarah. "I'm fretting about losing Mark to another woman. I can't stop my mind from going there."

"You must not dwell on Mark and other women. You're wasting your time. He's not interested in anyone but you.

If you treat him like you did at dinner today, you might turn him away. Be kind to him. He doesn't deserve your cold shoulder. Pouting isn't going to get you anywhere with him."

Grace quaked. It hurt when he spoke words of admiration for Eve. Jealousy was an ugly emotion. Her heart thudded. The thought of Mark pursuing Eve or any other woman sickened her. This was a small town. If he did choose someone else, she was bound to run into them at church and community picnics.

Showing interest in Mark had put her in a vulnerable position. The risk of getting hurt had been worth it. She had enjoyed getting to know him, having him look at her like she mattered and was pretty, and the hope it might turn into something more one day.

She closed her eyes for a moment and cringed. Her behavior had been childish this past week. Ashamed and embarrassed, she needed to talk to him. She hoped it wasn't too late.

Mark lay in bed early Tuesday morning and stared at the ceiling. Grace had avoided him and spoke little in his presence. Something was bothering her. He'd rehashed their conversations. He couldn't kumme up with anything he'd said or done to displease her. He didn't like this side of her. Honesty and communication were important to him. He'd ask her again today, but in a firm tone. He wouldn't let her dismiss the problem between them.

He washed at the sink, dressed, and advanced to the barn to find Noah. The young man worked hard and did everything Mark asked in a timely manner. Noah whistled while he worked, something Mark had never mastered.

His new friend worked hard and was a delight to have around. He told Noah he suspected an intruder slept in his barn and told him about the bag the man had left. "Keep an eye out for anything unusual. I don't want any harm to kumme to you. Maybe you shouldn't work here alone."

Noah paused and stood feet apart, head held high. "I'm not afraid. I can take care of myself. Please don't ask me to stop working for you. The money you pay me has made life easier for Mamm and me."

"Since the intruder hasn't hurt anyone, and you're a tall and strong man, I'll let you continue working. But again, please be aware of your surroundings." He smiled at the relief on Noah's face. "I'm on my way to the store. Anything you need?"

Noah unhooked a hammer off a rusted metal hook in the barn. He checked his tool belt. "No, I have everything I need to mend the corral fence. It will take me most of today to get it done. You have a pleasant day. Don't worry. I'll be fine."

Mark tipped his hat to Noah, readied his spring wagon, and headed for the store. The fields boasted of lilacs and scented the air as he passed. Everything appeared brighter and more brilliant since Grace had become a part of his life.

He went to the livery then crossed the boardwalk and opened his store. He had grown roots in Berlin. Strangers were now friends and neighbors. He had lost touch with his friends in Lancaster and it no longer mattered. Before he left, his time was spent working on the farm, hand-crafting furniture, and dealing with his parents' death and Abel's exit from the Amish life.

Grace had been quiet and distant around him recently. He was determined to find out before the day's end why she was upset with him. Unlocking the door to his shop, he contemplated when would be the best time to approach her.

For the next few hours, he greeted patrons. The clock in the corner of the store chimed noon. He penciled a note "Will return at twelve thirty" and posted it on the inside of the window.

Sarah popped her head around the connecting door. "I have vegetable soup warmed for dinner. Are you going to join us?"

"Jah. Danki." He followed her.

Grace stood at the counter. His beautiful Grace had had sad eyes for a week. Best to confront her while Sarah busied herself at the stove. "Grace, please tell me what's wrong, and don't say you're fine. You're not."

He waited.

Grace twisted her mouth then gazed at him. "It's not a subject I want to discuss with you. Please respect my wishes."

Mark crossed his arms and glared at her. "No, I won't respect your wishes. I care about you, Grace. I don't like this distance between us. Tell me what I've done to upset you."

Her face pinked. "I'm not proud of it." She squeezed her eyes shut for a moment. "I'm jealous of Eve. I'm afraid you might find her attractive and consider her for a potential fraa." She dipped her chin to her chest but looked up at him from beneath her dark eyelashes.

Jealousy of Eve was not what he'd expected would be wrong between them. He must not have shown Grace through his words and actions how much he cared for her. From now on, he'd be more mindful in doing so.

He was falling in love with her. She was softhearted, kind, and vulnerable. She was strong, determined, and spoke her mind. She looked at him with a gleam in her eye. It made him feel handsome and good about himself. She was far from lazy working as a midwife, managing a shop, and helping her parents at home. She didn't let her birthmark define her. He wanted a partner he could love and protect, but also consult about financial matters, problems at home and work, and share his ups and downs. He hoped Grace might be that woman.

He didn't want Grace to feel insecure, but safe with him. "I'm not interested in Eve. My interest is in you, and no other woman. Is this all right with you?" He grazed her hand with his fingertips.

Her chin lowered, and she gave him a shy smile. Her skin warmed to his touch. "I should've spoken to you about this earlier. I was embarrassed. I'm sorry."

"Jah, you should have. But I don't want you to shut me out when something is bothering you. Nothing good kummes from fretting over a problem alone. We should discuss our issues so we can resolve them."

Sarah joined them. "Sit, dinner's ready." She darted her eyes from Grace to Mark. "You both have somber faces. Have I interrupted a serious discussion?"

Mark waited for Grace to answer.

"I confessed my thoughts on Eve to Mark and apologized for giving him the cold shoulder this last week."

"It's about time." Sarah's mouth spread in a mischievous grin. "I don't want anything to get in the way of you two finding your way to happiness together. Let's eat."

Sarah and Grace were the two most outspoken young Amish women he'd encountered. Their sense of humor always proved entertaining. Mark chuckled. "Leave it to you, Sarah, to get right to the point and, in this matter, I agree with you." It concerned him he'd had to needle

Grace to get her to share her feelings concerning Eve. How would she handle the next problem they encountered?

He didn't want to have dissension each time a problem arose between them. It wouldn't be the life he had in mind for himself and a potential fraa. Her remorseful apology seemed sincere. He hoped she'd understood just how important voicing her concerns right away were to the success of their future together.

Chapter Five

Grace glimpsed at Sarah then Mark. She should've discussed her concerns about Eve with Mark early on. In minutes, he'd assured her she'd worried for nothing. She wouldn't wait to speak with him the next time something was on her mind.

Sarah sighed. "Let's discuss the Wittmers' barn raising. Mark, Levi said he mentioned it to you. Are you going to kumme to the Wittmers' tomorrow?"

"Jah, I'm bringing ten-inch oak pegs for the project. Levi told me over the past month a group of men have been preparing the roof and beams and other men have prepared the studs for the walls."

Sarah held her spoon in midair. "About ten of the men have already delivered the lumber and supplies to the site. They built and completed the stone and mortar foundation and corner posts four days ago. The Amish men in our community don't hesitate to help those in need. I'm glad you'll be joining them."

Grace pursed her lips. "Mark hasn't had his store open long. This may not be the right time for him." She considered him. "You're under no obligation to attend.

Everyone will understand." She wanted him to attend, but Sarah shouldn't put him on the spot.

"I'm looking forward to working on this project. Noah's already agreed to manage the farm, and I'll close my shop." He stood. "Will you two attend?"

"Yes, we'll be there to serve dinner and have jars of water on hand for the men."

He tipped his hat. "I'll meet you there in the morning." He looked at the clock. "It's time for me to get back to work. Danki for the fine dinner."

"See you tomorrow, Mark." Sarah turned and approached patrons entering the store.

Grace held his gaze until he shut the door behind him. She couldn't wait to watch him swing a hammer and help build the barn tomorrow. Maybe he'd work with her daed and they'd have a chance to chat and get better acquainted. She rinsed and dried the dishes and helped Sarah wait on customers.

Late afternoon, she whispered to Sarah, "We haven't had a minute to catch our breath all day. I'm not complaining, mind you. I've sold eight aprons and four quilts."

"I overheard a patron say something about heading west with a wagon train. Maybe they stopped in Berlin for supplies. I've sold three quilts and six bath towels." She eyed another woman coming in the door. "I'll wait on her."

Grace refolded quilts and stacked them in neat rows on the shelves. She grabbed a broom and swept the dirt off the floor then reviewed their sales for the day. She'd check with Mamm and other Amish women she'd hired to stitch for them and find out how much stock they had on hand. They may need to ask additional Amish women in the neighborhood if they were interested in sewing for money. She counted her supply of dry goods. More quilts, towels, and aprons were needed.

Thirty minutes later, Sarah locked the door and leaned against it. "Whew, I'm tired. The time is five. Let's go home. We've got a long day ahead of us tomorrow." She pinned a note on the door she'd written earlier to notify patrons the shop would be closed the next day.

She peeked in Mark's window. "He's waiting on customers. I won't bother him to say good-bye."

Grace strolled with Sarah to the livery, bid her farewell, and drove home. Wagons trailed in front and behind her on the dirt road. Were drivers guiding their horses slower than usual, or was she impatient? Sighing, she minded the road ahead.

A wild dog ran out ahead, stopped, snarled, and bared his teeth at her.

Her skin prickled, and her body quaked.

A gunshot rang out.

Her body jerked and her stomach clenched.

The wild dog thudded to the ground.

She whipped around. Her jaw dropped.

A woman with golden ringlets and a rose-colored printed dress nodded to her, stowed her gun, and went the other way.

Grace shouted and waved to her. "Danki."

Grace jiggled the reins and prodded her horse into a trot. The woman must practice shooting. Her aim was dead-on. Grace wouldn't complain again about other wagons in front and back of her on the way home.

At home a short while later, Mamm stood in the kitchen with flour in her hair and on her nose. Grace recounted her horrifying encounter with the wild dog and her rescuer. "It was frightening."

Mamm grabbed her shoulders. "Dochder, you've got to learn to shoot, for this reason. I worry about you."

"Daed's pressured me to learn in case I encounter wild

or rabid animals, but I have no desire. The two times I did go with Daed for target practice, I was a terrible shot. All I'm good for with a gun is to fire warning shots. I'll take my chances." She shook her head several times. "Enough talk about this. Do you have quilts, towels, and aprons already sewn?"

"Jah, I have plenty. Five of the other women stopped by today and dropped quilts and aprons off. They're over there." She pointed to a chair in the corner. "I paid them from the money you gave me to keep on hand for such occasions."

"Danki. Their timing couldn't have been better. We'll need them." Oatmeal, butter, and ginger cookies lined the table. Spice and sugar scents drifted from the oven. "You've baked a lot of cookies." No doubt Mamm baked the best cookies in the neighborhood.

Mamm's cheeks dimpled. "Men like to eat. Is Mark going to the Wittmers' tomorrow? I baked an extra batch so there'd be plenty for you to send home with him."

"Yes, he's coming, and he'd never turn down dessert." She loved barn raisings. Mark being there would make it even more enjoyable.

Grace carried a picnic basket and her medical bag Wednesday morning to the spring wagon. She followed Mamm and Daed outside. She recounted her story to Daed about the dog. She'd thought about telling him last night, but dismissed the idea. She was sorry she'd gone against her better judgment and said a word, as he badgered her the rest of the way on the importance of learning to shoot to protect our animals and ones we loved from those that meant to harm us.

Mamm eased her hand on Daed's for a moment.

"All right, I'll stop."

Smiling, Grace nudged her and whispered, "Danki."

Mamm then patted her dochder's hand. "I agree with him, but we've said enough on the matter."

Grace sniffed the honeysuckle and enjoyed the rest of the way.

Mamm wiped her brow with the back of her sleeve. "Some of my wood for the stove fire must've been damp. I had the hardest time getting a flame going this morning for warming breakfast. It put me behind. We'll be late."

"Don't worry. When you arrive with your fried chicken, they'll not mind you being late." Daed chuckled and winked at Grace.

Mamm wrinkled her nose. "I hope I fried enough chicken to please everyone."

Grace studied her parents. The love they shared showed in the words they spoke and the soft looks they exchanged. Would she enjoy a marriage like theirs someday? She thanked God often for such a loving mamm and daed.

Her eyes darted across the eight acres. Muscular horses were tied to shaded oak trees and eight of them grazed on the lush green grass in the larger-than-normal corral. Spring wagons and carts, some in better shape than others, were parked next to a good number of black buggies on a grassy area away from the plain white haus.

An angular pond sparkled. A goose and her four goslings paddled across the quiet water. She squinted at the old building. The tilted and weathered barn appeared rickety. No doubt a heavy windstorm would flatten it to the ground. She stretched her neck. "Where's the new barn's foundation?"

Daed gestured. "It's on the right side of the old structure, over there where Peter Zook is standing. He'll be the

man in charge. He's separated the men in groups already.
I should join them."

"Levi's in the group to the right." She searched for
Mark but couldn't locate him.

Bishop Weaver approached them. "Hand off your reins
to this young man, Wilbur Yoder. He's in charge of taking
care of the stable today."

"Good morning, Bishop." Daed passed the reins to the
red-haired, freckle-faced Wilbur. "Danki, Wilbur."

Wilbur gave him a curt nod and accepted the reins.
"Wilkom, Mr. Blauch."

Mamm jumped from the wagon. "I'm sorry we're late."
She grabbed her food basket from the back.

Bishop Weaver waved a dismissive hand. "You're for-
given." He pointed. "The women are putting their baskets
of food on the tables in front of the haus."

Grace looped her arm through her mamm's. She peeked
inside the basket and raised the dish cover. The food hadn't
spilled. *Yum*. Mamm had cooked a pan of chicken and
buttered noodles. She'd definitely spoon some of this
onto her plate at dinner. "Mamm, you outdid yourself on
this food."

Daed grabbed his wooden-handled toolbox. "I'm off
to swing a hammer."

Mamm tilted her head and dimpled her cheeks. "Don't
work too hard."

Grace smiled at the easy manner between her parents
and walked alongside Mamm to the outside table. She set
her dish on the table and pointed. "There's Mark."

"Good morning." Sarah placed her crate of covered
dishes next to Mamm's. "A lot of men showed up today."
She raised her hand and shaded her eyes from the sun.
"Mark and Levi are working on the wall frames."

"I'm going to love watching their progress throughout

the day." Grace picked up an empty pitcher off the table, crossed the yard, and pumped water into it. *What a gorgeous sunny day the Lord has provided.* She returned to the table and Sarah filled jars with water.

"Let's join the other women and gossip with them for a while."

A little while later, she put her mouth close to Sarah's ear. "Until dinner, there's not much else to do. Let's sit under the shade tree next to the pond for a few minutes. We can watch the men work."

Sarah pointed. "The kinner are playing hide-and-seek away from where we'll be sitting. We can chat and have a clear view for watching the barn raising."

They commented on the men's fast progress and talent.

Grace covered her eyes. "I like how they heave and lift the wall frame in perfect unison, but this part scares me. I'm always afraid the frame will fall on the men." She squeezed her eyes closed. "I can't look."

"I counted fifteen men holding the ropes on the left side of the frame and twelve on the right side ready to push it up with their poles. They've got plenty of men to raise the frame and place it into position. I'm sure it'll go without a hitch. This is my favorite part. The other men are in place, ready to connect it to the posts. Open your eyes, Grace."

Mr. Zook yelled, "Men, on the count of three, pull and push. One! Two! Three!"

She opened her eyes and squinted in the bright sun. The men had raised the wall into place. She flung her arm around Sarah and squealed. "They did it!"

Mamm waved them over. "The first wall frame has been hung. Your time under the shade tree has lasted long enough. Kumme help set the table for dinner."

Sarah sighed. "I wish Levi's parents could've been here

today. We're fortunate to have our parents. Levi's daed said raising a barn resembled putting a big puzzle together. He used to take charge."

"I remember. He was a respectable and compassionate man. It's like connecting all the pieces together to form a beautiful picture." She tilted her head. "I'm blessed Mamm and Daed are spry. I feel sorry for Levi and Mark for having lost their parents. I can't imagine something happening to Mamm and Daed." She shivered. "Let's not talk about this anymore. Kumme on, you can watch your husband work while we help set up. I'm definitely going to steal glimpses at Mark." She giggled.

They walked to the table and joined the women.

Grace removed dishes out of the handwoven baskets and peeked inside each dish. *Yum.* Peach tarts had filling oozing out both sides. Pickled cucumbers, beets, and eggs lined the second dish. Fluffy white corn bread occupied another. The women had outdone themselves bringing such scrumptious food.

Friends and neighbors arranged the dinner dishes on the right side of the food table and desserts on the left.

Mark headed toward her. She met him halfway. His sweat-stained shirt clung to his muscular body. No matter. She'd stand or sit next to him anytime.

"Your arms must hurt from hammering."

"I like the scent of wood and using my hands to create things. The men who prepared the oak girders, beams, posts, and studs did an excellent job. I'm impressed. They were precise when they cut and measured the joints. They're the best I've ever used on a project. We should have the rest of the walls with windows in place, roof on, and barn doors hung by four this afternoon."

"I noticed you paused to speak to the men several times. Were you instructing them on what to do?"

His chin lowered to his chest and he stared at the ground. "Jah. Mr. Zook asked if I'd direct the men in my group."

Mark certainly wasn't an arrogant man. Another trait she'd add to the list of what she loved about him.

"Don't be embarrassed. I'm certain the men are appreciative you're sharing your expertise."

"Danki. I wasn't sure how they'd take a newcomer telling them what to do, but they seemed to appreciate my guidance, which is a relief." His eyes drifted to the food. "My stomach has rumbled all morning. I'm hungry."

The bishop whistled. "Please bow your heads and join me in a word of prayer." He closed his eyes. "Dear Heavenly Father, danki for the men and supplies here today. Please protect these men from harm as they work to complete their task. Danki for the excellent food these women have prepared for us. All this we ask and pray in Your name, Amen." He raised his head. "Let's finish our meals in a short time and get back to work."

"Kumme and sit with me." She handed Mark a plate and scooped pickled vegetables, corn bread, fried chicken and buttered noodles, oatmeal cookies, and a peach tart onto hers. She noticed he chose the same. They joined Levi and Sarah.

Sarah passed two jars of water to her. "Taste the peach tart. It's scrumptious."

"Danki." She pinched off a corner of the tart and put it in her mouth. "I'm eating it first. It's mouthwatering delicious."

Mark winked. "I'm taking your advice and devouring my dessert first. The men are in a hurry to get back to work. I want to make sure I have enough time to eat my oatmeal cookies." He bit off a piece and moaned. "Yum, this cookie is scrumptious."

She slid a bag of cookies to him. "Mamm baked you an extra batch to take home." She sipped her water. "Have you met Mr. Wittmer?"

"Jah. Mr. Wittmer is a kind man. He sits in his chair and scrutinizes our every move. He hasn't wiped the smile off his face since we started at six. The minute we dropped our hammers, he got up, strolled to each group, and thanked us for our hard work." Mark hurried to eat everything on his plate.

"He's a sweetheart." Grace opened her mouth to speak again but closed it.

Mark didn't have much time to clear his plate. She'd give him time to finish his dinner. Mark's shoulder brushed hers. Her pulse raced. What would it be like to have his arms circle around her? She closed her eyes for a moment. What was she thinking? She mustn't entertain such thoughts. It wasn't proper.

Mark interrupted her musings. "The men are heading back to work already. I should join them. I'm glad we sat together, Grace. I'll share my cookies with them." He winked. "I'll find you before I leave."

Her breath caught at his smile and his promise. "I look forward to it."

Grace and Sarah helped the women rinse and stow their empty dishes in their baskets and transferred leftover food to containers. Sarah whispered in Grace's ear. "How are you and Mark getting along?"

"I think I'm falling in love with him."

"Do you think he's falling in love with you?"

She shrugged and smiled. "He said he's interested in me and not any other woman when we talked about my insecurities concerning Eve. We've shared our thoughts and feelings about friends and things that matter to us. I doubt he'd share this information with just any woman."

Sarah grinned. "He leans in when he talks to you, makes eye contact, and is in our shop for dinner often. You are his focus. I like him. I'm happy you and he have met and are attracted to each other. It will be interesting to see what the future holds for you and Mark."

"I appreciate your support, Sarah." She paused. "Is something wrong with Mr. Wittmer?"

Sarah craned her neck. "Let's find out."

Women and men were running to where Mr. Wittmer had been sitting.

Grace stopped Mrs. Beiler. "Has something happened to Mr. Wittmer?"

"Mr. Wittmer has fallen. He won't rouse."

Grace dropped the dish she held and wiped her hands on her apron. She heard Sarah's footsteps behind her, but she knew her friend couldn't run as fast. Grace had no time to wait on her. She followed a crowd of women. Where was Mrs. Wittmer? She weaved her way through the crowd and stared down at the widow next to her lifeless husband and Mr. Zook.

Mr. Zook knelt on the ground beside Mrs. Wittmer. "I'm sorry. He's gone. He groaned and clutched his chest then he slid out of his chair to the ground." His hands trembled. "I put my hand to his nose then my ear to his chest. His breathing and heart have stopped." The man's face paled.

Mrs. Wittmer didn't respond. She shook her husband's shoulder. "Wake up! Open your eyes this instant!" She grabbed both his shoulders and shook him again. "I said wake up!"

Grace eyed the worried faces among the crowd. She

wanted to block out their gasps. Her heart raced and she stood paralyzed. The woman's desperate pleas were more than she could handle. Tears stained her cheeks.

Bishop Weaver upstretched his arms. "Please stand back and give Mrs. Wittmer some air."

Mrs. Zook reached for the widow and eased her upright. "This has been a terrible shock for you. Let me help you. Kumme inside and sit."

Mrs. Wittmer allowed her friend to escort her inside the haus.

Wiping her tears, Grace moved away from the crowd and stood by a tree. She gave a shy smile as Mark approached.

His voice soft, he said, "Grace, sweetheart, God's taken him home. It's all right. He's in Heaven."

She trembled and her voice cracked. "Poor Mrs. Wittmer, she'll miss her husband."

"God will take care of her and so will her friends. Right now, you need to rest in the fact he's at peace this very minute."

She swallowed around the lump in her throat. "His sudden death shocked me. I'll be fine."

"It hurts me when you're upset. If I could hold you, I would. The chance someone will glance our way prevents it."

"Danki." She managed a weak smile. "I would wilkom your arms around me, but you're right. It's out of the question, even at a time like this."

Hammers hitting wood echoed.

She slid a hand in her apron pocket. "I should go inside and ask if I can do anything to help Mrs. Wittmer."

"I'll find you when I'm finished working." He brushed the back of her hand with his then joined the group.

She stroked her hand where he'd touched it. Her skin

tingled. She wished it would last forever. He'd rushed to her side when she needed him. He seemed like a compassionate man. She went inside the haus to find the bereft woman.

She found the widow with Mrs. Zook and Mrs. Beiler in the sitting room. Grace's heart ached, observing the woman's grief-stricken face. She knelt on the floor by Mrs. Wittmer, clasped her hand, and listened as Mrs. Zook and Mrs. Beiler comforted her.

Mrs. Zook circled her arm around Mrs. Wittmer. "I'll stay with you until the funeral is over." She gestured to Grace. "Would you mind getting a clean handkerchief for Mrs. Wittmer?"

Grace stood. "Yes, of course I will."

Mrs. Wittmer raised her head. "You'll find it on top of my dresser."

"All right." Grace padded to the bedroom. She had been in this room several times to visit the woman when she was ill. A simple maple bed covered with a faded dark blue and white wedding ring quilt caught her eye. She snatched the clean white handkerchief off the dresser then stroked the worn coverlet. What would life be like for Mrs. Wittmer to sleep and eat alone?

Grace pressed her hand over her heart. Mrs. Wittmer's life would be forever changed. Mr. Wittmer's chair would sit empty at meals. The couple would no longer talk about their day, solve problems together, reminisce about the past, or express their love for each other in many small ways. She couldn't imagine how sad Mrs. Wittmer must be at this moment. At least she could rest in the fact Mr. Wittmer was healthy in the presence of God. She wiped her wet cheeks and sat silent.

A few minutes later, Mr. Zook rapped on the door.

Grace startled. Her jaw dropped.

"I'm sorry, Grace. I didn't mean to disturb you. Mr. Beiler and I are going to take Mr. Wittmer's body to the funeral parlor. His fraa asked me to grab a coverlet and shirt and pants for him."

Grace wiped her face with a corner of her white cotton apron. "No, it's all right. Mrs. Zook asked me to retrieve a handkerchief for Mrs. Wittmer. I'm finished."

"Danki, Grace." Mr. Zook tipped his hat.

She returned to the sitting room and held up the delicate, handmade blue handkerchief. "Here you are."

"I appreciate your help, Grace." Mrs. Wittmer dabbed her wet nose.

Bishop Weaver entered and offered his condolences then stepped back. "Mrs. Wittmer, I'll tell friends and neighbors they may view Mr. Wittmer's body in your home for the next two days and the funeral will be held on Saturday as is customary."

Grace sucked in her bottom lip. Bishop Weaver could be direct. He shouldn't press her about this until later. Mrs. Wittmer might need time to gather her wits. The elderly woman had experienced a terrible loss this afternoon.

"Please, if you don't mind, Bishop Weaver, I'd like the funeral held on Friday at the church barn."

She understood the woman's request. Friday would be plenty of time to get ready for the funeral.

The bishop peered over his spectacles. "Please join me for a word of prayer and we'll announce this to everyone when the men are finished working." Bishop Weaver glanced at each of them. "Please bow your heads." He folded his hands. "Dear Heavenly Father, danki for taking our friend home. Please wrap Your arms around Mrs. Wittmer and comfort her. Give her peace and take care of her every need. We love You. Amen." He raised his head and expressed his condolences to the widow. "I'll check on you later." He excused himself and stepped outside.

Grace gently squeezed Mrs. Wittmer's hand. "Is there anything else I can do for you?"

"No, dear. I'm in excellent hands. Danki for your help."

Grace viewed the women entering the haus. "I'll leave and let your friends spend time with you." She darted her eyes from Mrs. Zook to Mrs. Beiler. "Mamm and I will assist you with whatever you may need."

Mrs. Zook's gaze met hers. "Danki, Grace."

She stepped outside and viewed the project site. The men heaved a framed roof angle in place. They made it appear easy, but she suspected the opposite was true.

Sarah joined her. "We got separated in the crowd. How is Mrs. Wittmer? I saw you go inside the haus."

"She's a strong woman and holding up well."

Grace's Mamm came alongside them. "I'll go in and offer my help and sympathy."

Sarah nodded. "I'll join you."

"I'll wait on the porch. I've already offered my sympathies."

"We won't be long."

Grace sat in a weathered white rocking chair on the porch and watched the men work. Many of them hammered on the roof. Her daed, Mark, Levi, and six others studied the barn doors that lay flat on the ground.

Mamm and Sarah returned.

"Mrs. Wittmer is doing better than I expected." Sarah sighed.

Shrugging her shoulders, Mamm cast eyes at the men. "I need to get home. Have you seen your daed?" She pointed. "Ah, here he kummes now."

Daed carried his dirt-stained toolbox as he approached.

"I'm exhausted. Mark and Levi will stay and help the other younger men hang the doors. Sarah, Mark's dropping Levi off at your place when they're finished, so you can take your wagon home."

Sarah nodded and bid them farewell.

Grace and her parents crossed the yard to their spring wagon. She untied the horse, hitched up her skirts, climbed in, and sat next to Mamm.

Daed flicked the reins. "It's a shame Mr. Wittmer didn't get to admire and use his new barn."

Patting Daed's knee, Mamm said, "He's got a better place in Heaven. He won't miss it."

Grace smiled. "What a sweet thing to say."

Mamm's positive outlook on things often brightened her and her daed's moods.

Mamm smoothed her apron. "Mrs. Wittmer is blessed to have the Zook and Pine families in her life. Their sons are digging the gravesite. I wonder if she already has a white shirt and pants for her husband."

"Yes. She asked Mr. Zook to retrieve her husband's clothes while I was there."

"Mrs. Wittmer said Mr. Zeller has constructed plain pinewood coffins for occasions such as this. He's offered her the box, and she accepted." Mamm held tight to the side rail as the wagon wheel hit a rut in the road.

Grace hung on to Mamm's arm. "Mr. Wittmer had a lot of friends and most everyone will want to attend the funeral. The crowd could be overwhelming on such an emotional day for her. At least the funeral will be at the church. It should take some pressure off Mrs. Wittmer not having to have it in her home."

Mamm rested her head on Grace's a moment. "You're sweet to worry about her, but the bishop is a step ahead of you. He stated the funeral will be held in the church barn since there wouldn't be enough room in the Wittmers' haus."

"The bishop is good man." Grace had an idea. She wanted to do something to help Mrs. Wittmer besides bringing food. Even better, she and Mark could do this together. She'd ask him about her idea first thing in the morning.

Mark guided his horse to Levi's haus. "I'm glad we were able to finish the Wittmers' barn today. If Mrs. Wittmer sells their place, the barn will bring her more money."

"It makes all the hard work we did worthwhile." Levi swatted a fly buzzing about his head. "It must be hard for her to lose her husband and remain here on earth alone. I remember when my daed died and then Mamm shortly after. Both passed from influenza but, in my opinion, Mamm died from a broken heart. I miss them, but I am comforted they're in Heaven."

Levi had become a good friend, but could he talk to him about anything? He'd find out. Mark stared at his lap. "I have a bruder. His name is Abel."

"Where is he?"

"He joined the Amish order at eighteen but departed from our community six months later to live in the world. The bishop in Lancaster insisted I have a full funeral service for him and place a marker on his grave. I found it more difficult to do than when I had to bury Mamm and Daed." He stared at the dirt road. "Sarah asked me if I had a bruder the first day I visited the shop, but I told her not anymore. She didn't pursue it. I spoke to Grace about him."

"Sarah told me you mentioned you once had a bruder. I wanted to wait until you were ready to bring him up, in case the subject was too painful for you to discuss. Most people in our community would scold you for speaking his name, but I'm glad you told me. I'm not offended. You're my friend. You can speak to me about anything. Were you close to him?"

Mark expressed a relieved sigh. "Danki, Levi. Yes. I pray often for God to protect him. My heart sank when he left. I hope he'll return someday. Noah often asks questions about the world. I hope he never leaves our community."

Levi put a hand on Mark's shoulder. "You're a strong influence on Noah. He'll be fine. If you need anything, think of Sarah and me as your family."

Levi's openness and willingness to let him talk about Abel put him at ease. They'd formed a true friendship. His bruder had chosen the wrong path in life, but this didn't change how much Mark cared about him. With his mamm, daed, and bruder gone, Levi's support meant a lot to him. "I appreciate your offer, Levi. You may kumme to me for anything you need as well."

Mark halted the horses in front of Levi's haus. "Did Sarah tell you what I found in my barn? I forgot to mention it to you."

"Jah. I figure he stashed it when he stayed a while back. I'm convinced the thief's gone. A box of matches and a jar of water wouldn't be worth returning for and risk getting caught. I'd say we're rid of him." Levi jumped out of the spring wagon.

"I hope you're right." Mark jiggled the reins. "Have a nice night." He went home, finished his chores, and then pumped water into two big pails. One in each hand, he carried them inside to the washboiler on the stove. He added kindling and lit a fire to heat the water. He wiped his brow and sighed. For a bath, this sure was a lot of trouble. He shed his sweat- and dirt-stained shirt, pants, socks, and underwear. Tossing his garments in a wooden box, he noticed his dirty clothes were piling up. He groaned. Washing clothes was his least favorite chore. Wrapped in a blanket, he sat at the kitchen table. Dirt stuck to his skin. He waited for the water to warm.

He grabbed his mamm's old, thick, worn pot holders and pulled the pots off the stove and carried them to the washroom to fill the tub. Soaking his weary body in the soothing water would relax his tired muscles.

He dipped his toe in the water. Satisfied with the temperature, he stepped in the tub. *Perfect.* He eased himself into the warm bath, grabbed his washrag, lathered it with soap, and washed his body. Resting his head against the rim, he shut his eyes. Grace came to mind. She had a compassionate heart. Her understanding about his bruder meant a lot to him. She didn't admonish him for bringing up the subject. Without hesitation, she listened and offered her support. He could trust her. She had his best interest at heart.

Mark rose Thursday morning to the sun shining bright through the window. He sauntered to the barn, fed the chickens, slopped the hogs, and milked the cow. His mind raced with thoughts of Mr. Wittmer on this day before the man's funeral. The death of Mr. Wittmer had weighed heavy on his heart. God had blessed him with a new home, a store, friends, and a church. He'd be mindful to not take these things for granted. The milk pail full, he carried it to the root cellar and covered it with a clean cloth. The cream would rise, and Noah could make butter later today. He returned to the kitchen and moments later, the door opened.

"Good morning, Noah."

"I'm glad you're still here. Mamm told me about Mr. Wittmer. I really liked him. He was a generous old man. Our plow horse died, and he bought us another one. He wouldn't let us pay for it." He smacked an ant on the floor crawling to his pant leg. "Do you mind if I attend the funeral? I'll return to do chores after the service and meal."

The stories about Mr. Wittmer's generosity impressed him. He regretted not having more time to get acquainted with the man before he passed. "You churn better butter than I do, so I appreciate your willingness to take care of it. About the funeral, of course you may."

"Danki, Mark."

"Do you mind getting out the bread and jam?" Mark set an iron skillet on the stove. He cut eight thick slices from the slab of bacon and threw them in the sizzling pan. *Yum.* He was going to devour this breakfast in no time. He turned over the bacon until it appeared crisp and brown. He slid the bacon onto a plate, threw eggs in the pan, and fried them.

"Not at all." Noah set the table, sliced bread, and opened a jar of blueberry jam. He sniffed the bacon. "Danki for breakfast. I left without eating this morning. How did the barn raising go?"

Mark poured a cup of coffee for Noah and refreshed his. He forked up the bacon and passed Noah eggs. He offered a prayer for their food and added a remembrance for Mr. Wittmer. "I've never worked with such an organized and efficient bunch of men. I'm glad I participated, but my muscles ache this morning." He paused and rubbed his legs.

Mark chewed and swallowed with silent gusto for a few minutes.

"I wish I could've been there. I would've liked to have helped with the barn raising."

"I should've brought you with me. I apologize. Next time, we'll go together." Mark finished his last bite and wiped his mouth. "Have you noticed any signs of the stranger I suspect left the bag behind?"

Noah wiped his mouth with the back of his hand. "No, but I check the trunk each day. It's still there."

"Levi has put the man out of his mind. I'm still leery he'll return. Be mindful of any unusual sounds or things out of place."

"I will. Don't worry. I'm keeping an eye out for him."

Mark patted Noah's back, grabbed his hat, and headed outside. He hitched his horse to his wagon and rode fast to town. Gray clouds rolled across the sky and hid the sun. Not a bright day, but a comfortable one. A deer scurried out ahead of him, and he jerked back on the reins in time for the graceful doe to scamper into the woods.

He nodded to friends and neighbors guiding their horses and buggies on the way to town. Time had flown since he'd moved here. He handed his horse's reins to the liveryman and headed to his store. As he turned the key and stepped over the threshold, he greeted Grace coming through the connecting door. "How are you this morning?"

Her disposition, unlike the gray morning, was sunny and warm. "I'm fine. Do you have a minute to spare?"

"Of course. Is anything wrong?"

Grace grinned. "No. I had an idea. No one mentioned constructing a grave marker for Mr. Wittmer."

"I'd be glad to do it. It wouldn't take much time. I have a nice piece of solid oak here. I'll work on it when I don't have patrons."

"Do you mind if I help you? I've already asked Sarah to mind the shop."

Did he mind? Of course not. He'd take advantage of any opportunity to be near her. "I'd enjoy constructing the marker together. I may have to stop to wait on customers, but it shouldn't take us long. I'll close my store while I walk to the bishop's haus and ask if Mr. Zeller or anyone else is taking care of it first."

"Kumme and tell me what you find out."

It touched him she wanted to work alongside him and share his interest in building something from wood. "I hope no one has started on this project. I like the idea of us doing this together, Grace."

Her face lit up, before she turned and departed. She had brought such joy to his life. A smile crossed his lips.

An hour later, Mark pushed the door open to Grace and Sarah's shop. He joined Grace. "The bishop said it had slipped his mind. Mr. Zeller was with him. He hadn't thought of it either. Kumme on over, and we'll get started."

"Sarah doesn't mind tidying up the shop by herself while we do this. I'll tell her I'm going with you." She padded to the back room.

Grace returned and Mark walked alongside her to his store. He selected an oak plank from a small, neatly stacked woodpile in the corner of the room. It was the perfect size for a marker. He cut the smooth, flat oak into the right shape. He removed a scrap of paper from his pocket. "The bishop wrote Mr. Wittmer's full name, birth date, death date, and age in years on this note." He measured and penciled the information neatly on the wood. He backed up and studied it. "Do the letters and numbers look even?"

"Yes. His name and the dates are straight and the right height." She moved closer to him. "What can I do?"

She hadn't spoken a word until asked. Consideration was a splendid quality to have in a partner someday. Another reason he found he loved her. "I'll demonstrate how to hold the chisel and hammer and form the first letter then you can carve the next one."

He hammered and chiseled the first letter, an *E*. He stifled his laugh. Her breath on his neck tickled, she stood so close. But he didn't dare tell her. Having her near and peering over his shoulder warmed and soothed every sore muscle in his body.

"All right, you try." He passed the chisel and hammer to her then moved behind her, keeping a safe distance between them, and wrapped his hand around hers on the tool. His breath caught. *Umm, her mamm must've baked cookies again. The cinnamon scent in her hair is sweet and nice. Her skin is soft and her hands dainty.* He had a wild notion to take her in his arms and hold her tight. He'd dreamt about it, but it was forbidden.

She didn't flinch or move. She tapped the chisel and cut a *Z*. A little crooked, but all right. *Impressive.* He could smooth out her flaws later.

"How'd I do?"

He held it up and blew off the chips and dust. "You do fine work, madam."

Her button nose wrinkled and her eyes squinted as she concentrated on each letter. She was so cute.

They continued working.

"*Ezra Wittmer* is centered and the dates and numbers are etched underneath his name perfectly. You're a natural. Would you like to work with me?"

She laughed. "I liked learning something new, and I would like to work with you but Sarah may have an opinion about my switching jobs."

They laughed and then quieted. His pulse increased.

He raised her chin and met her beautiful brown eyes then lowered his lips onto hers and kissed her gently. He let go of her slowly and put a little distance between them. "I'm sorry. I shouldn't have been so forward."

Her cheeks pink and her voice soft, she raised her eyes to him. "Don't apologize."

"I've wanted to kiss you for a long time. Your lips are softer than I had imagined."

"You're the first man to kiss me. I'm glad your lips were the first to touch mine."

His heart hammered against his chest. He thought it would explode. This memory would burn in his mind forever. He hoped to reminisce about it for years to kumme.

A patron entered. Mark stepped back quick. He strode to the customer. "Please kumme in. Are you looking for anything in particular?"

The gray-haired Englisch man tapped his cane and stepped to a potato box. "If you don't mind, I'd like to browse."

"Go ahead. I'm here if you need me." He returned to Grace and lowered his voice. "I'm glad he didn't knock on the door earlier."

She put a hand to her lips. "I'm relieved he or Sarah didn't ruin our special moment. I will treasure our first kiss for a long time to kumme."

"I will too."

A clang came from the corner of the room. Grace startled.

The patron apologized and righted the umbrella tin.

She blushed, cleared her throat, and brushed dust off her apron. "I wish we had more time together."

Mark tilted his head and grinned. "I don't want to let you go either."

The customer held up a wooden toy horse. "Excuse me, do you have more of these?"

Mark nodded. "Jah, I have more in the back room. I'll be with you in one minute."

Sighing, Grace clasped the connecting door's knob. "I should let you help your customer. I hope you'll join Sarah and me for dinner."

He winked. "I'll look forward to seeing you at noon." Grace held his gaze for a moment then returned to the store.

Mark answered his customer's questions, sold him wooden toys, and collected his payment. He waited on a steady stream of customers until noon, then went to join Grace and Sarah for dinner. "My morning went fast. How did yours go?"

"We haven't had a minute to ourselves. The rush of customers was good for business but has worn me out." Grace removed apples, cold pork sandwiches, and cherry tarts from the picnic basket and set the food on the table.

Sarah handed Mark a jar of water and sat. "Mark, would you offer a prayer for our dinner?" She bowed her head.

Mark prayed and thanked God for the food and to comfort Mrs. Wittmer. The three of them recounted their day at the barn raising, finished their meal, and returned to work.

At the end of the day, Mark locked his shop door. On the way home, he recalled the events leading up to Mr. Wittner's passing. It all happened so fast. The man's death brought back memories of his parents' funeral. He loved his parents and had enjoyed mealtimes, working alongside his daed and bruder, eating mamm's good cooking and treats. She had given the best hugs. He looked forward to having a family of his own one day.

Chapter Six

Customers trailed in and out during the long afternoon. Grace swept the floor and dusted off shelves to keep busy in between waiting on patrons. Tomorrow would be a hard day. Funerals brought tears and sad faces of family members and friends who would miss their loved one who had gone to Heaven. Poor Mark. It must bring back memories of his parents and bruder. He didn't have any idea if Abel was dead or alive. Did he experience loneliness? She must be a good friend to Mark and assure him she'd do anything for him. He had swept into her life and given her hope she might be his fraa someday.

The day dawned Friday morning. Grace rolled over in bed, sat up, slid her legs over the edge of the bed, and stood. She couldn't wait until this sad day ended. What a terrible thought. She shouldn't wish her life away.

After she dressed, she headed to the kitchen. "Good morning. Where's Daed?"

Mamm stood flipping pancakes in the skillet. "He's finishing his chores and readying the buggy for our trip to Mr. Wittmer's funeral. Sit and I'll put these on your plate."

Grace obeyed and poured maple syrup on them. "These look delicious."

Daed entered the kitchen. "I'm starved."

"Yours are almost done. Wash your hands and sit."

"Absolutely, madam." Daed laughed, did as Mamm asked, and sat with his fork in hand. "You make the best pancakes and everything else I put in my mouth."

Mamm slid his breakfast onto his plate. "It's easy to keep you happy. All I have to do is feed you several times a day."

They all chuckled and started chatting until they were finished with breakfast.

Daed wiped his mouth and stood. "I'll hitch the horse to the buggy and wait outside."

Grace carried the dirty plates to the counter. "I'll rinse the dishes."

"Danki, Grace." Mamm checked the basket. "On second thought, leave the dishes. Put the syrup away and kumme. We haven't much time."

Grace grabbed the glass container and dropped it. "Ack!" *Bang. Splat.* "What a mess." The thick brown liquid stained her apron. Broken glass pieces slid in the oozing, sticky mess and onto the floor. The syrup on the counter would reach the pie keeper if she didn't hurry.

Mamm put her basket on the counter and grabbed a cloth. "You change clothes. I'll hurry and clean this up."

"You go ahead without me. I'll take care of wiping up the syrup and change clothes."

"All right." Mamm peeked outside. "Your daed is waiting in the buggy. Be careful picking up the glass. Don't cut yourself." She retrieved her basket and headed outside.

Grace shut the door behind Mamm, grabbed some

rags, and sopped up the edges of the slow-moving liquid. Thankfully, Mamm had an extra pan of hot water on the stove that didn't get used. She filled a tub with soap and water, removed her apron, and left it to soak. Stepping out the back door, she grabbed an old wooden bucket off the back porch and filled it with the hot water and added lye soap.

This is an awful mess. Dipping a cloth in the water, she got on her hands and knees, gathered and discarded the broken pieces, and threw away before she mopped the wood floor. Her dress wet and dirty, she changed clothes and opened the door to leave.

Noah pulled in front of her haus. "Grace, I'm glad you're home."

"Why aren't you at the funeral?" She swatted at a bee flying in the door.

"Is Mrs. Blauch here? Mark has a high fever. I came to fetch you and your mamm to help him."

Grace's pulse raced. Her mouth dried. "Mamm and Daed left already. I'll kumme." She grabbed her bag and followed Noah outside. "You go on ahead. Mark shouldn't be alone. I'll be right there." She hurried to get her wagon and then rode to Mark's.

Noah accepted her horse's reins. "I'll put your horse in the barn. You tend to Mark. I'm worried about him. His fever's raging hot."

She threw the reins to Noah and dashed inside the haus to Mark's bedroom. Covers were stretched to the top of his head.

He groaned, moaned, and his legs moved beneath the blankets.

She peeled the quilt back a little and touched his cheek. "You're very warm."

He rolled to his side and blinked. "Grace, what are you doing here?"

His face pale and his eyes glassy, she swallowed hard. Beads of sweat coated his forehead and his hair was damp. He must've had a fever off and on through the night. "Noah came to fetch Mamm and me, but she has already left for the funeral. I'm going to take care of you, and don't argue with me about it. How long have you been ill?" She shouldn't be in his bedroom alone, but she didn't care. He had no one. She wouldn't leave him. He needed her.

His lips quivered and his body shivered. "I've been miserable all night."

She stepped to a table in the corner of the bedroom and poured water from the pitcher into a bowl. Then she grabbed a clean cloth from the pile on the table, dipped it into the tepid water, and wrung out the excess. Hopefully, cooling his body would help. She couldn't stand for him to suffer. A high temperature could be dangerous. Dragging a chair to beside the bed, she draped the cloth over his forehead then untied her medical bag and removed a bottle of aspirin powder. "I'll be back. I'm getting a spoon and a glass."

Mark's body quaked.

She returned, grabbed the pitcher, and filled his water glass. He had gone to bed in his work clothes. He must've been sick not to change into something more comfortable. She measured the powder and added droplets of water to it. "Can you raise yourself?" She held a spoon filled with the medicine.

He eased up on his elbows and opened his mouth.

Carefully, she tipped the spoon into his mouth.

Shuddering, he motioned for the water. "Aspirin is the nastiest medicine to swallow."

She held the glass to his lips. His teeth chattered against

the glass. She'd rather it be her sick than him. Maybe the medicine would work and lower his fever. "Put your head on the pillow. Close your eyes and rest."

"I appreciate your help, but don't miss the funeral on my account. I'll be fine."

His clammy hand, warmer than normal, worried her. "I'm not going anywhere until you're better. You don't have any blotches on your skin, and you aren't scratching your face or neck. No measles or chicken pox as far as I can tell. Hopefully, the medicine will work and your condition will improve."

"Grace, you must go. You shouldn't be alone with me. It isn't proper, according to Amish law." He drew in a deep breath. "I don't want you to get what I have. Please, tell Noah not to kumme in again. He mustn't catch this either."

Noah peeked in the door. "How's Mark?"

Grace moved her chair to address him. "I've given him aspirin powder. It will take time to work. I'll stay with him. You can finish your chores."

"May I attend Mr. Wittmer's funeral?"

Mark raised his head. "Jah, Noah, you go."

"I'll pass along your condolences and apologies for your absence to Mrs. Wittmer."

"Danki, please take the marker for Mr. Wittmer's grave. It's by the door." Mark coughed and covered his mouth.

"I will." Noah gave him a reluctant look then departed.

Mark beheld Grace with pleading eyes. "Please go, Grace. What will your family and friends say? And what punishment will the bishop bestow on you if he finds out. Think of the dire consequences."

Pursing her lips, she threw back her shoulders. "So be it. I'd rather be scolded than to leave you here alone sick. I'll speak to them about this later." He was right. If anyone found out, she'd be shunned for a period of time for staying with Mark in his haus alone. It wasn't proper, since they were unmarried. She wouldn't abandon him. Getting caught was worth the risk. "Mark, I'll return in a minute."

Grace bolted outside and found Noah. "Don't tell anyone where I am. Tell my parents I'll explain my absence from the funeral when I arrive home."

"I understand. I wouldn't have told anyone anyway. I'm glad you're here to help Mark. I'm worried about him. I'll return after the funeral and spend the night if he needs me to."

"Danki, Noah."

"Take care, Grace." He secured the grave marker in the wagon and untied his horse.

She went inside the haus and entered Mark's room. She approached the side of his bed. Putting a hand to his cheek, she found he remained very warm. She poured water in a bowl and dipped the cloth in it and then gently dabbed his face over and over. Her heart hurt. His restlessness and quivering showed his discomfort, and she felt helpless to ease his pain.

A few hours passed, and his fever broke. She relaxed, rolled her shoulders, and sat quiet. He dozed in and out the rest of the afternoon. His restless legs stilled beneath the covers.

She startled when he touched her. "I must have fallen asleep. I'm sorry. How are you feeling?"

"You're an angel to care for me like this." He attempted to sit up.

Mark's hand had cooled and his eyes appeared less cloudy. The medicine must've worked. She pointed her finger. "No. You stay put. Noah will do the chores, and you need your rest. You're weak and it will take a day or two to regain your strength." She pushed the chair back. "Now that's settled, do you want anything to eat?"

"Bread with peach jam slathered on top and coffee?"

Grace waggled her finger. "Not a good choice, since you're sick. Settle your head in the pillow. I'll bring the appropriate food on a tray." She left the room.

In the kitchen, she found what she needed in the cupboard and prepared his meal. She carried it to his room. She gasped. "Get back in bed. What are you doing?"

He sat on the edge of the bed, still in his work clothes from the day before. "I'll join you at the table."

She set the pinewood tray on the bedside table. Why wouldn't he cooperate? His body must be weak. She couldn't stay much longer. Didn't he realize he could get sick again if he didn't listen to her? "You are a difficult patient. I'm trying to help you, but you're exasperating."

He scooted back on the bed and sat. "I apologize. I appreciate what you're doing for me."

She softened. Maybe he wasn't as stubborn as she feared. His face was contrite as if guilty. She had to stand her ground and have him take her seriously. "I fixed you chicken broth and bread and butter. Get back in bed."

He pushed his suspenders off his shoulders and pulled the covers over his pants and shirt. "This will hit the spot." He sipped the broth. "This is what I needed. Danki."

She sucked in her bottom lip. Her parents must wonder why she hadn't shown up at the funeral. They might be worried she'd cut herself with the glass from her earlier mishap. She should head home and explain her whereabouts. It wouldn't be an easy conversation. She hoped they'd be empathetic. The last thing she wanted to do was worry Mark about this. She'd keep it to herself. "I need to help Mamm and tell her you are good. Noah's going to stay with you tonight. Now stay in bed."

"Danki, Grace." He reached for her hand and kissed it. "Again, you're my angel."

His words warmed her from head to toe, and her hand tingled from his touch. It washed all the worry from her mind. Her face warmed. "I like being your angel." She nervously twisted her kapp ribbons around her finger. "You scared me. I can't stand the thought of anything happening to you." She gave him a sideways endearing glance. "I'm glad your fever has gone, but I won't relax until you have fully recovered. Please stay home tomorrow."

He mumbled, "Be careful going home. Danki, again, my beautiful Grace."

She smiled at him, as he closed his heavy eyelids. She tiptoed out of the room and went outside to ready her horse and wagon. His barn and haus were much the same as her parents' property, but his fields and pond were larger. The water glistened in the sunlight. Rows of vegetables in perfect lines looked pretty in his colorful garden. She breathed in the scent of honeysuckle growing wild near the barn, climbed in and sat on the bench seat. Reins in hand, she headed home. She hoped Mark would sleep the remainder of the day and get a good night's rest. She had liked taking care of him, although she didn't relish facing her parents' displeasure when she told them she'd been with Mark alone and why.

Grace urged her horse into a trot. The barn doors were open. She chilled. Her parents had returned from the funeral sooner than she'd expected. No reason to wait to tell them where she had been today. Her hands quivered as she climbed out of the wagon. She took her time stowing her horse, then stared at the ground and took heavy footsteps to the haus. She entered the kitchen and cleared her throat.

Mamm faced her and put her hands on Grace's shoulders.

"Where were you? Noah said you'd explain when you arrived home. Your daed and I were frightened you were hurt or sick. Then I thought you may have been asked to help birth a boppli."

"I'm fine. I told Noah not to tell you where I was so I could explain. He came to fetch you and me to help Mark."

"What's wrong with Mark?" Daed's eyes narrowed. "Did you go to his haus alone?"

"No, Noah stayed with me until he left for the funeral. Mark had a high fever. I gave him medicine."

Hands on hips, Daed stood in the kitchen doorway. "Is Mark doing better?"

"Yes, his fever broke. I'm hoping the food I prepared will give him strength."

Her daed frowned and his eyes squinted.

He crossed his arms. "Am I to understand you stayed with Mark after Noah left?"

"Yes. His fever spiked dangerously high, and I had to make sure it broke before I left." She put her quaking hands in her dress pockets. Her knees threatened to buckle. She stepped back.

He glared at her and stood, feet apart, shoulders straight. "I'm ashamed of you, Grace. You disobeyed Amish order."

Mamm tapped her right foot. "Grace, you must mind your actions in the future. You don't want friends and neighbors to gossip about you or Mark. If someone had caught sight of you alone with him, the bishop would ask our friends and neighbors to shun you for a period of time."

"I understand." Cringing, Grace shuffled her feet. She got caught up in the moment, and only saw that Mark needed her. She should've handled it differently, and had

Noah tell Mamm at the funeral she needed her to kumme to Mark's.

Daed stared at her, mouth shut in a grim line. "Enough said on the matter. Mind what your mamm tells you. I'll speak to Noah and Mark about their part in this tomorrow."

"Noah and Mark aren't at fault. Mark begged me to go home for my reputation's sake. They did as I asked."

"They shouldn't have listened to you. Noah should've fetched your mamm from the funeral to help. She would've obliged. Mark should've ordered you to go home." He pushed the door open with force and strode outside.

She should've considered her reputation and Amish law when making the decision to care for Mark alone. Nonetheless, she didn't want her daed to hold Mark or Noah responsible for her actions.

Mamm pursed her lips. "Don't argue or speak about this again with your daed."

"All right." Noah would probably take it in stride, but would her daed's disapproval put a wedge between Mark and her parents? They had gotten along so well. This wasn't good. She mustn't push her mamm any further. Tired, she wanted to rest, but she should make peace with Mamm first. It would be rude not to ask Mamm about the funeral. "How did Mrs. Wittmer hold up?"

Mamm rolled her shoulders and rubbed her neck. "She misses her husband but says she finds comfort knowing he's in God's arms."

She would want time alone when her parents joined God in Heaven. Even though friends and neighbors meant well, it would be too painful to speak to them about her loved one for a while, she just knew it. She shivered. She didn't want to think about this anymore. "She's a sweet woman."

"I do like the custom of burying our deceased in white clothes to symbolize their passing on to eternal life."

Grace plucked an apple from the fruit bowl. "How long did the bishop preach?"

"About an hour and a half, I'd guess. The women prepared a superb funeral meal." She sat next to Grace and clasped her hand. "I like Mark. In spite of your error in judgment today, it tickles me to see you taken with him."

Grace swallowed the bite of apple in her mouth. "I'll be disappointed if he isn't your son-in-law one day."

"God hears your prayers and mine about Mark for you and your happiness."

Grace hoped to mend fences with her daed this easily. She wondered what he would say to Mark.

Mark woke Saturday morning to a noisy woodpecker. He blinked. Stretching his arms above his head, he yawned. Fever gone, he sat up then slid out of bed. No dizziness today. He wished Grace's mamm had kumme with her yesterday. It wasn't good she and he were alone in his haus. What did her parents say when they found out? He would stop and visit Grace at the store this morning.

He dressed and went to the kitchen. Oatmeal, bread, and apple butter would go well together for breakfast. He readied the stove and prepared his meal.

A few minutes later, he burped and covered his mouth. *Excuse me.* He'd eaten too much. He found Noah in the barn. "I'm leaving for work."

"Are you feeling better?"

"Jah. Whatever sickness I had has passed. Danki for your help, Noah."

Mark wondered if the man who'd snuck into his barn and slept there weeks ago had returned for his bag he hid in the trunk in the corner. He opened the lid and searched for it. "Noah, the flour sack the intruder stuffed in my trunk a few weeks ago is gone. Have you found anything missing or out of place in here?"

"I haven't noticed anything different in the barn, and I didn't move the flour sack. Let's search for the bag again."

Noah rummaged around inside and held it up. "I found it. It's here on the side."

"Danki, Noah."

"I doubt he'll return."

"I hope not. Have a pleasant day." He climbed in his wagon and steered his horse to town. He was weak but felt much better. An eagle perched on a tree limb spread its wings and soared to the sky. The wildlife was a joy to watch on his way to work. The eagles were the most fascinating.

After arriving in town and dropping his horse and wagon at the livery, he opened the shop. Not quite as strong as usual, he moved about a little slow. He worried Grace wouldn't understand and would scold him for not heeding her advice and resting at home today, but staying in bed wasn't something he could afford to do. He'd never witnessed her temper until yesterday. No doubt it could be a problem when she found out he didn't honor her request.

He stepped inside and met her cold eyes. "Good morning."

Grace approached him, her face red. She eyed Sarah heading for a customer coming in the door and lowered her voice. "What are you doing here? We have to keep our voices low. I don't want Sarah to find out I tended to you. She wouldn't approve."

He agreed Sarah shouldn't discover she'd been at his haus alone, but her reprimand about his being at work was ridiculous. He didn't owe her an explanation. She had taken excellent care of him, but he decided what he would and wouldn't do. He'd had enough of her bossy tone and glare. "I won't say a word to Sarah." He crossed his arms. "My being here is not up to you." He huffed. "I have to earn a living. Enough said on the matter."

She crossed her arms and tapped her left foot. "You're pale and your voice is weak. You have no business being here. You're as stubborn as a mule."

"Grace Blauch, you shouldn't speak harsh to me. It isn't proper." He removed his hat. "I'd like us to resolve this awkwardness between us. I've recovered, and there's no reason I shouldn't be working. Furthermore, it was sweet of you to help nurse me back to health, but it's not your decision whether I stay home or manage my shop." He held her angry gaze.

She shoved her hands in her apron pockets and dropped her chin to her chest. She remained silent for a few moments then raised her head. "I'm sorry. I shouldn't have spoken to you in such a way. Speaking my mind has gotten me in trouble more than once. Forgive me?"

She'd put her hand on her cheek. A gesture she did to hide her birthmark when something upset her. Even though her temper had flared, she hurried to apologize. His worry she'd be stubborn and hold on to anger eased away. This was a good sign they could resolve conflicts. A trait he wanted in a potential fraa. "Of course I forgive you. Can we put this behind us?"

"Yes." She stared at her feet. "Mark, my parents are upset about my caring for you alone. Daed may visit and scold you. I'm sorry. I hope you won't allow his disapproval to change anything between us."

He put on his hat. He didn't want to kumme between

Grace and her parents. He'd do his best to calm her daed about this matter. "Don't fret. I respect his objection to you being at my haus alone with me. As far as we're concerned, you have nothing to worry about."

Grace gave him a shy grin. "Danki."

Sarah peeked in a basket. Mark doubted she'd over-heard their conversation. They'd been cautious and whispered.

Sarah turned around and held up a dish. "I bought some delicious bread pudding from the bakery. I'll share a scoop with you and Grace after dinner. Kumme back about noon."

"I never pass on dessert." He paused. "The bag the intruder left behind in the trunk weeks ago is still there. There's no sign of him being there."

"I'd put this man out of your mind. Throw the bag away or use what's in it." Sarah straightened a quilt hanging on the wall.

Grace nodded.

"Noah agrees with you. To be on the safe side, both of you still be careful."

They both murmured they'd be watchful.

Satisfied they'd heed his advice, he pushed the intruder out of his mind, bid them farewell, and headed to his store. He was late to open. Grace's demeanor had changed for the better since their conversation. If any other woman had spoken to him as harshly as she had, he would've changed his mind about pursuing her, but not Grace. He loved her, and odd as it was, he also loved her reckless determination to speak her mind. She was sweet and tenderhearted but, at the same time, strong and opinion-ated. He'd always know where he stood with her. He hoped not to experience her directness *too* often. If so, it could be a problem.

When would Mr. Blauch visit him? If he didn't kumme to his store before the end of the day, Mark would go to the Blauches' haus and ask to speak to him. He had settled his differences with Grace, and he needed to settle differences with her parents.

Chapter Seven

Mark shut the door behind a patron and gazed at his shop. He picked up a knife with a small blade and chose a thick piece of oak. He sat and imagined a miniature toy bear. Slivers of wood flew off as he whittled and waited for another patron to visit the shop. The bear's round belly, four legs, and head took shape.

Mr. Blauch entered. "Good morning. Are you feeling better?"

Mark stood and placed his knife and unfinished toy on the table. "Jah. Danki for asking. I was going to kumme to your haus after work to speak to you about Grace tending to me during my sickness. Please don't be angry with Noah or Grace for wanting to help me."

Mr. Blauch's jaw clenched. He stood, feet apart, with arms crossed and head tilted. "Noah knows better than to listen to Grace. He's an Amish man and has been taught our laws. He shouldn't have taken her to your haus or left her alone with you, and you should've been more persistent with her and sent her home."

The man's statement came across direct and to the

point. Mark would never forgive himself if this incident severed his relationship with Grace and her parents. "You're right, Mr. Blauch. I apologize for not demanding she go home. I hope you can forgive me."

Grace's daed stared at him. "Don't let it happen again."

"Jah, sir."

"Is Noah working at your place today?"

Mark wouldn't let Noah take the blame for what happened. His friend had the best intentions in going to get Grace. "Please don't blame him. I'm the one at fault."

"I accept your apology." He paused. "I'll not speak to Noah myself about this, but I trust you'll speak to him as to the proper person to alert should a situation present itself such as this again. Remind him of Amish law and his responsibility to uphold it. I expect you to do the same. Understood?"

It would've bothered him if Mr. Blauch had expressed his displeasure to Noah after all his friend had done to help him. "I understand, and I'll do as you ask." He scratched behind his ear. "Is everything all right between us?"

"I said what I had to say. I still think you're a good man, but I won't be as forgiving if you disappoint me again where Grace is concerned. I'm giving you leniency since you were sick and not yourself."

"Danki, Mr. Blauch."

"Good day, Mark."

Mark let out a sigh and watched out the window. Mr. Blauch headed for his wagon. He peeked at the clock. *Noon already?* Where had this day gone? He entered Grace and Sarah's shop.

Grace carried a quilt, put it aside, and stopped. "Is it time for dinner already?"

He should inform her of his conversation with her daed,

but he must relay the information out of Sarah's earshot. "Jah, where's Sarah?"

"She went to the post office to mail a letter. You're frowning. Is something wrong?"

"Your daed came to visit me. He expressed his displeasure about you being at my haus alone with me."

Grace gasped and put her hand to her cheek. "What did he say?"

He recounted his conversation with Mr. Blauch. "I'm grateful he's letting me speak to Noah. I feel bad you and Noah got into trouble with your daed because of helping me. I'm glad he's being reasonable." He put his hands in his pockets. "I fretted he wouldn't allow you to talk to me."

"I've been nervous and worried wondering when he'd approach you about this. I'm glad it's over. Now we can move past it."

Grace taking care of him alone in his haus could've turned her daed against him for good. Time with Grace had been precious and his love for her grew each day. He didn't want anything to hinder their future time together. He was thankful Mr. Blauch had given him another chance.

Sarah came in smiling. "I'm hungry. Let's eat." She served them and they sat.

Mark listened to Grace and Sarah chatter about the new wedding quilts they'd sewn and hung on display this morning. He studied their handiwork. They were quite talented. He finished his meal and bid them farewell. His limbs hurt walking back to his shop. Mr. Blauch's words weighed heavy in his mind. He dreaded having to discuss Mr. Blauch's concerns with Noah. If he closed early, he'd catch Noah still at his place. He waited on customers until midafternoon then went home. Guiding his horse down the lane, he waved at Noah taking a seat in his wagon. "Noah, wait."

Noah got out of his wagon, holding his horse's reins. "You're home early. Are you ill again?" He accepted Mark's horse's reins. "What do you need?"

Mark got out of his wagon and faced him. "Mr. Blauch came to visit me today. He reprimanded me for not telling Grace to leave my haus the other day when she tended to me. I apologized to him."

Noah's forehead wrinkled and his eyes read concern. "Did he leave annoyed, or did he accept your apology?"

"He accepted it, but he intended to discuss his concerns with you. I asked him to let me speak to you about it, and he agreed."

"I wouldn't do anything differently. You needed help."

Noah was a close friend. Mark cared about him. Sometimes he didn't agree with Amish law concerning these types of situations either, but he understood the importance of being obedient to their Amish order.

During his life in Lancaster, he had let Abel stay overnight in his haus, and he'd given him money for his gambling debts. He had been wrong to do so, but he loved and cared for his bruder. He didn't understand Abel's enthusiasm for the outside world. He could never abandon his faith in God or leave his Amish life.

He hoped Noah would determine it was in his best interest to stay in Berlin. "I appreciate your concern, but we must obey God and our laws. Sometimes it's difficult, but hard choices must be made in certain situations. If something like this should happen again, please alert Levi or Mr. Blauch."

"I understand Mr. Blauch's point of view. I'm glad he let you speak to me rather than him. Don't worry. I'll be mindful of Amish law in the future. I wouldn't want to get Grace or anyone in trouble."

Noah's response gave him peace of mind. He understood Mr. Blauch's concern and showed a willingness to respect the Amish law.

Hairs on the back of Mark's neck bristled on Monday morning as two men barged into his store. The rough-looking men sported scruffy beards, fierce scowls, and gun belts with pistols on their hips. They bore down on him. Mark tightened his grip on the counter. "May I help you?"

"Why I believe the man can help us. Don't you, Buck?" The foul-smelling stranger stood tall and his spit tobacco-laced saliva on Mark's clean floor. His thick dark tangled hair hung to his shoulders, and his cold menacing eyes put Mark's teeth on edge. The intruder turned his sign. "I'll turn this here sign to closed and lock your door. I don't want no customers comin' in and interferin' with our little discussion." He snapped the lock in place and sneered at Mark.

"Let me have a go at him, Skinner." Buck pushed past his partner and poked a finger hard into Mark's chest. The man's rotten teeth were sickening. "You don't have a choice, Amish man."

Mark's jaw clenched. Buck stood inches from him, face hard and eyes threatening. Skinner was shorter than Buck, but no less mean. He had a deep scar on his left cheek and mangy brown hair and beard. Did they mean to rob him? "What do you want?"

Buck gripped him by the collar, knocked off his hat, and shoved him against the wall. "Where's your good-for-nothin' brother?" The stranger glared at Mark. "Abel

King owes my partner and me money. We aim to collect it one way or another. Don't matter which way, long as we get what's owed to us."

Mark winced at the man's fowl-smelling tobacco breath. These men had murderous eyes. They meant business. Buck jammed a gun into Mark's side. Never in his life did he think he'd find himself in such jeopardy. His life might end today. He flinched. How much money did Abel owe them? Maybe he could pay them off. "I haven't seen Abel for six months. I don't know his whereabouts." If he did, he wouldn't tell these scoundrels. "Who told you I'm Abel's bruder? How did you find me?"

Skinner stepped alongside Buck. "Abel said he was Amish and from Lancaster. Claimed you gave him the money he owed us last time. We went to the post office and asked for your address. The clerk told us you're his friend. He told us you'd moved and planned to open a furniture store in Berlin. We searched your place lookin' for your good-for-nothin' brother. We thought you might be hidin' him. You got some fine property. I'd hate to see anything happen to it." He snickered. "You sleep sound, but you snore like a freight train."

The two men squinted and laughed. Skinner stepped back and kicked over a footstool. "Abel owes us forty dollars. You gonna cover his debt again?"

Buck pushed the gun harder into Mark's ribs. "Skinner, should I shoot him in the arm or leg soin' he gets we're serious?"

"Nah, I'd wait for him to turn over the money he has in his cashbox 'fore we do any shootin'."

Mark's heart thudded against his chest. These thugs could've murdered him in his sleep. What if they'd stopped by his haus during the day and harmed Noah? He'd never forgive himself if something happened to his friend. His answer might get him killed. He swallowed around the lump in his throat. "Abel borrowed twenty dollars back then. The truth is, I don't have forty dollars. Let go of me so we can discuss this in a reasonable manner."

Buck shoved him. "This is as reasonable as you're gonna git from me, Amish man."

Mark regained his balance, picked up his hat, put it on, and crossed his arms to hide his trembling hands. He glanced out the window.

Buck scoffed. "I've been keepin' a lookout. Nobody's walked past your store since we been here. Town's quiet this morning. You're on your own. Nobody's comin' to rescue you." He slammed his handgun into its holster and glared.

There was nothing more to negotiate. Mark returned the man's threatening stare. "I can't help you. Please leave."

"Buck, this here Amish man's gotten tough all of a sudden."

"His pasty face says otherwise." Buck paced, stopped, and whirled on Mark. "We'll leave, but we're comin' back if we don't find your brother." He picked up a carved train on a shelf and held it up. "Best get busy carvin' a lot more of these and savin' your money."

Skinner picked up a toy engine and laughed. "This Amish man might need a little more convincin'."

Buck grabbed Mark's shirt collar again. "If your brother shows up here, you tell him we're lookin' for him. He knows to find us in the gamblin' hall in Lancaster." He leaned close to his ear. "If Abel don't pay up, he's a dead man." He jerked the toy engine away from Skinner and threw it against the wall. He stared at Mark then turned on his heel and followed Skinner outside, slamming the door behind him.

Mark dashed to lock the door and leaned against it to

catch his breath and held his bruised side. He'd never
encountered such cruel men. They had no scruples or
conscience. They were frightening and ruthless.

If Abel showed on his doorstep, he doubted he could
turn him away. He had built a life here and agreed to obey
the Amish law, but he loved his bruder. He worried these
gunmen would find him. He bowed his head. "Dear
Heavenly Father, please protect Abel and help him to see
the error of his ways. Guide me on what You would have
me do in all situations. Danki for all You have done for
me thus far. Amen."

Mark opened the door to Grace and Sarah's shop. He
peeked around the doorframe. They were smiling and
speaking with customers. He counted five other women
shopping and chatting throughout the store. He closed the
door quietly and blew out a pent-up breath. Grace, Sarah,
or her patrons mustn't have been alerted by the thugs. He
prayed they wouldn't be bothered or hurt by these hooligans. *What more trouble will Abel bring down on my head?*

A man peered in Mark's front window and rapped on
the door. Mark unlocked it, turned his sign, and waved the
patron in. He forced a smile and straightened his shoulders. "Wilkom. May I help you?"

The Amish man proceeded to browse the store and chat
about the weather and his vegetable garden. He carefully
examined an oak bed frame and a quilt rack. "I'd like to
purchase these for my fraa."

He pushed his unpleasant encounter with the ruffians
to the back of his mind, collected his money, and helped
carry his purchases to the man's wagon. The kind customer
had boosted his mood and momentarily distracted him.
Someday he hoped to shop and buy things for a fraa, his
fraa, namely Grace. Her insecurities and innocence tugged

at his heart. She had just the right amount of softness and strength he wanted in a partner.

Mark rubbed his aching head and groaned deep. He had held up well, despite his recent illness, but he was ready to go home and rest. The intruder who'd hid the bag at his place and the thugs barging into his store could potentially harm him or someone he loved. He didn't like not having control over either of these situations. He stepped to the front door intending to lock up and close the shop.

Mr. Blauch motioned for him to let him in.

The man's worried face sent Mark's heart racing. *Has something happened to Grace?* He opened the door and waved him inside. "What's wrong?"

Grace's daed bent to catch his breath. "Jonah's missing. I bumped into Grace on her way home and told her. Levi, along with other friends and neighbors, is already out searching for him. Grace said you were still here when she left. We need all the men we can gather. There's a lot of ground to cover."

Mark felt light-headed and his stomach clenched. He had grown fond of Jonah. The boy could be hurt.

"Jah, of course. Let's go find him."

He followed Grace's daed out and locked the door. He had gotten his second wind. "I'll fetch my wagon."

"I'll meet you outside the livery."

Mark crossed the boardwalk and retrieved his wagon. What were the details of Jonah's disappearance? He hadn't dared to take the time to ask. They didn't have a minute to spare. He gestured to Grace's daed, prodded his horse to a gallop, and followed Mr. Blauch as they left town.

They reached a familiar large area of dense woods not far from Jonah's haus. They each tied their horses to a shady oak tree. "Does his mamm or daed have any idea where he might be?"

"Mr. Keim told us Jonah asked his mamm if he could go search for blackberries and to the creek to skip rocks in the water. She said no and instructed him to stay close to the haus. She stayed outside to pick green beans. Time got away from her, and she blames herself for not watching him."

"Which direction should we head?"

"She's taken him to several places in these woods. The creek is wider and deeper than most. It stretches far. Mr. Keim and some of his friends fetched their fishing boats to paddle along the river and search for the child." He pointed. "The rest of the men are on foot checking the north and south woods. You and I can check the east woods."

Mark paused and cupped his ear. Distant muffled voices were calling Jonah's name. The trees must be blocking the volume of the men's shouts.

Mark groaned when he considered how terrifying this ordeal must be for Mr. Keim. What could be more horrible than a daed finding his lifeless son? A picture of the child floating facedown in the deep water came to mind. His eyes pooled with tears. Bowing his head, he whispered a prayer. "Dear Heavenly Father, please lead us to Jonah. Protect him from harm. Danki. Amen." He lifted his head, and Mr. Blauch stood in front of him with head bowed.

Grace's daed put his hand on Mark's shoulder. "Thoughtful prayer, son. Let's go locate him." He untied two shotguns from his saddle and handed one to Mark.

Mark accepted the gun. "Danki." They'd be prepared if they encountered dangerous wildlife. They tromped through tall grass, weeds, and brush.

Mark shouted, "Jonah!" He waited for Mr. Blauch to do the same and then repeated the child's name several times. Why didn't the child answer? His heart sat heavy in his chest, and he pushed his weak body to prod ahead through the woods alongside Mr. Blauch for over an hour. It would take days to search these woods. No matter. He wouldn't rest until he held Jonah.

"Grrrr."

The hair on Mark's neck quilled. "Do you see any-thing?"

Mr. Blauch cupped his ear. "Sounds like a bear."

A child's terrified scream rang out. "Somebody help me!"

Mark's heart thudded against his ribs. The shriek was definitely a child's in obvious distress. Something had happened. He pointed to a spot beyond a cluster of trees and headed for it. "It came from over there. Let's be as quiet as possible."

He took a step at a time then stopped. He held his breath for a moment. Beads of sweat formed on his upper lip. He put his palm out to stop Mr. Blauch and then put a finger to his lips.

Jonah sat hugging his knees to his chest with his back against a tree. The young boy's face was deathly white, and his eyes were wide with fright.

Mark raised his gun and aimed at the bear.

Mr. Blauch didn't move or make a sound.

A black bear, on all four legs, lifted his head and growled at Jonah. His large mouth opened, and the animal bared his fangs. The bear sniffed then stood on his hind legs and growled louder, this time whipping his head to and fro.

Mark couldn't afford to miss. Jonah had invaded the

bear's territory, and the animal didn't like it. His shirt stuck to his back, soaked with the perspiration of raw fear.

"Mark! Help me!" Jonah, face as pale as milk and eyes as big as silver dollars, struggled to stand.

Mr. Blauch yelled, "Be still, Jonah."

Jonah pressed his hand against the tree and stood anyway.

The bear growled again at Jonah.

Mark held his breath and squeezed the trigger.

The animal dropped to the ground with a thud and lay still.

Mark exhaled and lowered the shotgun.

Jonah ran and jumped into his arms. "You saved me! I was so scared! I thought the bear was going to attack me." He buried his head in Mark's shoulder, his small body racked with sobs.

He rubbed the young boy's back. "I've got you. The bear can't hurt you. You'll be snug and safe at home soon."

Mr. Blauch accepted Mark's gun, walked over, and prodded the bear with the barrel of his gun. "He's dead." He wiped the sweat from his brow and aimed his gun at the clouds. "I'll shoot twice to alert the other men we've found you. Cover your ears."

Jonah squinted and covered his ears. He buried his head farther into Mark's shoulder.

Mr. Blauch stepped away and shot twice toward the sky. "I'm not a great shot. I'm thankful you are. You acted fast. Good job, son."

Other searchers joined them, expressed their relief the boy had been rescued, and then gathered around the bear.

Mark touched Jonah's leg. His hand was sticky and stained red. "Did you hurt yourself?"

Jonah straightened his legs, ready to stand, as Mark

put him down. "I caught my leg on a tree branch. It scratched me."

Inspecting the wound, Mark studied the injury. "It doesn't appear deep, and it's not bleeding much." He tugged a plain white handkerchief out of his pocket and tied it around Jonah's leg to slow the bleeding. "This should do until you get home. Your mamm can put a proper dressing on it later."

Mr. Blauch rubbed his arm. "What were you doing in the woods alone?"

Jonah bowed his head and stuck out his bottom lip. "I asked Mamm if I could go berry pickin'." He shuffled his feet and kicked a stone. "She said no, and I went anyway."

Mr. Blauch narrowed his eyes and waggled his finger at the child. "You mustn't ever disobey your parents. If you go away from home, it must be with an adult and only with your mamm or daed's permission. Understand?"

A tear trickled down Jonah's dirty cheek, and he met Mr. Blauch's gaze. "I'm sorry. I won't ever do it again. I'm scared to go into the woods. The big bear Mark killed might have a friend."

"You might be right." Mark gently tapped the boy's nose. "Let's get you home." He carried him a few steps.

Mr. Keim dashed to them. "Jonah!" The look of relief on the man's face was heartrending.

Friends and neighbors followed behind Jonah's daed.

The man took his son from Mark's arms and hugged him tight. "You scared me! We must go to your mamm. She's worried sick about you. You must never go into the woods alone again."

Jonah's eyes got big. "Mark saved me. He shot the biggest bear in the whole world."

Mr. Keim thanked Mark and the other volunteers. "I'm thankful I heard your signal shots out on the water. I came as fast as I could. I'll never be able to express to you in words how much saving my son means to me. Danki." His eyes swam with tears. "I should take him home. His mamm must be frantic."

Mr. Blauch asked, "Would you like me to fetch your boat and bring it to you?"

"Danki, but two of my friends are already taking care of it." He bid them farewell and headed home with the boy grasped tight in his arms.

Mark and Mr. Blauch studied Mr. Zook and Mr. Pine alongside two other men scrutinizing the bear.

Mr. Zook approached Mark. "I overheard the boy tell his daed you killed the bear. We appreciate what you did for Jonah. Danki." He cocked his head. "Are you interested in the bear? If not, I'd like to have it. Several of the men have offered to help me with it. We'll sell the hide and donate the money to the Amish community fund for those in need. We'll deliver the meat to the widows."

"I like both your ideas. You're wilkom to the carcass."

"Danki." Mr. Zook returned to his friends.

Mark drew a breath. He thanked God for Jonah's safe return to his parents. He hoped Mr. and Mrs. Keim would punish the boy. Jonah must understand the importance of obeying his parents. He and Mr. Blauch returned through the woods to their wagons.

"Son, danki for coming with me to find Jonah. Would you care to go target shooting sometime? I'd like you to give me some pointers on becoming a better marksman. Are you as good with a rifle as you are with a shotgun?"

"My daed was an excellent shot. When I reached eleven, he showed me how to use a shotgun, rifle, and pistol. We practiced every chance we got. We really had a good time. The woods in back of our haus provided the perfect place for target shooting. He'd save and line up empty tin cans on fallen trees. When I had mastered hitting them, he moved the cans to a spot farther away. His method is what helped me improve my distance shooting."

"It must've been hard to lose him at an early age. Sounds like you were close."

"Jah, I miss him. We were close. He was a good listener, teacher, friend, and confidante, in addition to being a loving daed."

"If he was anything like you, I'm sure he was a fine man." He swiped a hand through his hair. "I'm serious about having you show me how to improve my marksmanship. I'll visit you at your store in a week or two, and we'll pick a day."

Mark's heart leapt. He had not been in a favorable place with Grace's daed a few days ago. He had worried it would be difficult to regain Mr. Blauch's confidence. It was a blessing Grace's daed had chosen him to partner with to find Jonah. They had gotten better acquainted. Shooting targets in the woods would be a way for them to cultivate a friendship. If Mr. Blauch didn't kumme to the shop in a week or two, he'd approach him about setting a time for target practice. He'd start saving empty cans tomorrow.

He pictured how Grace's lovely face would look when he told her about his afternoon with her daed. He had no doubt her face would beam. Laying eyes on her face couldn't kumme soon enough.

Chapter Eight

Grace paused on the boardwalk Tuesday morning. Who was the woman running out of Mark's shop with him? Something must be wrong. She ran to meet them.

"What's the matter?"

Mark appeared happy to see her. "Mrs. Oyer came into my shop by mistake. She got flustered and thought she had gone into your store. What a relief to find you coming up the boardwalk. She needs your help."

Mrs. Oyer squinted and her lips trembled. She grasped Grace's arm. "Please kumme with me. My dochder, Marie, is having her boppli. Hester is on another call. Marie's husband is with her. She's bleeding and in pain. I'm afraid something is wrong."

Mark faced her. "Grace, I'll go with you. I can fetch water and sit with her dochder's husband. I'll lock my store and get our horses and wagons."

Mrs. Oyer untied her horse from the hitching post outside Mark's store. "I'll wait here." She climbed in her wagon.

Grace ran to the shop and stuck her head in the door.

"Sarah, I'm needed to help with a birth. I might go home after I'm finished."

"I understand. Don't worry about returning here. I hope everything goes well."

"Danki." Grace darted outside and met Mark and Mrs. Oyer. She dropped her bag in the wagon.

Grace motioned for Mrs. Oyer to go ahead, and she and Mark followed in their separate wagons. Mark didn't have to kumme. She had helped many a mamm birth their boppli. His assistance wasn't necessary. She didn't like taking him away from his shop. But again, he'd jumped in to assist her.

Mrs. Oyer stopped in front of a small white haus with a garden to the side.

Grace grabbed her bag out of her wagon.

Mark jumped out of his and accepted the reins from both women. "I'll take care of the horses."

Screams rang out. Grace lifted her long skirt and bolted inside, behind Mrs. Oyer, to Marie's bedroom. Marie had sweat-matted hair and thrashed in her soiled gown on bloodstained sheets.

The terrified woman pressed her hands on her stomach. "Something's wrong. Please help me. I've been with child only seven months. It's too early."

A man stood and hugged his arms to his sides. "This is my wife, Marie, and I'm her husband, Joel Brandenburg. Please help my fraa." His face filled with fright and he kissed his fraa's damp forehead. "I'll be in the kitchen or outside."

"I'm Grace Blauch. I'm a midwife. I'll do my best for your family."

Mrs. Oyer knelt by her dochder's bed. She dipped a cloth in a bowl of water sitting on a bedside table and wiped Marie's forehead. "Try and stay calm, my dear dochder." Her pleading gaze held Grace's.

Grace bit her tongue to hide her concern. *Seven months.* The boppli would be at risk. She poured witch hazel from her bag onto a clean cloth to clean her hands then checked Marie. *Oh no,* the infant's feet were where the head should be in the birth canal. "Mrs. Oyer, please hold Marie's shoulders firm against the bed. I need to reach in and turn the infant into position. Marie, what I have to do will hurt, but it must be done." She eased her fingers as far inside Marie as she could and worked fast to turn the small body.

Marie gripped the white cotton bedsheet and paled.

Mrs. Oyer's lips trembled. "The pain will be worth it once you lay eyes on your new little maedel or boy. Please take a deep breath and keep still to help your child."

Marie whimpered, groaned, and cried but didn't scream or kick.

Grace concentrated on the boppli and worked as fast as she could.

"You're doing a fine job, Marie." She eased her hands out. "I'm going to count to three. On three, push as hard as you can." She nodded to Mrs. Oyer. "Ease her shoulders up to help her with this." With arms out, Grace counted. "One, two, three, push."

The new mamm grunted and her cheeks turned bright red. Beads of sweat dripped from her face.

The infant's head emerged. Grace gently moved the infant's shoulders and the rest of the tiny lifeless body slid out in her hands. The infant's legs and arms twisted in the wrong direction. The little maedel's right hand showed two fingers missing, and the left hand had none. The head appeared misshapen and her mouth twisted. Her color was ashen and her body limp. No movement or sound came from the newborn. Her tiny, grotesque, delicate body was like an injured bird. Tears pooled in Grace's eyes. She closed them for a moment and fought to keep from trembling. She blinked several times and faced the distressed woman.

"Do I have a maedel or a boy?"

"You have a dochder."

"Why hasn't she cried or moved?"

Grace didn't answer. She had to check the infant for her peace of mind and to stall for strength to tell Marie her boppli was stillborn. She held the infant with one hand and grabbed her stethoscope out of the bag with her other. The tips in her ears, she pressed the metal pad to the infant's chest and listened for a heartbeat. She swallowed around the lump in her throat, removed her stethoscope, and set it aside.

The two pale and stricken women stared at her.

She held the newborn low, so they couldn't see her. "I'm sorry. Your dochder is lifeless."

Mrs. Oyer and Marie sobbed and held each other.

Grace's tears dripped onto her cheeks. "Would you like to hold her? Her face and body aren't normal."

Marie parted from her Mamm's arms and wiped her eyes. "Please give her to me."

Grace held up her palm then carried the infant to a small table. "I'll clean her first." She grasped the pitcher and poured water into a bowl then washed the infant and dried her.

Marie's voice quivered. "Please wrap her in the white cotton blanket on the dresser. Mamm sewed it for her." She slumped back against her mamm. Marie looked like a picture of hopelessness.

Mrs. Oyer stroked her daughter's hair. She let her tears fall. "I'm sorry, my sweet child."

Would Marie be able to handle the sight of her abnormal

child? She guessed some people might be repelled by her. She had empathy for the infant and couldn't turn her head from her. Grace touched her downy cheek. Maybe her birthmark allowed her to gaze upon the newborn's imperfections without wincing. All she felt was a deep sadness. She'd not faced a more disfigured boppli than this newborn. She placed the swaddled infant in Marie's outstretched arms and waited.

Marie gasped, closed her eyes, and passed the bundle to her mamm. "I'm sorry. I can't stand the sight of her." She hung her head. "I'm so ashamed."

Grace blinked back stinging tears. Marie had suffered losing her child and might be haunted by the sight of her for a time. Mrs. Oyer passed the bundle back to Grace and comforted and supported her dochder with love and compassion. How blessed Marie was to have such a loving mamm. Mark and the new daed came to mind. "I'll find the stove and warm the water. I need to remove the after-birth and clean you. Are you ready for your husband to kumme in?"

The bereft mamm cowered. "Jah."

Grace left the room and entered the kitchen. Mark and Mr. Brandenburg sat at a round maple table.

The new daed stood and stared at Grace with worry in his eyes. "How's Marie? How's my boppli?"

Grace paused. It was hard enough telling Marie about her dochder, and now she had to repeat the sad story again. She swallowed. "Marie is fine physically. She's upset and needs you. I'm sorry. Your dochder didn't live. I suspect she died in the womb sometime during your fraa's pregnancy." She paused and swallowed hard. "I think it's only fair to warn you that your dochder was born abnormal. Her head is misshapen, her hands are missing fingers, and her arms and legs are disfigured. I just want you to be prepared."

He groaned, tore at his hair, and paced. "No! No! No! It can't be! We've waited a long time to have kinner." He strode to the bedroom door, pushed it open, and rushed to Marie.

Mark came alongside Grace. They watched the couple through the open doorway, both silent.

Mr. Brandenburg held Marie then stood. He stared at the infant. He gasped and ran from the room, past Grace, and out the back door.

Startled, Grace glanced at Mark. She opened her mouth, but no words came to mind. What should they do?

Mark whispered, "Are you all right?"

She twisted her hands. "Yes."

"I'm sorry you've had to endure this hardship. I admire your strength and compassion, Grace. Stay here. I'll go speak to him."

What would she have done without Mark today? He never hesitated to kumme to her aid whenever she needed him. She could count on him to handle any situation. How would he find the words to say to the man?

At the stove, she poured clean warm water from the large pot into a smaller one to clean and wash Marie then carried it to the stricken woman's bedroom.

Marie lay quiet and pale and stared at the ceiling with desolate eyes.

The infant lay in the oak cradle in the corner of the room, and Mrs. Oyer prayed to God to comfort the bereft parents and welcome the boppli into His loving arms.

Grace paused and bowed her head until the prayer ended. She approached Marie. "I wish I didn't have to disturb you, but I must massage your stomach and remove the afterbirth."

Marie didn't take her eyes off the ceiling.

Mrs. Oyer wiped her damp cheeks. "Can I help?"

"You're already helping by soothing your dochder. The calmer she is, the easier my job will be. I'll not be long." Grace worked to remove the afterbirth, inspected it, and ensured it was intact. She discarded it in an empty flour sack she'd brought and then covered Marie. She left to wash her hands in the kitchen then returned to bathe the heartbroken woman with the clean water.

She undressed and redressed Marie with Mrs. Oyer's help into a clean gown. "I'm going to escort you to the chair. You can rest there while we change your bedsheets." Grace circled her arm around Marie's waist and guided her to the chair.

She and Mrs. Oyer changed the bloodstained and soiled bedding.

Marie and her mamm had worried and pain-filled faces. Mrs. Oyer's cheeks were blotched. Marie's were as white as snow. Tension and sadness swamped the small room. Shoulders slumped and her body heavy, Grace placed the dirty towels, bed linens, and gown in a tub and carried them to the kitchen. She poured the dirty water out the back door, pumped clean water in the tub in the kitchen, and added soap overtop the linens to soak.

The door banged open and the men came in. She stole a glance at them. The new daed and Mark appeared calm.

Mr. Brandenburg patted Mark's shoulder. "Danki for your time and advice."

"I'm glad I could help."

The daed approached Grace. "Danki for everything you've done."

Grace gripped her apron. "You're wilkom."

The man left to join his fraa. A few minutes later,

he brought the infant to Mark. "Do you want to lay eyes on her?"

Mark held out his arms and accepted the light bundle. He peeled the blanket from the infant's face and body. A tear escaped his eye. He didn't cringe or turn from her. "I can't imagine the anguish you must be going through. I'm sorry."

Mr. Brandenburg gently reached for the lifeless tiny body. "You and Grace have eased our sorrow a little by being here with us. Danki."

Mark's gentle gaze at the malformed infant was another reminder of his compassionate heart.

Mark swiped his cheek. "I'll ready our wagons and wait for you outside."

"I won't be long." Grace gathered her things, bid the family farewell, and joined Mark out front. "I'm thankful you came with me today. What did you say to calm Mr. Brandenburg?"

"I prayed with him and told him Marie would need him now more than ever. I said I understood his sadness, but it was important for them to get through this together. He loves Marie very much, and he hadn't thought of how his running out of the room might have affected her. Joel's a good man."

"I've not assisted in the birth of a boppli as disfigured as Marie's newborn."

"Now she has a healthy body and is in Heaven. A picture of her smiling and normal is what gets me through a wrenching experience like this."

"Yes, I agree. I'll do the same." She stared at her feet and moved her shoe over a patch of thick green grass. "Do you want kinner someday?"

"Jah, I want a family. Do you want kinner?"

"Yes, at least two. A boy and a maedel would be perfect.

And I'll love my boppli whether he or she is healthy or not. My birthmark is insignificant compared to this infant's infirmities, but it stands out as different from other women. The infant's list of abnormalities reminded me I should be thankful and not complain about a painless birthmark on my face."

"It doesn't bother me a bit. You're beautiful, Grace."

Her face warmed and she stared at the ground. Could he have said anything better? She thought not. "Danki." She looked at her feet then back at him. "If you don't mind my asking, Mark, how did you get the scar under your eye? I noticed it the first day we met. It's not unappealing, but interesting. I'm curious as to what the story is behind it."

He stared at the ground and rolled a small stone with his foot. "Abel and I were out playing. We were kinner. He had a slingshot, and he'd set up cans as targets. I dashed outside unaware of what he had in mind and got in the way. He blamed himself, but he shouldn't have given the incident a second thought. I should've paid more attention. The wound didn't hurt much at all. Sounds strange, but I'm glad I have it to remind me of our good times together."

"It adds appeal to your handsome face. Your attitude toward it is a lesson to me not to wallow in pity over my birthmark."

"It adds to strength to your character. You are intelligent and willing to do far more than most Amish women in working in a shop and assisting with birthing bopplin. I suspect your birthmark has made you stronger in coping with unkind people. It's a trait I admire in you." He lifted his eyebrows. "We haven't talked about Jonah's incident. Did your daed tell you how we found him?"

She patted her heart. "Yes! I understand you saved him by killing the bear. It must have been a tense situation." She gazed at him. "Daed told me he asked you to take him target shooting. He was impressed with your aim and the way you handle a gun. Sounds like you two are becoming good friends."

He grazed her hand. "Jah, I'm hopeful."

She smiled. "I shouldn't keep you any longer. Are you going back to the store? If so, would you mind telling Sarah I'm taking her up on her offer and heading home? I'm worn out."

He reached for her bag and secured it in her wagon. "I'll pass your message on to Sarah. If you need me, please don't hesitate to ask."

How had she gotten so fortunate to meet a man as kind as Mark? She never thought she'd be blessed to have a man like him in her life. He empathized with her, Mrs. Oyer, and the Brandenburgs. She had no doubt he'd support his fraa and put her first in any given situation.

After witnessing his compassionate heart and integrity, his ability to get along with friends, neighbors, and customers, his patience and kindness, she wanted him to ask her to marry him soon. She loved him. He listened to her joys and her concerns, offered constructive advice, and she could be herself with him. She could trust and depend on him if they experienced hardship or a loss of a loved one. "Danki, Mark."

"I'll wait and leave with you." He untied her horse and handed her the reins.

"No, you go ahead. I need a minute, then I'll head out."

He paused, then nodded.

She waited until he departed and climbed in the wagon. She bowed her head and prayed. "Dear Heavenly Father, please forgive me my sins. Please give this family the strength to overcome this infant's loss. My heart breaks for them. I love You, and I praise You. Amen."

She would never grow accustomed to the sad and forlorn face of a mamm holding her lifeless infant. She drove to her favorite spot near the creek in the woods by her home. She got out and secured her horse then sat near the water's edge not far from a covered bridge. She plucked a full dandelion from the ground and blew the seeds. She followed them as they danced in the air. A cottontail hopped a few feet away. The timid creature paused and stared at her. She wanted to reach out and touch the animal's soft coat but refrained.

The water moved over stones in the shallow end of the river. Birds perched on tree branches were chirping and a chubby brown squirrel unburied a nut. Did Mark have a plan for them? She bowed her head. "Dear Heavenly Father, danki for bringing Mark into my life. Amen."

A menacing grunt came from behind a cluster of trees. The hairs on her head and neck stood straight up. She gasped, ran, and hid behind a thick tall tree. A bear had its back to her a short distance away.

She brought her hands to her mouth and stared.

The bear stood still for a moment. Two cubs joined her.

Grace stiffened and held a knuckle between her teeth to keep from screaming. The bear went in the opposite direction with the two little cubs tumbling behind her and disappeared in the woods.

She waited then peered around the trunk again. Her close call was a sign she should be more careful. She'd had more than enough excitement. She untied her horse, climbed in the wagon, and headed home. *What a day.* Life could change in an instant.

* * *

Mark rode toward town. He uttered a prayer for the bereft family and for Grace. He couldn't imagine what she must be going through after birthing a lifeless, deformed infant. He respected Grace's ability to control her emotions and to put others first.

He left his horse and wagon at the livery and crossed the boardwalk to Grace and Sarah's shop. Glancing over his shoulder, he shrugged. There weren't many shoppers milling about today. He opened the door. Sarah stood alone at the counter.

She pushed a stack of aprons aside. "Did Marie have a little boy or maedel?"

Mark frowned. "I don't like having to deliver sad information. Oh, Sarah, it was awful. The poor infant's disfigured body shocked the parents. They're grief-stricken, of course."

Sarah gasped. "Oh no! They must be devastated! Poor Grace. I'd fall apart at the seams, but Grace is strong in difficult situations and puts her heartache aside to focus her bottomless compassion on the mamm. I've witnessed her having to deal with a stillborn boppli more than once. It's one of the traits I love about my dear friend."

"Jah, you're right. She performed her midwife duties and comforted Marie as best she could. I tried to lend support to Grace and the daed. I hope I don't experience this." He held his hat to his chest. "Grace is exhausted. She's gone home. I came back to work the rest of the day, and then I'm going to do the same."

He bid Sarah farewell and went into his store. He slid a knife and small chunk of pinewood off a small table and sat to whittle a lamb. The Oyers' dochder would be a sad memory he'd never forget. He'd expected to share in a joyful moment with the young daed, but instead, it had been dreadful. He bowed his head. "Dear Heavenly Father, bless the Oyer family. Strengthen and comfort them in their time of sorrow. We don't understand why this happened, but we trust in Your divine will. Amen."

A young couple wandered in the store. Mark met the couple halfway. "Kumme in. How can I help you today?"

The Englisch woman wouldn't look at him, and the man gazed at her with a sparkle in his eyes. "I'm Wallace Brownstone." He circled the young woman's shoulders. "Meet Tillie. She's my wife."

The man was proud of his pretty fraa. They both glowed around each other.

"I'm Mark King. I'm glad you stopped in today. Is there anything in particular you had in mind?"

"We got married yesterday. I built a small house on the outskirts of town, and we'd like to purchase a bed frame and dresser. Friends have provided a settee and kitchen table and chairs." The young man reached in his pocket and pulled out coins. "Here's what I have to spend." He held up the money. "Do you have a set for a reasonable price?"

Mark guessed the couple to be around seventeen. His heart went out to them. They couldn't take their eyes off each other. He stroked the simple maple frame and matching dresser he was willing to let go for less than what he had in it. "Do you like this furniture?"

Mrs. Brownstone stroked the finish and bobbed her head, looking at her husband.

"Is this enough?"

Mark nodded and accepted the payment. He would've given it to them without charge, but he didn't want to injure the man's integrity. "Would you allow me to help you load it into your wagon?"

"Yes, please." The man threw back his shoulders and circled an arm around his fraa's waist.

Mrs. Brownstone bounced on her toes and hugged her husband's arm. "Thank you, sweetheart."

Mark and Mr. Brownstone carried the furniture to the couple's wagon. The man removed his hat and wiped perspiration from his brow before he shook Mark's hand. "Thank you for your help."

"You're wilkom. Best wishes to you and your fraa." He waited until the couple drove away before returning to his shop. He envied their openness in showing affection for each other. More than once, he'd wanted to hold Grace's hand, trace her cheek with his finger, and kiss her full lips when there were too many people around. He wished the Ordnung didn't dictate the Amish not do so. His mouth formed a mischievous grin. He had managed to slide his hand across Grace's a time or two when no one was looking. He loved her soft skin and dainty hands. And their first stolen kiss was something he'd never forget.

He blinked a few times and rubbed his forehead. It had been a long day. He closed the store early and locked the door. He stopped to glimpse in Grace and Sarah's shop window. Empty. Sarah must've gone home already.

On the way to the livery, he passed the saloon. A man tumbled out and bumped into him. He steadied himself and moved away. A second man picked the first one up by the shirt collar and punched him in the face. Mark quickened his pace. He wanted nothing but distance from their dispute.

The cruel men who had threatened him came to mind. He must speak to Noah. His friend shouldn't be working for him alone during the day. Those men could decide to visit and question him. He didn't want to put his friend in harm's way.

He arrived home and found Noah washing his hands

using the outside pump. "It's time for you to go home, but can you spare a few minutes before you leave? I'd like to speak to you about a matter."

Noah dried his hands on his shirt. He bit his bottom lip. "Is everything all right? Did I do something wrong?"

Mark patted Noah's shoulder. "No, you do an excellent job for me. It's about your safety. Kumme inside."

Mark filled two jars of water and passed one to Noah. "Have a seat." He gestured toward the kitchen table. "Noah, I'll get right to the point. Two menacing men confronted me at my shop. They're looking for my bruder, Abel, who left the Amish life in Lancaster to live in the world."

Noah pushed his back against the chair. "I'm surprised you have a bruder. Do you have any idea where he is? What did you tell them?"

"I never told you about Abel, since Amish law forbids me to mention him. I had no choice but to talk about my bruder with you now because these men might kumme here searching for him." He drummed his fingers on the table. "They are aware of where I live and have already been here. I'm not comfortable with you out here alone. It would be best if you didn't work for me."

Noah frowned and his pleading eyes watered. "You need me. You can't handle the farm and store yourself. We discussed my continuing to work here when you found evidence a stranger had hidden in your barn." He leaned forward. "Please, Mark, I need this job. I'm not afraid. I always keep my shotgun loaded to fire warning shots to the neighbors. If I need someone, they'll kumme running."

Mark's shoulders slumped and he closed his eyes for a moment. Noah had a point. What should he do? He understood Noah's dilemma. Eighteen years of age, Noah would soon choose a fraa and have a place of his own. If his loyal friend wanted to stay and work for him, he should honor his request. The thugs might never show up. He would pray for God to protect Noah. "The intruder hasn't done anything to threaten us. I have firsthand knowledge the hooligans who roughed me up are dangerous." He paused. "All right, you can continue to work here, but please be mindful of your surroundings. Don't let your guard down."

"Don't worry. Mr. Pine and Mr. Zook stop and check on me now and then. I'm sure Mamm has asked them to keep an eye on me."

Mark sipped his water. "Mr. Zook's and Mr. Pine's visits ease my mind a bit, but you'll be here alone most of the time. Be alert."

"I will. Danki, Mark. Your trust and confidence means a lot to me. I'll be fine. Don't fret."

Mark bid farewell to Noah, lit the stove to warm left-over stew, and slumped heavily in a kitchen chair. Why couldn't life be simple? He liked living in Berlin, and he'd met beautiful Grace, benevolent friends and neighbors, and enjoyed a profitable living farming and running his store. He didn't want any trouble.

After he finished his meal, he went to check for signs of anyone who may have been in his barn. Opening the trunk, his head jerked in surprise. A yellow scarf lay on top of the bag. He picked it up. Had the stranger staying in his barn been a woman? The scarf's threads had been woven from fine silk. Not the type of material an Amish woman would wear. This elegant piece of clothing would've been expensive.

He pushed it aside and held up the stranger's bag. Blood stained the side. He untied the bundle and found the Blue Diamond matches were inside, but the jar of water was empty. *What's this?* Fabric tied in a knot containing money lay inside the bag. The stranger had to have returned and put it there, along with the scarf. Not wanting to remove the money, he fingered the coins through the material and guessed the thin bag contained about three dollars. He set the illicit stash back where he'd found it.

He pinched his chin. Had a woman taken refuge in his barn? Where had the blood on the bag kumme from? Again, he hadn't heard a sound. Noah hadn't either. He dropped the bag back in the trunk and laid the scarf on top.

Mark inched his way through the crowd outside his store on Wednesday morning and unlocked the front door, and men and women flooded in. He answered questions and hurried to accept money for his products. Moving to the left or right, he bumped into shoppers.

A burly Englischer tapped his shoulder. "I visited your store a while back and told my friends about your fine furniture. We came together to buy furniture and goods for the new homes we built. Our wagons are outside."

"Danki for spreading the word about my store."

"Do you have another potato box? My friend and I both want the one you have in the corner."

"Jah, I have another potato box under the shelf over there." He pointed to the back. The number of customers wanting to purchase goods overwhelmed him. He wondered if Grace and Sarah were busy. Men and women waited for his attention. If he didn't have help, patrons might get frustrated and leave. He peeked around the door between their shops. Grace stood folding quilts. "Grace, would you mind helping me? I have a lot of potential buyers in my shop."

She dropped the quilts on the counter. "Sarah, I'm going to assist Mark. He's overrun with shoppers."

"Go ahead. We're not busy. I can manage."

Grace rushed to him and entered his shop. "Your display cabinet filled with boxes of Blue Diamond matches and assortment of knives is getting a lot of interest. There isn't a bare spot left on the floor for another person to stand!" She greeted and waited on patrons, while he did the same. Noon passed, and they were too busy to pause for dinner. He couldn't believe his good fortune.

He noticed men and women bought some of his miniature wooden toys for their kinner, and others browsed and left without buying anything. Grace spoke highly of his handcrafted toys and sold a small lamb to a mamm holding a little boy's hand. He stole glances at Grace.

Mark was delighted Grace was there with him. Was there anything she couldn't do? He didn't think so.

The last customer departed. "Danki for rescuing me."

She laughed and stretched. "You've had a profitable day."

"Jah. I sold a lot of high-priced items, plus my display cabinet is about empty."

"I'm not surprised. You do exquisite work and offer an assortment of useful household items as well as essential furniture. I'm delighted for you. Each shop owner longs for a day like the one you've had today." She checked the clock. "Since the patrons have dwindled here, I better return to Sarah."

"Oh no, I shouldn't have taken you from her for so long."

"I'm sure Sarah's fine. She wouldn't hesitate to kumme and get me if she needed me."

"I've got disturbing news. The stranger came back." He described the scarf and blood on the flour sack.

She opened her mouth in surprise. "I would never have guessed a woman would be stowing a bag in your trunk. How did blood get on the bag? She mustn't have been too hurt to walk, or she would've still been there. Did you notice blood on the ground?"

"No. There wasn't any sign of blood on the trunk, barn floor, or outside."

She tapped her lip with her finger and raised her eyebrows. "I'm baffled."

He shrugged. "I left the sack in the trunk. Maybe she'll kumme back for it." He hesitated and then told her about the thugs visiting his shop and why. "Grace, please be mindful. If any men kumme into your store and sound like the description I've given you, grab Sarah and run through our connecting door."

Grace wrinkled her nose. "They didn't bother us. I doubt they'd have any reason to kumme into our store." She wrung her hands. "I'm worried about you and your bruder."

Her concern warmed him. Her fearlessness scared him. "I'll be all right." He couldn't put Abel out of his mind. "Sounds like Abel's up to no good from what these ruffians told me, but there's nothing I can do but pray for him."

"I'll pray for his safety and yours."

A man came in.

Mark whispered to Grace, "It brightened my day to have you by my side. I appreciate your help."

She waved as the Englischer approached him.

He listened to the door shut behind him. He missed her when they weren't together. He could talk to her about anything, and she understood. She hadn't scolded him for bringing up Abel, even though it was forbidden. Grace wasn't a judgmental person, but a compassionate one. There were so many reasons why he loved her. Her physical beauty sent his heart racing. The sound of her soft voice, her gaze into his eyes said she cared about whatever he had to say, good or bad. He admired her midwifery and manager skills. It set her apart from other Amish women in the community in his eyes. The more he learned about her, the more he loved her.

The man strolled around his store, picked up toys, and slid his hand across the wooden frames and household products. Weak from missing dinner, Mark wished the patron would make his selection and leave, but the shopper asked lots of questions.

The Englischer held a small oak footstool. "I like this fine piece."

Mark collected his money and wished the man a pleasant day.

His store's appearance was a mess. Sighing, he grabbed a broom and swept dirt off the floor and out the back door, straightened toppled toys on the shelves, and righted quilt racks turned sideways.

Outside, he locked the door. Grace and Sarah had left. Surveying the area, he didn't catch sight of the menacing men searching for Abel. He sensed he hadn't seen the last of them, though. The scent of fried chicken drifted from the Berlin Restaurant. He crossed the boardwalk and stepped inside. The bell clanged overhead and the restaurant buzzed with conversations of men and women filling the round oak tables and chairs. Amish waitresses jotted customers' orders and bustled back and forth to the kitchen. A display of delicious desserts on a tray caught his attention. He found a seat across from a small window.

The young maedel set a glass of water in front of him. "What would you like to order? Our special is shepherd's pie."

"I'd like the special and bread pudding, please."

She jotted the order on paper and went to the kitchen.

Mark watched the men and women passing the restaurant, bags in hand. He'd had a busy week at the shop, and he missed dinner with Grace and Sarah. What a profitable week both their shops had experienced. Wagon trains and travelers from all over had kumme through town and kept them busy.

He was certain the mystery woman would return to collect her money. It didn't make sense she had such an expensive scarf but needed to sleep overnight in a barn. Perhaps she was hiding from somebody. Why not go the sheriff if she was in danger, or was she hiding from the law?

Mark finished his breakfast. Four days had passed, and there had been no sign of the stranger. He hoped whoever had been stowing the bag in his barn was long gone. He didn't want anything to interfere with his life in Berlin and with Grace. He'd missed her this week. His stock had gotten low, and he'd had to forgo dinner with her and Sarah to work in his back room on replenishing his stock by constructing potato boxes and wooden trains. He breathed deep and smiled. She'd be at church today. They'd have a chance to talk at the after-service meal. He looked forward to it.

He readied himself for church. He went to the barn where the Amish community gathered to worship. The bishop hadn't asked the members to accept him officially into their Amish order yet. In his mind, he'd proved himself responsible. He was in love with Grace, and being voted into the membership of the church would have to happen before he could ask her to marry him. He had no intentions of ever leaving. The church and his commitment to God played an important role in his life.

Inside the church, he chatted with Grace, her parents, Levi, and Sarah. He winked at Jonah sitting with his mamm and daed. The boy's face beamed. Comfortable and feeling like he belonged sitting with the men, he took a seat and waited for the bishop to deliver his sermon.

The elderly and stout man opened his Holy Bible. His baritone voice rang out as he spoke. "Obedience to God and our Amish laws is not easy, but it is important for each of us to strive to follow this law according to our Bible and the community Ordnung."

Mark's chest tightened and his upper lip beaded with sweat. The man's words pricked his conscience. He didn't want anything to jeopardize his reputation with Grace, her parents, the bishop, and his new friends.

The scarf he found meant trouble, and so did the intruders who confronted him at his shop. None of which would go over well with anyone in the community. Let alone the ruffians' connection to a bruder he was supposed to consider dead.

He closed his eyes for a moment. He couldn't do anything about these predicaments. He would take it a day at a time and deal with the intruder or the thugs as they presented themselves.

The bishop called his name. "Mark King, will you join me at the front, please?"

Mark jerked his head up and stood. His heart pounded as he approached the bishop.

"Please face the members."

The bishop's tone sounded serious and his mouth formed a grim line.

Mark scanned the sea of men and women dressed in black. Faces stared back at him, some with smiles and others somber. His vision blurred and his armpits dampened.

The bishop's hands rested on his shoulders. "This fine Amish man has proven his loyalty to our order by giving his time to those in need in the community. He's been faithful in church and he's managing a plentiful crop and furniture store. I'll ask him questions, he'll answer them, and then we'll vote on whether to accept Mark into our membership."

The bishop asked Mark questions concerning his faithfulness and dedication to God, God's Son, Jesus, and the Amish law and the Ordnung.

Mark swallowed hard. He spoke a firm answer to each inquiry, while facing the members. Sweat dripped down his back. He suspected warm air and nerves were to blame. He meant what he said to the bishop and members, even though Abel's face stuck in his mind. His devotion to God never wavered, but he wasn't sure he wouldn't bend the rules to help the bruder he loved.

The bishop upstretched his arm. "Men, please raise your hand if you are in favor of accepting Mark into our Amish order."

Mark gazed at Grace. She smiled and there was a sparkle in her eyes. She sat on the edge of her seat in anticipation. He couldn't help it. His grin broke out.

"Every man raised their hand, unless I've missed someone. Anyone opposed?"

Mark skimmed the congregation. No one opposed. He let out a sigh.

The bishop stepped in front of Mark. "It's settled then.

Mark, wilkom to our Amish order. Let's pray." The bishop knelt with Mark and asked the members to do the same. After the prayer, he dismissed them for the Sunday meal. Grace, Sarah, and Levi rushed to join Mark.

Grace's eyes gleamed. "I wanted to raise both hands, and I would've if the bishop allowed women to vote."

"Me too." Sarah bounced on her toes.

Levi gave him a friendly pat on the arm. "Congratulations, my friend."

Friends and neighbors swarmed around Mark. They expressed appreciation for Jonah's rescue, helping with the Wittmers' barn raising, and offering them discounts on furniture from his store. He thanked them for their kind comments. The building emptied, and he joined Levi at the dinner table.

Grace passed him a full plate of food. "Is there anything else I can get you?"

"No, danki. You didn't have to do this. I would've gotten it. Kumme sit with us."

Grace filled her plate and sat between Mark and Sarah. "Here kummes Mamm and Daed. Did they speak to you yet?"

"Not yet." He stood and gestured to the bench. "Mr. and Mrs. Blauch, we can make room for you here."

Mr. Blauch waved a dismissive hand. "We wanted to congratulate you and say how pleased we are to have you join our community. The Zooks have saved places for us at the end of the table."

Mrs. Blauch's eyes sparkled. "I'm delighted to have you join our Amish order, Mark." She leaned to his ear and whispered, "Grace is too."

Grace chuckled. "I overheard your comment, Mamm."

Mr. Blauch had already walked away, and Mark laughed with Mrs. Blauch and Grace.

Mark pointed to a big oak tree offering shade. "Let's take our plates over to the tree, Grace. We'll be in sight but can talk privately."

Kinner raced past them. Grace's plate wobbled, but she steadied it.

Mark paused. "Are you all right?"

"Yes."

"Kinner, please be mindful of others." He held her plate while she sat then passed it to her. "Your parents are welcoming and gracious. You're blessed to have them."

"I agree. I'm sorry you have no immediate family, but I hope you will consider my parents and the Helmuths your family now."

He sat next to her but left a respectful distance between them. Coming to Berlin, he had no idea what to expect. He'd never anticipated falling in love with a beautiful woman and acquiring close family like the Blauchs and Helmuths. He'd been truly blessed. He whispered in her ear. "Grace, it's only been a short time since we met, but you are very important to me. I love you."

She blushed and stared at her feet then looked at him. "I love you, too."

"I'm giving your daed time to get over the incident of you caring for me alone at my haus before I ask for your hand in marriage. I had planned on asking him first, but I can't wait any longer. Grace, will you marry me if your daed gives us his blessing?"

"Yes!" She covered her mouth and beamed. "It's difficult to stifle my excitement."

He wanted to hold her. "I want to hug you. This is when I really envy the Englischers' freedom to show affection to the one they love in public."

She chuckled. "At this moment, I would agree with you."

"I'll ask your daed soon."

She bowed her head but not before he glimpsed her sparkling gaze. "It can't be soon enough for me."

His heart swelled at her words. Mr. Blauch had wanted to go target shooting. It would give her daed and him another chance to build their friendship. He'd have to figure out some dates when he could close his shop for a few hours and then approach Mr. Blauch to see which ones suited him.

Chapter Nine

Grace gazed at Mark sitting next to her under the tall, shady tree. The birds were singing as if they were sharing in her happiness. She couldn't wait for him to ask her daed for her hand in marriage. She loved him so much she thought her heart would burst. He gazed at her as if she were flawless with his big brown eyes over and over again. He cared about what she had to say about any given subject. He had stepped in and helped her without her having to ask. Like with the Oyers. He loved her back and told her not just with words but in his actions. Sharing life with him was what she wanted to do more than anything. Shouting their news from the mountaintops was what she wanted to do, but she mustn't utter a word to anyone. Her friends and family were gathering their baskets. "Pass me your empty plate, and I'll rinse it." She stood.

He got to his feet. "Danki, but it's not too dirty. I'll take it home and rinse it. I'll walk with you to your parents."

Grace was thrilled the men had crowded around Mark and shown their support of him today. Her parents had expressed their congratulations. He had treated her with respect and kindness, despite her strong opinions at times.

He was a good provider, hard worker, and a fine, upstanding man. She admired his love for God and his openness to share his feelings about matters of the heart with her.

Sarah approached them. "Would you, Mark, and your parents like to have supper at our haus tomorrow evening?"

Grace glanced at Mark and he nodded his agreement. Her friend's haus would provide a comfortable setting for Mark and her parents to get better acquainted. "Yes, danki. What can I bring?"

"You don't need to bring anything. I'll cook supper and dessert. Levi and I like Mark, and we want your parents to like him too."

Mark grinned. "I appreciate all the help I can get, Sarah. Let me bring something."

"No, it's not necessary."

"I'm certain Mamm and Daed will kumme. Mamm will insist on bringing something. Do you have any special requests?"

Hands on hips, Sarah rolled her eyes. "No, tell her to take advantage of this opportunity to not have to cook."

"I'll tell her, but don't be surprised if she walks in holding a dish. What time should we arrive?"

"I won't turn her food away. She's the best cook in the community. Kumme around six thirty. That will give me plenty of time to prepare our meal after we close the shop."

Grace chatted with Mark, Sarah, and Levi for a short while. What a wonderful day this had been. She sucked in her top lip. Hopefully Mark wouldn't mention Abel tomorrow. Her daed might not like him referring to a bruder he was supposed to treat as dead. He and her daed had gotten along so well over Jonah's rescue, and she didn't want anything to stir the pot again.

"There's Daed and Mamm fetching the wagon." Grace walked with Mark to meet them.

Mark kept pace with Grace. "I'm looking forward to supper tomorrow night. I'd like to sit down with you, your parents, Levi, and Sarah. We'll have a good time."

"Levi and Sarah's support means a lot to me."

"Our friends have bent over backward to make things easy for us. Giving me another opportunity to be with your parents at their haus is really thoughtful of them."

Grace warmed at his remarks. Sarah and Levi were her best friends in Berlin, besides Hester. If she and Mark married, it was nice to know he and her friends liked each other. "Oh, Mark, I'm so thankful you chose Berlin to start a new life. Everything is working out wonderfully."

Mark exchanged pleasantries with her parents, and then she stepped into the wagon.

Mark called out, "See you in town in the morning."

She grinned and put her hand on her mamm's knee. "Sarah's invited us to supper tomorrow night at six thirty."

Mrs. Blauch's cheeks dimpled. "What a dear. I'll bring a sugar cream pie."

"She wants you to take the night off and not cook."

Her mamm wrinkled her forehead. "I can't go there without taking something. She can save my dessert and serve it after supper on another day."

Her mamm's determination to not go empty-handed squelched Grace's desire to argue the matter. She would've liked Mamm to use the time to do something she'd enjoy, but Mamm wouldn't listen. She didn't go to anyone's haus without offering a gift. Grace looked at the sky and hoped the conversation between her parents and Mark would be a stepping-stone to building a positive relationship between him and them.

Grace greeted and waited on customers during the morning hours on Monday. She watched the clock tick by. Having dinner at Sarah's with Mark and her parents this evening rolled around in her mind and brought joy to her heart. Concentrating on work was another story.

Two women admired a friendship keepsake pocket quilt on the wall and chatted.

"Are you in need of any help?"

The tall, elegant woman stared and winced at her. "No, we're browsing."

Grace ducked behind the counter and retrieved a biscuit and jar of water out of her dinner basket. The woman's impolite dismissal of her hadn't bothered her. She shrugged her shoulders. Maybe she had finally grown accustomed to ill-mannered customers. Time would tell.

Mark poked his head around the door. "Grace, are you and Sarah doing all right? I've been busy, but it finally let up."

"We've not had a minute to ourselves until a few minutes ago. Did you have time for dinner?"

"I brought a small pot of beans and rice and ate it cold." Several patrons entered Grace and Sarah's shop. "I should let you get back to work. I'll meet you at Sarah and Levi's tonight." He nodded then shut the connecting door.

Her heart raced. Tonight at supper, would her parents consider him a potential husband for her? She bowed her head. "Dear Heavenly Father, please forgive me for worrying about things. Please fill Daed's heart with compassion and understanding toward Mark and the hardship he is experiencing in missing his bruder, Abel, should the subject be mentioned. Danki for Your mercy and love. Amen."

She and Sarah sold their textiles to a steady stream of purchasers the rest of the afternoon. Finally the last woman left. Grace then counted the coins and raised a hand to her open mouth. "Sarah! We collected fifteen dollars today."

Sarah leaned against the counter and hugged herself. "Word has spread about our keepsake pocket quilts. Women are coming from other towns to buy them. The five ladies we have making them are doing a splendid job. Charity Lantz can stitch a quilt together faster than anyone. Her handiwork is beautiful. I love busy days. Time goes fast." She tilted her head toward Grace. "Are you nervous about supper at my haus tonight?"

"Yes, but excited, too. I'm certain Mark will leave a good impression on Mamm and Daed."

"Maybe someday soon he'll ask your daed for your hand in marriage."

Grace's face warmed and she stood. "I wouldn't be opposed."

Mark rode home. He'd missed having dinner with Grace today. Tonight, he, Grace, and her parents would be in a relaxed setting at the Helmuths' haus. It would provide a time for her parents to ask him questions. What a relief he and Mr. Blauch had shared the experience of rescuing Jonah. Otherwise, he'd be more nervous. If Mr. Blauch asked about siblings, he'd tell him the truth but not expound on Abel. The least said the better.

He reminded himself to check the trunk. Finished with

his horse and cart, he opened the trunk lid and the bag lay undisturbed. The scarf sat on top where he'd placed it. Maybe he'd seen the last of the intruder.

Crossing the yard, he went to his workshop and grabbed a plain but smooth oak bread box for Sarah and Levi and set it by the barn. He and Levi had become best friends. He valued his opinions and trusted him.

He pumped water in a large metal basin and poured it in the tub inside the haus. He added soap and bathed. The cool water soothed his tired body and washed the sweat and dirt away. Refreshed, he stood, toweled off, and put on a pair of clean, older pants to shave and comb his hair.

Time had flown by since he left the shop. He should get going. A good impression was important tonight. No time to dawdle. He dressed in fresh, clean clothes, strode outside, and picked up the bread box. He secured his horse to the spring wagon and departed.

He caught a whiff of hyacinth along the way and sneezed. The patches of mixed flowers decorating the landscape along the way lifted his mood, but their fragrance sometimes irritated his nose and throat. He arrived at Levi's and caught sight of his friend on the front porch.

Levi approached him. "Good evening. Grace and her parents are inside. I hope you're hungry. Sarah made enough food to feed ten people."

Mark retrieved the bread box from the wagon and passed it to Levi. "I can exchange this gift for something else if you already have one."

"Ours is falling apart. It belonged to Sarah's grossmudder. Danki. Sarah will love it. She's been nagging me to build or buy a replacement for weeks. I kept forgetting to tell you, and I haven't had time to visit your store." He gently slapped Mark's back. "Are you nervous about talking to Mr. Blauch? Mrs. Blauch is a sweetheart. You don't

need to worry about her asking you awkward questions."
He laughed. "She'll leave those to her husband."

Mark chuckled as they secured his horse. "I wasn't
nervous, but I am now after your keen insights."

"I'm teasing you. He's a fair and kind man. Sarah and
I want you to relax and enjoy the evening. We are certain
this supper will enhance their already good impression
of you. We'd like nothing more than if you and Grace
would wed."

"I would like to ask Mr. Blauch if I may wed Grace,
but I want them to learn more about me first."

Levi's mouth flew open. "Congratulations on your decision. Don't worry. I'll keep this information to myself.
I admire your patience. Your wisdom in waiting to ask
Mr. Blauch at the right time is an excellent decision. He'll
respect you for it."

Mark walked alongside Levi toward the haus. "Danki,
Levi."

Sarah opened the door. "Wilkom. Kumme in and take
a seat. Supper's on the table." She narrowed her eyes.
"Levi, what are you carrying?"

He held up Mark's present. "Mark brought us a new
bread box."

Sarah led Mark and Levi to the sitting room. "Mark,
how sweet of you! Danki. Levi's been in trouble over not
replacing this one." She gave the leaning box a soft kick
and winked at her husband. "He's back in my good graces
danki to you."

"Jah, danki, Mark."

"I'm glad you both like it, and if I helped my friend get
out of trouble with his fraa, all the better."

They laughed.

Mark approached Grace and her parents. "Good

evening, Grace, Mr. and Mrs. Blauch." He exchanged a winning glance with Grace.

Mr. Blauch extended his hand. "Good to see you, Mark."

Mrs. Blauch grinned. "Save room for dessert. Sarah baked blueberry tarts."

"I might want those first."

Mrs. Blauch's cheery disposition was uplifting.

Mark slid a chair next to Grace and sat.

Leaning close, Grace whispered in his ear. "You're so thoughtful, but you didn't have to bring a gift."

"I wanted to, and I wouldn't miss the opportunity to spend time with you for anything." He sniffed the fragrant scent coming off the food centered on the table. "Sarah, this turkey, carrots, boiled potatoes, and green beans make a pretty picture on your table. I'm anxious to sample each of them."

"Danki, Mark, but there's enough for you to spoon heaping portions on your plate. Don't be shy. Would you like to pray for us?"

Mark bowed his head. "Dear Heavenly Father, danki for this food and bless Sarah for preparing it for us. Danki for Your love and mercy. Amen." He raised his head and picked up his fork.

Mr. Blauch sat across from him. "How is your store doing?"

"Better than I anticipated. My regular customers must've spread the word."

"How's Noah working out for you?"

"Noah and I have become good friends. He's a wonderful and hardworking man. You did me a favor recommending I hire him. He's talented and a perfectionist when taking care of the farm. I'm blessed to have him working for me."

"Noah's an inquisitive young man. I worry about him."

Mrs. Blauch sipped her water then held the glass. "His mamm told me Noah asks a lot of questions about the outside world. She's afraid he'll leave our faith."

"Jah, he is curious about life outside our community. I'm doing my best to discourage him from leaving us. I hope he'll stay here and settle down." Mark scooped more potatoes onto his plate.

"Did you like living in Pennsylvania?" Mr. Blauch helped himself to a slice of turkey.

Grace's daed wasn't shy. Mark stifled his chuckle. Putting a carrot in his mouth, he had little time to chew his food before answering the man's questions. Was he sizing him up for a potential husband for his dochder? Mark hoped so. "I liked Lancaster very much, but I prefer Berlin."

"Good." He forked a carrot.

Mrs. Blauch passed him a bowl of potatoes. "Would you like more?"

He'd already had plenty, but he accepted it. "Danki."

Levi wiped the corner of his mouth. "How's your vegetable garden doing, Mrs. Blauch?"

"The vegetables are plentiful, and the animals have left them alone this season. I'm so pleased. I plant marigolds around my vegetables and it keeps those pesky bugs away."

Sipping his water, Mark was grateful his friend had given him a little break from Mr. Blauch's inquisition. He set his glass on the table.

Mr. Blauch held his fork in midair. "Do you have siblings?"

Levi's attempt to change the discussion hadn't worked. This was it. The question he'd been dreading. The question he wasn't sure how to answer. "My bruder, Abel, joined the Amish order then left to live in the world."

Mrs. Blauch frowned. "You're young to suffer the loss of your entire family. I'm so sorry." She set her knife on the edge of her plate. "Anything you need, you don't hesitate to ask. Any one of us would be glad to help you. Consider us family."

Grace, Sarah, and Levi nodded in agreement.

Mark met Grace's daed's gaze then waited. The man's face had grown serious. What thoughts were running through his mind? He wished he'd say something.

Mr. Blauch pushed his half-empty plate inches in front of him and leaned forward. "My fraa is right. Anything you need, don't hesitate to ask, but please don't mention your bruder again."

"I understand." Mark appreciated the soft tone the man used to deliver his message.

Mr. Blauch sniffed. "My nose tells me blueberry tarts might be for dessert. Am I right, Sarah?"

Mark relaxed. Grace's parents were compassionate and kind people. Her daed had put him at ease and ended the subject of Abel. He respected the man.

Sarah stood. "Jah, you're right."

Grace scooted her chair back. "I'll help you serve."

"No, you sit. It won't take me a minute."

Mark asked Levi and Mr. Blauch how their crops were doing, and they discussed the possibility of an early fall.

Mr. Blauch folded his hands on the table. "Mr. Peter Lehman's fraa died this morning. The man has five kinner. He's distraught and needs help. I'm going to take care of his animals in the morning. The Pine and Zook families are tending to the Lehman farm and garden."

Grace frowned. "She's young to pass at the age of thirty. The kinner are all under the age of eight."

Mamm held a palm to her heart. "A group of us have

already coordinated taking food over for the next month or so."

Sarah carried a tray of tarts in and put them in the center of the table. "How did she die?"

Grace shook her head. "The doctor isn't sure. She passed in her sleep."

Mr. Blauch cut a corner of his dessert. "Her husband said she had complained of a bad headache for several days. He'd coaxed her to go to the doctor, but she wouldn't listen."

Mark couldn't imagine losing a fraa and raising and providing for five kinner alone. What an undertaking it would be for a daed. "What can I do?"

Mr. Blauch reached for the napkin. "He has enough help right now. You have a full schedule running your property and store. A fraa would make your life and Mr. Lehman's easier." He finished his blueberry tart.

Mrs. Blauch nodded.

Grace blushed.

Sarah and Levi chuckled.

Mr. Blauch's comment about his needing a fraa hadn't escaped anyone's attention, least of all his. He'd take it as a good sign Mr. Blauch's caring words meant he'd found favor with the man. Jah, he'd say this evening was a success.

The women cleared the table and headed to the kitchen to wash dishes. He joined Levi and Mr. Blauch on the porch. Stars sprinkled the sky and the full moon provided natural light. The air was pleasant.

He pushed his chair between Levi and Grace's daed.

They sat silent and listened to the frogs croaking and watched the fireflies light the night.

Mr. Blauch crossed his legs. "When do you want to go target shooting, Mark?"

"Friday would be a good day for me. Levi, would you like to join us?"

"Jah, Levi, kumme with us."

"I'd like to, but Friday is my day to help Mr. Lehman. Don't wait on me. Go and have a nice time."

Was Levi giving him time alone with Grace's daed? Maybe it was a good idea. "I'm sorry you can't join us. Maybe you can join us another time."

Mr. Blauch outstretched his legs and crossed his ankles. "I've got to get home soon or I'll fall asleep in this comfortable chair. What time should we meet and where?"

"Six o'clock? I'll meet you at your haus."

"All right, I'll be ready. I'm going to corral my fraa and dochder."

Levi stood and whispered in his ear. "Target shooting with Mr. Blauch is a smart idea."

Mark went inside with Levi and bid everyone farewell. He exchanged glances with Grace before he followed Levi outside to get his wagon. Mark nudged Levi's arm. "You're bowing out of target practice to give me time alone with Mr. Blauch, right?"

Levi gave him a sly grin. "Of course. I told you, Sarah and I are doing everything we can to help you foster a positive relationship with Mr. and Mrs. Blauch. We think you and Grace would make a good couple, and it's obvious you and she care for each other."

Mark put his hand on Levi's shoulder. "I can use all the help I can get. Danki."

Mark rapped on the Blauches' door early Friday morning, and Grace answered. Her birthmark was more prominent this morning. Maybe it was the way she turned her head. He had gotten used to it, and it did nothing to diminish her beauty to him. He loved her sweetheart-shaped face and sweet lips.

She opened the door and gestured him in. "Good morning. Daed's ready to go shooting. He's been cleaning his gun and talking about it since our supper at Sarah's the other night."

"This will be pleasurable for me as well. I haven't taken time to go target shooting for a while. The sport relaxes me."

Mr. Blauch came to the door. "Mark, would you like some breakfast before we leave?"

"No, danki. I had breakfast at home."

"I've got my rifle, shotgun, and supplies. If you're ready, let's head out."

Before following her daed out the door, he leaned close to her ear. "I have high hopes my time with your daed today will foster our friendship leading to my asking him for your hand soon."

She blushed. "I hope so."

He left and crossed the yard to his wagon. "I've got a bag of empty tin cans we can use for targets."

Mr. Blauch patted a large gunny sack. "I brought some too." He pointed. "Let's go over there."

Mark untied his horse and took his seat next to Mr. Blauch in the wagon, and then he directed his horse to a thick grassy patch down the road for his animal to graze. "Let's walk east. No one should be there, and it will be a safe place for us to shoot."

Securing his horse, Mark watched Mr. Blauch grab his gun, target cans, ammunition, and canteen. Mark did the same, and they trudged through the dense woods.

Mr. Blauch gestured to a large dead tree on its side.

"This area looks perfect for setting up our targets." He

untied his bag and lined the cans on the tree. "You go first." He stepped behind Mr. Blauch, showed him how to aim his shotgun, allowing for windage and distance, and then backed away.

Mr. Blauch aimed and fired. A can flipped off the log. "It worked. Danki."

For the next hour, they practiced. There was little left of the pellet-riddled cans when they finished the last of the shotgun shells.

Mark liked being with Mr. Blauch. The man's relaxed grin, exclamations of success, and praising him for his pointers brought smiles to his face.

Mr. Blauch swiped sweat off his forehead with his shirtsleeve. "I'm tired. Let's sit for a few minutes."

Mark found a rock-free area. "This is a large enough spot."

Mr. Blauch rattled his canteen. "Mine's empty."

Mark handed his canteen over. "Take mine. I've had plenty."

Mr. Blauch thanked him and drank. He screwed the cap back on and passed it to Mark. "I've had a splendid time this morning. Danki." He wiped his brow with a handkerchief. "Mark, you're not getting any younger. Have you thought about finding a fraa?"

Mark choked on his saliva. He didn't know what to say. "Jah." He silenced for a moment then cleared his throat. "Marriage and family are definitely something I'm considering in the near future."

"Glad to hear it." He checked his timepiece. "We better head back. We both have chores to do."

Mark swallowed. Had he passed up a perfect opportunity to ask for Grace's hand? No. Today was about concentrating on his friendship with Mr. Blauch. He didn't want him to think he'd brought him shooting as a ruse. It was important Mr. Blauch understand he truly liked being with him. He bit his lip. His patience would run out soon. Each time he set eyes on Grace, he found it more difficult to wait.

Mark followed Mr. Blauch to the wagon and drove him home. The man looked tired. He bid him farewell. "Please give my best to Mrs. Blauch."

"I will. Danki, Mark, for a nice day."

"Wilkom. Take care." Mark guided his horse to the store. Asking for Mr. Blauch's blessing would be a big step. The timing and setting must be perfect for the occasion.

Chapter Ten

Mark finished working at the store, went home, and fixed soup and buttered bread for supper. He had fretted about closing during the morning to shoot with Mr. Blauch, but a steady stream of customers relieved his mind in the afternoon. His regret was not getting to spend much time with Grace. He'd had a few minutes to open their connecting door and say hello. She, too, had been busy.

He pictured them living life and working out problems together. She had a strong will he suspected would challenge him at times, but he liked having a woman not afraid to speak her mind. She'd be a good partner to consult with. No doubt she'd be a good mamm. He'd witnessed her way with kinner. Jonah adored her. Of course, who wouldn't?

He strolled outside to the barn and looked around. Lifting the trunk lid, he peeked inside. The bag appeared undisturbed. It'd been days since he found the scarf. She mustn't be coming back. He shrugged his shoulders. Something rubbed against his leg. Glancing at a dog, he breathed a sigh of relief.

He petted the scraggly, dirty black mutt. "Do you belong

to someone? Are you lost? Since you're rail thin, you've probably gone without food for a while."

The dog tilted his head from side to side and wagged his tail.

He'd noticed dogs playing with kinner in the community, but not this one. "You must be hungry, but we better bathe you before I offer you food. You're filthy."

He pumped water into two big washtubs and added soap to one. He grabbed a towel from a shelf in the barn and threw it over his shoulder. He set the dog into the soapy water and washed him then moved the animal into the tub with plain water. "Good boy. You're obedient. You and I will get along fine."

"What should we name you?" He rubbed his chin. "I'll call you Dusty."

The dog jumped out of the tub and shook.

Mark laughed and held up his hands. "Hey, you're getting me all wet." He grabbed the towel off his shoulder.

Dusty stood and licked his face while he toweled him off.

The medium-sized dog had the softest coat of black fur. "You're a handsome animal when you're clean. Let's fatten you up."

Mark led him in the haus and offered him a plate of leftover food. He cut up chicken and scooped leftover potatoes in a bowl and pumped water in another bigger bowl.

Dusty jumped on his hind legs and scratched at Mark's knees. He barked.

Mark pointed. "Sit. Be patient." He put the bowls on the floor, and Dusty stuck his nose in the food and didn't raise it until he'd licked the bowl clean. He then drank the water.

Mark watched him and waited for a minute. "You

downed your supper too fast. You're not going to get sick on me, are you?"

Dusty tilted his head as if he understood.

Satisfied his new furry friend wasn't going to get sick, he readied for bed and climbed in.

Dusty jumped up and snuggled next to him. His soft fur tickled Mark's nose, but he liked having a new pet. He'd never had a dog. The animal obeyed, was friendly, and was good company in the short time they'd spent together. He hoped Grace would like him. He wouldn't want to have to give him away when he and Grace got married.

Mark woke with a start to Dusty's loud barking.

Dusty paced the floor and barked over and over.

"What's wrong, boy?"

A loud snap came from outside. Light flickered in the window. It hadn't been dark all that long. He climbed out of bed and dashed to the window. "Fire!"

Dusty ran through the haus barking.

Mark's heart throbbed against his chest. He hurried to the door and opened it. "I've got to alert the neighbors." He rushed back inside, grabbed his shotgun off hooks above the door, and ran to the front yard. He pointed to the sky and fired off two shots then put it by the door. Flames flickered and crackled. Black smoke billowed out between burning wall planks.

He opened the barn door, blinded, and urged the horses out first. He turned them loose in the corral a safe distance away. Back inside the burning building, he got the rest of his livestock out. Friends and neighbors, who'd arrived within minutes of the gunshots, worked along with him to save his livestock.

Dusty barked and herded the animals to the far end of the corral.

Chickens, hens, and the rooster squawked and carried on. The dog herded them into the enclosed chicken-wire area and nudged the door shut with his nose.

Relieved to find the fire stayed on the left side and not the right, he hoped it was manageable. Men and women filled every tub and pail they could find and helped put out the blaze.

Mark caught sight of Grace, her parents, Levi, and Sarah. They had formed a line with several others and were throwing one pail after another on the fire. He joined them. It was working. The fire had diminished. He bowed his head. "Dear Heavenly Father, danki for saving me, my animals, and my dwellings. Danki for kind and helpful friends and neighbors. Danki for Your love, grace, and mercy. Amen." He trembled. His livestock might have been killed and everything he owned destroyed. God had been good.

He, Levi, Mr. Blauch, Noah, and other neighbors lugged wooden planks he had in his workshop to the barn and repaired the damaged areas by lantern light.

Mr. Blauch clapped the dirt off his hands. "The barn should air out in a couple of hours, and then you can put your animals back inside. The damage isn't too bad. Earlier, I worried you'd lose the entire structure. Do you have any idea how this happened?"

"I didn't see anyone, and I didn't leave a lantern on. I have no idea."

Mr. Zook greeted Mark and Mr. Blauch. "Sorry about the fire, Mark. I'm glad your livestock survived and there wasn't more damage. Your furry friend did a fine job helping corral the animals."

"Danki. He came in my barn earlier. I'll keep him, unless someone claims him."

Mr. Zook and Mr. Blauch nodded to Mark then got in conversation about their hay fields.

Mark approached Grace. "Danki for kumming."

Grace wiped her wet forehead. She was pretty, in spite of her dirty apron, the smoke scent, and her sweat-stained face. "It's over, and the barn is still in good condition. I'm relieved your animals are unharmed. What caused the fire?"

"I wish I knew."

Dusty joined them.

Grace petted him. "Who is this handsome boy? He's quite helpful and smart. I was impressed and stunned by his heroics."

"His name is Dusty. He showed up in the barn earlier this evening. We're becoming fast friends. I'm surprised at what he did for me tonight too."

Dusty licked her hand.

"He's a pretty dog." She giggled. "He's friendly, too."

The Helmuths, Blauches, and many friends and neighbors surrounded him. They asked if they could do anything else, and if not, they were headed home.

"No. I appreciate your help more than I can say. Danki for your quick response." He waited until the others turned their backs to leave, then exchanged a look with Grace and mouthed the words, *Danki again for your help.*

He waited until the last person had departed and then checked on the animals. He'd keep his gun handy in case a coyote threatened to harm them. The soft breeze would help rid the barn of smoke.

Monday morning Mark fed the animals, milked the cow, petted Dusty, and went to work after chatting with Noah a minute. He grabbed and pushed a broom across the floor of his store and familiar voices drifted his way minutes later. Icy dread crawled up his back and neck. He held the broom tight. "What do you want?"

The thugs bore down on him.

Buck stood inches from his face. "How'd you like our warning?"

Mark winced at his putrid alcohol breath, stepped back, and gritted his teeth. "You started the fire? Why?"

The man sneered. "Call it a warning." Buck knocked the broom out of Mark's hands. "We haven't found your brother, and we want twenty dollars to tide us over until we do."

"I don't have twenty dollars on hand."

Skinner brandished a knife from his boot. "Maybe you need a little more convincin'." Skinner stepped in front of Buck and pressed the sharp blade to Mark's throat. The man narrowed his eyes. "Give us what you've got then, or you're a dead man."

Heart thundering against his chest, Mark stared at the man. "Let go of me and I will."

Skinner poked the knife against Mark's neck then lowered it. "Make it quick."

Mark reached in his pocket and pulled out three dollars in coins and passed the money to Skinner. "You've taken all my money. Now leave." His legs threatened to buckle, and he hoped the fear rising in his chest wouldn't show.

Skinner scoffed and curled his fist around the coins. He held them to Mark's nose. "You think this is enough?" The thug smirked. "Buck, the Amish man isn't moving to open his cashbox. Guess we shoulda lit his house on fire." He pressed the knife once again to Mark's throat and pricked the tender skin. Blood trickled down Mark's neck.

Buck crossed his arms. "Maybe you didn't make

yourself clear, Skinner." He crossed the room, and Skinner stepped back.

"We can sure take care of putting some fear into him." Buck grabbed Mark's shirt and held up his fist. "You tell me, Amish man. Do I need to knock you around to get our point across? My friend, Skinner here, would like nothing better than to drive his knife into your side. I might let him do it if you don't cooperate. Where's your money box?"

Mark held his breath a moment then let out a ragged sigh. "Under the counter."

Buck pushed Mark. "Come on, Skinner. Let's see what the Amish man's got hidden in his treasure box."

He had taken his earnings to the bank on Friday. Glad the men wouldn't get a substantial amount of money, he worried their tempers would flare. He slid back the curtain under the counter and removed the metal box.

Buck grabbed it from his hands and opened the lid. "Not much in here." He counted the money. "Five dollars in coins." He snorted and pinched his lips together. "This will have to do for now."

Buck socked Mark in the stomach. "We'll be back for more if your brother doesn't show his face soon. You can count on it."

Mark gasped for air, moaned, and doubled over. "Get out."

The scoundrels left, slamming the door.

He looked out the window. The men crossed the street to the saloon. It wasn't the Amish way to notify the sheriff about trouble from Englischers, but he couldn't put up with these ruffians harassing him. He thought they would've been tired of searching for Abel in Berlin and moved on. He'd settled into Berlin, gained friends, and was about to ask Grace's daed's permission to marry her. He didn't want to create a stir about this. He'd wait.

Mark rose to a gray sky on Sunday morning. There had been no encounters or sightings of the menacing men the rest of the week. He hoped not to lay eyes on them again. He shrugged into his clothes, hitched his horse to his buggy, and rode to church.

He caught sight of Grace the minute he entered. He adored her beautiful face, waved to her, and sat next to the men on the other side. Eager to see her, he struggled to pay attention to the bishop's message for the first few minutes.

Bishop Weaver held up his King James Bible. "Please turn to the Book of Luke, chapter six, verses twenty-seven, twenty-eight, and twenty-nine." He adjusted his spectacles and read. *"But I say unto you which hear, Love your enemies, and do good to them which hate you. Bless them that curse you, and pray for them which despitefully use you. And unto him that smiteth thee on the one cheek offer also the other; and him that taketh away thy cloak forbid not to take thy coat also."*

Mark stared at his hands. This was a difficult message to adhere to these days. He bowed his head in prayer. *Dear Heavenly Father, forgive me for wanting to harm the men who came in my shop. Protect Abel in spite of his shortcomings. Prick his heart and conscience. Help him find his way back to You. Please give me the right words to say to Grace's daed. Amen.*

He raised his eyes at Grace and her family. Enough time had passed. He would ask Mr. Blauch for his dochder's hand in marriage. He was ready to move on with his life and put the past behind him.

Outside, after the service, Jonah hugged Mark's legs. "Play hide-and-seek with me."

"I'll help the women set the table and then I'll fix you a plate." Grace strolled toward the food table.

"Danki." Mark chased Jonah and played the game with him for a while. "Everyone's gathering around the table. We should fill our plates before the food is gone." He escorted Jonah to his parents then returned to Grace. "Would you like to join me at the small table under the oak tree?"

She carried two jars of water, and he carried their filled plates of food. She squinted at the bright sun. "I watched you with Jonah. I'm not sure who was having more fun, you or him."

"He's a well-behaved boy. I like having him around." He sat across from her. "I can't wait to have kinner."

"Me too."

He paused, leaned in, and met her eyes. "Grace, I'm in love with you. I can't imagine spending the rest of my life without you in it. I'm going to ask your daed for your hand in marriage tomorrow. He and I have spent enough time together to know and trust each other. I don't want to wait any longer." His mouth curved in a teasing grin. "You haven't changed your mind about marrying me, have you?"

"Of course not!" She squirmed. "I'm anxious to marry you. I'm nervous but confident my parents won't have any objections."

Her sweet expression confirmed her love for him. He reached out to touch her hand but withdrew it. "I have the hardest time not wrapping my arms around you and planting the biggest kiss on your sweet lips."

She blushed. "Oh, Mark, I've longed to have your arms around me. If we were alone, I wouldn't push you away."

"Sarah and Levi are coming. I've been itching to tell them about our plans, and you must be also, but let's not say anything until I've had a chance to talk to your daed."

"I'm bursting at the seams to tell Mamm and Sarah. You must kumme for supper tomorrow. Mamm loves cooking and having people over for meals. It will give you a chance to talk to Daed in private."

Her enthusiastic response and providing the perfect opportunity to carry out his task thrilled him. He wouldn't forget her expression for the rest of his days. If Mr. Blauch agreed to his request, the Blauch family would soon become his in-laws. It would be comforting to have parents again.

On the way home, Mamm patted Grace's knee. "I rocked for a few minutes on the porch this morning and delighted in the sunshine, watched squirrels chasing each other up and down the trees, and listened to the birds chirp. I thought about how happy you have been, and it warms my heart."

Daed nodded. "You deserved a few minutes to yourself. You work hard. Your food tasted delicious, as always. I'm pleased to find our dochder smiling a lot these days too."

Grace stared off in the distance. She would be a bride soon. *Mark's fraa.* He hadn't appeared uneasy asking her to marry him. A sure sign he was certain about her and their future together. She had no qualms about spending the rest of her life with him.

Grace listened to her mamm's chatter but couldn't concentrate on what she was saying.

"My dearest dochder, you haven't paid attention to a word I've said, have you?"

"No, I'm sorry. Tell me again."

The wagon wheel jostled when it hit a rut in the dirt road. Mamm clasped Grace's arm for support. "What's got you preoccupied?"

Daed laughed. "Not *what* but *who* would be the appropriate question."

Mamm patted Grace's hand. "It's all right. I'm pleased our dochder and Mark have a spark. This is an important time in her life." She nudged his arm. "I remember when I swooned after you."

Daed chuckled and scoffed.

Grace said, "Speaking of Mark, he's coming for supper tomorrow."

"Good. I'll take venison out of the icebox." She winked. "This might be a very special occasion."

Daed halted the horse and jumped out of the wagon. "He's wilkom to our haus anytime."

Grace climbed down and grabbed a dish. She avoided Mamm's gaze. The words on her tongue begged to be spoken, but she mustn't say anything. The joy she'd felt since Mark proposed had put a smile on her face. Mamm must suspect something. Nonetheless, she'd honor Mark's wishes.

Grace opened a jar of peach jam and emptied it in a small dish Monday evening. Mark would arrive any minute. This had been the longest day. Would her daed have any reservations about Mark's proposal? She was certain he'd be delighted to have Mark for a son-in-law. "Mamm, what else can I do?"

Mamm bustled about the kitchen. "The table is set, and food is done, and ginger cookies are ready for dessert. You've been as jumpy as a cat today. Is anything bothering you?"

Tempted to tell Mamm Mark had proposed, she stifled her excitement. "I'm fine. I'm anxious to have Mark join us for supper."

Voices came from the sitting room. She went to greet Mark and waited. Her daed welcomed him with a grin and handshake. This night was off to a great start.

"Kumme in, Mark. Take a seat. Let's have supper while the food is hot. I'm pleased you could join us this evening." She poured water in their glasses.

Grace couldn't sit still. Food sat heavy in her stomach, and she struggled to clean her plate. Glancing at the mantel clock, she willed the minute hand to move faster.

Mr. Blauch asked Mark how his store was doing, and they discussed his latest handcrafted items to sell.

Mark asked, "Mrs. Blauch, what would you shop for in my store?"

Being asked her opinion brought dimples to her cheeks. "I would seek out potato keepers, bread boxes, and mending chests large enough to hold material and supplies." She blushed. "Danki for asking my opinion."

"You've provided a new idea for me. Mending boxes are something I can add to my inventory. Danki."

Grace passed Mark the carrots. "Would you like more?"

"No danki, but it was delicious."

They chatted a little while longer about church, the weather, and how well Jonah had recovered from his incident in the woods. She squirmed in her seat. Her patience had run out.

"Let's save apple pie for later." Mamm carried the dishes to the kitchen.

Grace wasn't sure her nerves could take another minute of sitting still. She was more than ready for Daed and Mark to go off alone to discuss what would be a life-changing and memorable occasion for her.

Daed pushed back his chair. "Mark, join me on the porch. The night's quiet and the stars are shining bright tonight. We can chat while the women clear the table."

Grace caught Mark's wink. This was it. Her hands trembled as she dried the dishes Mamm handed her. Straining to listen to the men's conversation, she couldn't understand a word they were saying.

Mamm paused, dried her hands, and slipped her arm through Grace's. "I have an idea what's going on here tonight. What are we doing in the kitchen?" She gave her a playful grin. "Let's go to the sitting area. The door's open. We can eavesdrop."

Grace's mouth flew open. "You don't miss a stitch." She laughed and gently squeezed her arm.

They sat in the chairs closest to the door. She cast her eyes on Mark through the open doorway.

Mamm leaned forward. "I wish they'd speak up."

"Me too!"

Mark stood and shook her daed's hand. They came inside.

Her daed directed his attention to Mamm. "Mark's got something he'd like to say to you."

"Mrs. Blauch, I asked Grace to marry me. She said jah, and your husband has given us his blessing. Do you?"

Mamm jumped up from her chair and put a hand to her heart. "I'm thrilled! Grace hasn't wiped the smile off her face since meeting you. She has a lilt in her voice and a bounce in her step, and I credit both to how happy you're making her."

Grace rose and stood next to Mark. "Danki, Mamm and Daed, for your blessing. This is the happiest day of my life." She gazed fondly at her future husband.

"Why don't you two take a walk? It's a beautiful night, and I'm sure you have a lot you'd like to discuss."

She grabbed a lantern and walked outside next to Mark. Out of her parents' earshot, she paused. "How did it go with my daed?"

"He was gracious and kind. He didn't hesitate to offer his acceptance of me as a son-in-law. Spending time with him rescuing Jonah and going target shooting was a good idea. We've grown close, and he's had a chance to find out what kind of man I am. I promised to love, honor, and protect you."

Grace bubbled with excitement. "Mamm shocked me. She figured it out. Like a schoolmaedel, she wanted to overhear your conversation with Daed. I did too, but we couldn't understand your conversation. I had no doubt she'd be pleased for us."

He led her to the barn, hidden out of sight from her haus, set the lantern on a tree stump, and put his arms around her.

Her heart raced and her knees weakened. Not sure what to do, she placed her hands on his shoulders.

He gently raised her chin and leaned close to her face.

Her body melted with excitement. He was going to kiss her. The moonlight hid his eyes. She held her breath for a moment.

"I love you, Grace." His lips met hers.

Mark's lips were soft and the swell of delight went from her head to her toes. His kiss was so much better than she'd imagined it would be. Nothing like the brief, stolen kiss in his furniture store so long ago.

He rested his forehead on hers and hugged her closer. "My heart is about to jump out of my chest."

"I can hardly speak. I don't want our time together tonight to end." She thought her heart would melt.

He'd said what she wanted to hear, and she had no doubt he meant it. Words she hadn't expected to hear from a man. Not with her ugly birthmark marring her face. Mark had looked past her flaw and taken the time to find out what was on the inside.

"I love you so much. I want to climb the highest mountain and shout to the world I'm marrying Mark King!"

"I'd stand beside you and shout our news too." He caressed her cheek. "When would you like to get married?"

"Tomorrow!" She laughed. "In all seriousness, we must check the bishop's schedule. This is a busy time for you with farming and the store. I'll leave the wedding date to you."

"I, too, would like us to marry as soon as possible." He kissed her nose. "I'll speak with the bishop and schedule the date, then we can look forward to him announcing it to the membership."

His touch and smallest kiss sent a thrill through her. She didn't want to wait. "Because of the harvest season, November is popular for weddings. I'm not sure I can wait."

He stepped back and held her hands. "I'll ask the bishop for a date in early November." He swung her hands a little. "As much as I don't want to wait, our friends and family will enjoy our day more after the harvest. They will also have more time to help us."

"Good idea. Thursday is a popular day for weddings. It allows us one day before to prepare and gives everyone two days before Sunday to catch up on chores."

"Will you tell Sarah right away?"

"Yes, she and Levi won't share our wedding plans with anyone until the bishop has a chance to announce it."

"I'd like them to know now." He gently squeezed her. "I'm so anxious to begin our life together." He embraced her and kissed her again.

She closed her eyes for a moment and willed herself to remember the way his lips touched her mouth, his arms circled around her waist, the perfect night air, and the stars lighting the sky. "I've been praying for a man like you. God sent you into my life when I least expected it."

"Since losing my parents and Abel, I've anticipated finding a fraa but never found the right woman, until I met you. Now I understand why. God had you in mind for me." He caressed her soft cheek. "We should go back. I don't want to have you out here too long. The last thing I need is for your daed to catch me kissing his dochder!"

She laughed, and they went inside. Mamm and Daed sat across from each other in the sitting room drinking lemonade with Bibles in their laps.

Mark said, "I wanted to say farewell and danki for the meal and your blessing."

Mr. Blauch stood and patted him on the back. He glanced at Mamm who joined him. "We couldn't be happier."

Mamm handed him a container. "Here's a bag of short-bread cookies and some leftovers to take home."

"I'd never turn down your cooking. Danki."

Watching her parents, Grace hugged herself. This night had surpassed her expectations. She walked outside to bid Mark a private farewell then stepped in the haus.

"When will Mark speak to the bishop?"

She stifled her giggle at Mamm's enthusiasm. "Tomorrow. It's no secret I'm not a patient woman. Waiting for my wedding day to arrive will be my hardest challenge yet."

The three of them shared a warm laugh.

Daed kissed their foreheads. "I'm off to bed. I'll leave the two of you. You have a wedding to plan."

Mamm returned to her chair. "Of course, you'll make

your dress. Do you and Sarah have light blue fabric at the store? It would be perfect."

"You and I have the same idea. If we don't have enough of what I'd like, I have time to order the material."

"Grace, I'm so elated for you and Mark. He fits in well with us and the community. I'm looking forward to helping you with your dress, cooking for the wedding, and whatever else you need."

"Danki. You've set a good example of what a good fraa should be to her husband."

"I fell in love with your daed the first day I met him. Taking care of you and your daed makes me happy. I want the same for you." She reached across the short distance between them and squeezed her hand gently. "I love you, Grace. It warms my heart you're happy."

"I'm not going to sleep a wink tonight, I'm so thrilled. I've waited a long time for this moment." She hugged her mamm. "I'll see you in the morning." She went to her room and shut the door. After attending a number of weddings, she'd be the bride this time. She'd stitch her wedding dress instead of one for a friend who couldn't sew, stand with Mark in the church, and exchange vows with him.

She undressed and shrugged into her nightclothes. She'd be a mamm someday. A pang of guilt went from head to toe. She'd doubted God at times. She knelt beside her bed, folded her hands, and bowed her head. "Dear Heavenly Father, I'm sorry I doubted You in my prayers to provide a husband for me. In my heart, I thought I'd be a spinster. Mark is an even kinder, gentler, stronger, and more loving man than I'd pictured marrying. Danki for mercy and grace. Danki for Mark and my parents' acceptance of him. Amen."

Pushing herself up, she stood. Sharing their wedding

day with friends and neighbors would be a pleasure. She wished she could tell everyone her news now. They were supposed to keep their secret until a month before the ceremony, but she'd tell her best friend. Sarah would be delighted.

She fingered the quilt over her chair in the corner. She took a bottle of ink and a piece of paper and wrote Mark a letter. Tucking it inside, she wondered when she should give it to him. She could give him one before and the other after the wedding. He'd have the note in the pocket to read and remind him of her before they were married, and the other as a keepsake to read on their anniversary date for years to kumme. It would be her way of telling him she loved him every day.

Becca would be happy for her, but how could she tell her without getting in trouble? She'd visit Hester and ask if she needed help. At the same time, she'd tell Hester she was getting married. No doubt Hester would pass her news on to Becca. This day had been special, and she couldn't stand to have it end.

Chapter Eleven

Grace arrived at Hester's haus on this bright and warm Tuesday morning. A red fox scurried in the brush, and a fish jumped out of the pond, making a splash. She climbed out of the wagon and tied her horse to the hitching post. She flinched. A little gray mouse crossed in front of her feet.

Hester stood fastening a sheet to a clothesline. Her long dark braid hung down her back. Her calico dress fit pretty on her tall thin frame.

Grace tiptoed and snuck up behind her. "Good morning."

"What a nice surprise!" Hester quickly turned and circled her in a hug. "It's been a while since I've laid eyes on you. Have you been busy at your shop?"

"Our shop is making a profit this year. Have you delivered any bopplin lately?"

"No, but children hurting themselves have kept me busy patching them up." She gestured to the porch. "Let's sit outside in the rocking chairs. I need a break." She paused. "Would you like lemonade?"

"Get some lemonade for you, but I'm all right. I won't

be here long. I must get to the shop. I have something exciting to tell you." She sat.

Hester put hands on her hips. "What is it?"

"Mark King proposed to me. I'm getting married!"

Her friend's eyes sparkled. "I'm thrilled for you, Grace. Tell me about him." She slid her rocker closer to Grace's and sat.

"He's everything I want in a husband. Kind, compassionate, and handsome with thick brown hair and beautiful eyes I get lost in. He stands tall next to me, and his scent is a pleasant one of cedar. He's a talented man. He handcrafts furniture, household items, and toys. He owns a furniture store in town next to Sarah and me." She loved talking about Mark. What she couldn't say was how the joy of his touch and thoughts of him were with her every waking moment.

Hester said, "I recognize the name. I've walked by his store in town."

"Mark's talking to the bishop today about our wedding date. I wish you could attend."

"Since I'm an Englischer, I'm blessed the Amish let me teach you midwifery and let us work together. Your community appreciates my help, but I understand not being included in their social lives. It's all right."

Grace paused and nervously fingered the string on her kapp. "Can you tell Becca I'm getting married the next time you write or visit her? I can't be in contact with her any longer."

Hester covered her hand. "Of course I will. She'll be happier than a bee in a pot of honey."

"I miss her, but I'm pleased she's happy." She paused. "Do you have any mamms expecting bopplin soon?"

"I'm not aware of any. I'll visit the shop and tell you if I hear of pregnant women needing us."

"I'm ready to help whenever you need me." Grace stood. "It's so good to see you, but I should get to work." She winced. "Mark and I can't tell the Amish community we're getting married until the bishop announces it. Please keep the news to yourself until then, except for telling Becca."

"I'm good at keeping secrets." She crossed her lips with her forefinger. "My lips are sealed."

"Danki. Take care of yourself." She hugged Hester and drove to work.

On her way to town, the sky darkened and the wind threatened to blow her kapp off. She hurried to beat the rain sure to kumme soon. Arriving at the store, she went inside and peeked through the middle door to Mark's shop. Dark and quiet, he wasn't there. Maybe he was meeting with the bishop at this very moment. She ducked back into her and Sarah's shop.

Sarah entered minutes later, shaking out her black umbrella. "The rain came down with a vengeance. Water is pounding the dirt."

"I've been anxious for you to get here."

Sarah's concern shadowed her face. "Why, what's wrong?"

"Mark asked me to marry him. I said yes! Mamm and Daed gave their blessing last night at supper. Mark's going to ask the bishop for his blessing and set a date for the wedding."

Sarah reached for Grace's hands. "I couldn't be more thrilled. I understand I mustn't tell our friends and neighbors yet, but may I tell Levi?"

"Yes, please inform him."

"He'll be thrilled. We've been praying for this to happen. What can I do to help?"

"I haven't been able to think straight, I've been so

excited. First, I need to check our fabric supply. I'd like light blue for my dress. Mark will need a new white shirt and black pants. I'd love it if you'd stitch my white kapp."

"I'd love to. Danki, Grace."

Grace slipped her arm through Sarah's as they strolled to the back. She pulled a box from a shelf and rummaged through the stack of fabrics. "Look, I found the perfect shade of light blue for my dress."

"I like it." Sarah unfolded white material. "Here's enough to make Mark's shirt." She fingered black fabric. "There's enough black cloth to make a pair of pants."

"Not having to order and wait on fabric is a big relief. I can get started on my dress tonight."

"When is Mark talking to the bishop?"

"He's not in his store yet. I'm hoping he's visiting him as we speak. I hope the date will be sooner than later. I'm itching for it to happen so I can share my wedding date with our friends."

"I'm already counting the days." Sarah put her hand on the middle door. "Let's see if he's here yet."

Mark woke with Dusty snuggled up against him. He glanced at the clock and groaned. "It's late. I overslept." He patted his pet and swung his legs over the side of the bed. Standing up, he stretched, washed his face, combed his hair, and dressed.

Grace entered his mind. Anxious to talk to the bishop, maybe he should go visit him first. He was hoping for the early part of November. He was anxious to share his life with her. Soon, they'd live together here in his haus.

He downed a few bites of buttered bread and drank half a cup of coffee.

Noah pushed the door open. "Mark, I'm surprised you're still here. I thought you'd be at work."

"I'm running late today, but the shop can wait to open. I've got an important errand to run before I go to town." He rested his hand on Noah's shoulder. "Can you keep a secret?"

Noah squinted. "Jah, you can trust me."

"I'm getting married!"

Noah pushed his back against the chair. "Congratulations, I hope you and Grace will be very happy together. When's the wedding date?"

"I'm on my way to the bishop's haus to ask when he can perform the ceremony."

"I couldn't be happier for you."

"I'm having a difficult time keeping this information to myself. I want to shout it all over town."

Mark pulled back the window curtain. "The rain has ceased. I should hurry to the bishop's haus. I hope we don't get another downpour."

"Again, I'm thrilled for you, Mark."

"Danki, Noah. You're an important person in my life. I wanted to tell you before anyone else did."

Mark left and rode straight to the bishop's haus. He rapped on the door, and raindrops fell.

The bishop answered with surprise on his face. "This is an odd time of day for you to visit." He gestured him inside. "Is everything all right?"

"Everything's more than all right. I asked Grace Blauch to marry me, and she said jah. I'm here to ask your blessing and to schedule a date for our wedding."

"Congratulations, and I'm pleased." He pushed his spectacles back up on his nose. "Have you asked Mr. Blauch for his approval?"

"Jah, he and Mrs. Blauch are in favor of our impending union."

"I really didn't have any doubt they would grant you their permission. I've observed you chatting with them at church. You all appear to get along well." He leafed through the pages of his calendar. "November fifteenth is available."

"November fifteenth it is then. Grace and I want to get married as soon as possible. We're ready to experience life together."

Bishop Weaver adjusted the spectacles on his nose. "Let's meet Tuesdays and Thursdays at five at my home for premarital counseling. Is this time all right?"

"We'll be here."

The older man shook his head. "I didn't offer you anything. Would you like to visit for a few minutes? I have lemonade."

"No, I should get to the shop. I'm late opening today. Danki."

The bishop patted his back. "I'm sure our members will rejoice when they hear of it. I'll announce it sometime in October."

"It will be a very memorable and important day for Grace and me. I'm anxious to marry her."

Bishop Weaver laughed. "Your enthusiasm is infectious. I doubt I'll stop smiling the rest of the day." He patted Mark's shoulder. "Take care. Give Grace my best when you see her."

"Will do. Danki again." The rain had disappeared and white puffy clouds parted in the sky. A vibrant rainbow arched. Grace's family and the bishop had been receptive to their impending marriage. He couldn't have asked for things to go any smoother.

A short time later, he strolled into Sarah and Grace's shop.

"Mark, did you visit Bishop Weaver?" Grace bit her lip in anticipation.

Sarah hugged the quilts in her arms. "Congratulations! Grace told me you're getting married. I can't wait to tell Levi. He'll be happy for you."

"Danki, Sarah. And jah, Grace, I did visit the bishop. November fifteenth is our wedding date, and we will meet Tuesdays and Thursdays at five for our premarital counseling meetings at the bishop's haus."

Grace's face glowed. "November fifteenth is perfect. It gives us enough time to prepare, and we don't have to wait as long as I'd feared."

Sarah set the quilts on the counter. "All the women will want to cook and take part. A wedding brings such joy. I can't wait."

A customer came in. "Can someone show me what you have to offer in aprons?"

Sarah rushed to her. "I'll help you."

Grace pressed her hands together. "Mark, danki for taking care of this so soon."

Mark looked at the Englisch woman and Sarah. They had their backs to them. He brushed her hand then stepped back. "Talking to the bishop was the first thing I thought of the minute I woke up this morning. Time is going to tick by slow for me until we are in front of the church saying our vows, although I'm thankful for the date the bishop gave us."

Her eyes sparkled. "This is wonderful. I wonder what the bishop will say to us during our counseling meetings. I'm a little nervous."

Mark shrugged his shoulders. "There's nothing to

worry about. I'm sure he'll stress how important the sanctity of marriage is and for us not to take our commitment to each other lightly. I have no reservations about marrying you."

"I'm committed to you and have no doubt you'll be a loving husband, and I will work hard to be the very best fraa to you."

He scanned the room then leaned close to her ear. "Soon your name will be Grace King."

She blushed. "I like my new name."

He wouldn't want anything to spoil their joy. "I don't want to leave you, but I should get back to work." He lifted his shoulders. "I'm counting the days until I can call you my fraa."

He entered his store. The hours passed slowly as he waited on customers the rest of the day. He'd been busy and hadn't noticed it was half past five. Opening the connecting door, he found Grace and Sarah's shop locked. They must've gone home. She wouldn't have bothered him if he'd been waiting on customers. He frowned. Too bad he'd missed her.

Mark went home. Noah had already left. Dusty ran to greet him, wagging his tail. "Good boy." He smoothed his hand over the dog's soft black fur and eyed his food and water bowls. "Noah takes excellent care of you. You won't go hungry while he's working here." Something on the table caught his eye. "He must have something to tell me. He left a note."

He picked up the paper and stared at the signature. *Abel.* A chill coursed through him.

Mark, I'm in town. I'll return around six tonight.
I'll come through the back door, so no one will
spot me.

Mark slumped in a chair, wadded the paper, and pushed it aside. It was after six. Abel could arrive at any moment.

The fateful day he'd rolled over in his mind time and time again had kumme. He had no idea how to handle this. Should he speak to him? Should he risk everything by letting him in his haus and disobeying Amish law? He had to inquire about Abel's well-being and tell him Buck and Skinner had been searching for him. What if those ruffians found him, while he was out? Would they kill him? There was nothing for him to do but wait.

He warmed boiled ham and beans, sat, and spooned a bite in his mouth. He finished half the serving on his plate and pushed it aside. Stomach tense and head throbbing, he poked his head out the door. No sign of Abel. He could tell him what he had to say at the door. Letting him inside put everything he had with Grace at risk.

Choosing a container, he stored the leftover food in the icebox and washed and dried his dish. The back door banged open then shut. He stiffened.

Abel swayed and caught the counter. "Hey, bruder, how are ya?"

Dusty jumped to his feet and snarled.

Staring at his bruder, Mark swallowed the lump in his throat and calmed Dusty. He was relieved Abel was alive. He studied his bruder's bloodshot eyes and too-relaxed manner. He was drunk. Abel had no regard for him or he wouldn't barge in and put him at risk of losing Grace and his respectable reputation in the community. "How did you get here?"

He pulled out a chair and sat. "I hid my horse in your barn so no one would see you have company." He held up the flour sack and scarf. "Thanks for storing my stuff."

He pulled out the scarf. "This is a present for my special lady."

"I had no idea it was your bag. Have you been hiding in my barn? Why?" Mark narrowed his eyes and crossed his arms against his chest. "Why not barge into my haus like you are now?" Mark gritted his teeth in anger.

Abel hung his head. "I'm sorry. I haven't hid in your barn much. I had to find places to hide for a while. I thought as long as you or anyone else didn't see me, you wouldn't get in trouble with the bishop or the community. I came inside now because Buck and Skinner, the same thugs I owed money to before for a gambling debt, are after me again. I used the money you gave me a while back to pay them off. This time I owe them even more money. Will you give me forty dollars?"

"You hiding in the barn and coming here puts me at risk of losing everything. You left to discover the world. I didn't. It's wrong of you to put me in this position. Furthermore, Buck and Skinner showed up at my store searching for you and demanded I pay them money you owe them from a gambling debt. They stole what I had on hand, but they weren't satisfied. They're still looking for you."

Abel straightened. "What! Oh no! I didn't think Buck and Skinner would find you here." He stared at his feet. "When I paid them the money you gave me the first time to satisfy my gambling debt, they beat me until I told them where I got the bag of coins. I had to tell them I got it from you when you lived in Lancaster. I had no idea they'd find out you moved to Berlin."

The reason Amish law was necessary to shun family members who left the community to join the outside world had never been clearer to him than at this moment. "Buck and Skinner learned my whereabouts from the postmaster in Lancaster. I'd left my forwarding address at the post office. Since my full name is the on my shop and matches your last name, it was easy for them to find me. They charged in and demanded I tell them your whereabouts."

"Mark, these men are dangerous. They've killed men for looking at them the wrong way. I'm sick I've put you in harm's way."

"You're right. They are dangerous. They also asked the clerk where I lived. They set fire to my barn to show me they mean business. They aren't going to stop harassing me until I pay your debt. There's no excuse for your behavior. Did you steal things from other homes in the community?"

"Jah, I'm sorry. I don't know what to say."

"Why was there blood on the sack?"

"I cut my hand opening a can of beans."

Mark splayed his fingers on the table. "I'm sickened at your lazy attitude and arrogance to consider no one but yourself." He straightened and picked up the Holy Bible. He was desperate for his bruder to show remorse and want to change his life. "Stay and ask God and the community for forgiveness. You can live with me and work in my store. We can earn a profitable living together. We'll ask the bishop what we should do about these men. Maybe the sheriff can help."

Abel sneered. "This life isn't for me." He folded his hands on the table. "You should join me. The world outside this community is a more interesting place. Gambling, alcohol, and scantily clad women provide great entertainment."

His bruder hadn't listened to a word he'd said. He looked at his gray shirt and then at the man before him, wearing a garish red shirt, big metal belt buckle, and fancy leather boots. The stranger sitting before him was no longer the bruder he recognized. His bruder had turned his back on the Amish life and showed no regret for his actions. Until Abel desired to turn his life around, there was nothing more he could do for him but pray. "Since you won't stay and ask forgiveness, you must leave. I'm getting married. I won't let you ruin what I have with her."

Abel stood and narrowed his eyes. "I'm sad for you. You'll be stuck with one woman the rest of your life. Don't say I didn't warn you when life gets boring." He smacked the table. "I need money to pay these men. Give me what you can, and I'll not bother you again."

"Please reconsider. This is where you belong."

"No, I told you. I'm not coming back. Please give me any money you can spare. Maybe it will satisfy them until I can pay them the rest."

Abel had definitely succumbed to the world's temptations and had every intention of still giving in to them. "These men you owe money to are too unpredictable. Go to the sheriff."

Knock. Knock. Mark and Abel gasped and froze.

Dusty ran to the door and barked.

Mr. Blauch was staring at them through the window. Mark winced. *My worst fear is coming true. Mr. Blauch won't like this one bit.* No use hiding inside and not answering the door. Mr. Blauch had caught him with his bruder. Abel's red buttoned shirt, cowboy hat, and square metal belt buckle gave away his choice to live his life as an Englischer and they were standing right within Grace's daed's view. Mark took heavy steps to the door and opened it.

Mark shuddered as Abel met Mr. Blauch's eyes then fled out the back door. He trembled and heaved a big sigh. "Please kumme in. What brings you here?"

"Mrs. Blauch made an extra batch of potato soup and asked if I'd drop it off to you." He handed Mark the container. Stepping inside, Mr. Blauch's eyes bore down on him. "Who was the Englischer?" He narrowed his eyes. "He resembles you."

Mark swallowed hard and gestured to the chair.

Dusty snarled.

"It's all right, boy. Sit."

Dusty stayed by his side.

Thoughts ran rampant in his mind. He didn't know what to say. "Jah."

"I need an explanation, son. Is the Englischer related to you? What is he doing in your haus? More importantly, why did he run out the back door like his feet had stepped on hot coals?"

Mr. Blauch's clenched jaw and stern tone told him the man had already passed judgment on him. The truth would make things worse. Everything he'd done to earn a good reputation shattered in a split second. "The man who rushed out of here is my bruder, Abel. He's in trouble and came seeking my help. He owes money to thugs. They're searching for him."

"You shouldn't have let him in your haus. You told me your bruder left our community to live in the outside world. Our laws are meant to protect us from Englischers, such as the men who are after him." His face red, he huffed. "I no longer trust you. I'm withdrawing my blessing for you to marry Grace."

Mark gasped. He couldn't breathe, and his body shivered. Grace would never become his fraa. They couldn't go against her daed's wishes. He blamed Abel. No, it was his fault. Even though he didn't invite his bruder in, he should have sent him out the door the minute he entered.

He had to do something to set this right with Mr. Blauch. "Please, let me explain!"

The man turned on his heel, slammed the door, and departed.

He closed his eyes and fell to his knees. What had he done? His dreams of life with Grace had been crushed. Would he be able to repair it at some point? He had to believe God could work a miracle in Mr. Blauch's heart. "Dear Heavenly Father, I beg You, please forgive me for my transgression. I'm so ashamed. I leave Abel in Your hands. Please protect him and change his heart to want to kumme back to You. Please have mercy on me and change Mr. Blauch's mind. Please help him to find it in his heart to forgive me. Danki for Your love and mercy. Amen."

Dusty jerked his head up and barked.

Mark bolted outside and searched for Abel. No sign of his bruder. Trudging back to the haus, he hoped Abel would stay away. If he had caught sight of him, he would have demanded his bruder leave. The disappointment and anger in Mr. Blauch's face seared his senses. He'd worked hard to gain the man's trust and friendship. The loss of Grace and the parents he'd anticipated becoming his family devastated him.

He and Dusty walked inside the haus.

"You may be the only friend I have left when the news of Abel kumming here spreads."

Clenching his teeth, he gripped the arms of the chair. Why did Abel want to stay in the outside world where trouble plagued him? It made no sense to him. Boasting of what the world had to offer, Abel hadn't benefited from what he could tell. The man's life was a mess. Now his bruder had turned Mark's life upside down. In spite of the awful position Abel had put him in, he didn't want any harm to kumme to him. He loved Abel. But from this moment on, he must consider him dead.

What would Mr. Blauch tell Grace? He'd have to find a way to talk to her. He went to feed his animals. Going through the motions, his mind raced. He was certain Grace would be upset but forgive him. She was understanding and kind. Her experience with her best friend, Becca, had been as heart-wrenching for her as his bruder's leaving the Amish life had been for him. Not quite the same, though, with his bruder coming back and bringing trouble with him.

Finished, Mark crossed the yard to the haus and slumped in a chair.

Dusty sat next to him and rested his head on Mark's leg.

Mark stroked his furry friend's back. "You're a comfort, boy. I'm blessed you wandered into my life. What am I going to do, Dusty?"

Stretching his arms, Mark yawned and blinked several times early Wednesday morning. He glanced at Dusty beside him. "We should've gone to bed after I finished chores. My back and neck will be sore all day, and I've got some important business to attend to."

He fixed breakfast and took a few bites then pushed his plate aside. He had to ask Grace's forgiveness. Even if they couldn't marry in the near future, it was important she understood how sorry he was and that he'd always love her. Giving up wasn't an option. No matter how long it took, he'd pray for God to intervene on his and Grace's behalf. He shrugged into his white shirt and black pants and snapped his suspenders in place. Hat in hand, he drove to town.

Entering Grace and Sarah's shop, he approached her.

"Grace, may I talk with you privately for a few minutes outside?"

She put a hand to her heart. "Mark, I was hoping you'd seek me out today. Sarah hasn't arrived yet. Before you say anything, Daed told me about taking Mamm's soup to you and about finding you with your bruder. I'm sick he's judging you for speaking to Abel. I'm not done pleading with him to understand your dilemma and change his mind about withdrawing his blessing for us to wed."

He hadn't thought he could love her more than he already did. At this moment, he loved her more than he could possibly put into words. Her forgiveness eased his mind. "Grace, I'm relieved you understand. I'm sorry I disobeyed our laws and disappointed your daed."

"What did Abel say? What did he want?"

"He's in trouble. The men Abel owes money to barged into my shop searching for him this week. The Lancaster postman told them where I'd moved. I left my forwarding address in case Abel came looking for me. My bruder told the men I'd given him money to pay his debt the first time. They assumed I'd pay his debt again. These villains stole what money I had in my cashbox, and they're searching for Abel for the rest he owes to them."

"Is your bruder at your haus?"

"No, he rushed out when your daed came inside. Grace, I didn't invite him in, but I should've asked him to leave the minute he came through the door."

Her lovely eyes showed deep concern. "What will you do if he returns?"

"Send him away." He twisted the brim of his hat. "I asked him to seek forgiveness. If he would agree, I said he could live and work with me. He refused." His heart hurt looking at his beautiful Grace. The woman he'd lost. He had to tell her the whole story. She deserved to know every detail. "He confessed to hiding in my barn and stealing from community members and me while we were away. He gambles and associates with dangerous men. Other than praying for God to protect him and change his heart, I've done all I can. It's up to him to turn his life around."

"He might return and beg you to take him in. You love him. It will be hard for you to say no."

"I do love him, but I won't allow him to ruin my life. If I have any chance at all of making this right with your daed, I have to turn Abel away. I never should've disobeyed the Amish law and spoken to him. I did so because he is my flesh and blood. The only family I have left. Nonetheless, the fault is mine. I won't further jeopardize you or the members in the community. He must deal with his problems on his own. I suggested he go to the sheriff for assistance."

"I'm sorry Abel put you in this predicament. I'll pray for him, too."

The door whooshed open. *Mr. Blauch.* Mark swallowed the lump in his throat. Standing next to Grace was the last place he'd wanted Mr. Blauch to find him. "Good morning, I came to check on Grace. I mean no disrespect."

Grace's face blanched. "Daed, please don't be angry. I invited Mark in. Sarah will be here any minute. We needed to discuss our situation."

"Nothing either one of you say will change my mind. Mark, I'll give you until the end of the day to relay your transgression to the bishop. If you don't, I will take it upon myself to do so."

The man's fury and determination was daunting. He stood tall with his eyes squinted and lips pinched.

"Please. Hear me out."

Mr. Blauch interrupted him. "You have brought trouble

to our community! Therefore, you are no longer wilkom in our home and stay away from Grace."

Grace wiped tears from her cheeks. "Please, Daed, don't be so hard on Mark. He loves his bruder. There was nothing wrong with Mark asking his bruder to repent and return to our faith. Give him another chance."

"You watch your tongue, dochder. I have made my decision, and you will abide by it."

Lips trembling, she stared at her feet.

Mark's heart ached for her. One bad decision had caused him and Grace more pain than he could've imagined. Observing her daed admonish her was awful. Grace shared a close relationship with her daed. Mark had caused trouble between them. It pained him. Even though he'd ruined her life, Grace still forgave him. She astounded him. "Again, Mr. Blauch, I'm sorry."

"Please leave."

His heart heavy in his chest, Mark went to his store. It was time to open, but he didn't want to face customers. Eyes pooling with tears, he blinked them back. His chance for a happy married life with Grace was over. Mr. Blauch had made this very clear. It wouldn't be easy telling his story to the bishop. He might be shunned or, even worse, asked to leave Berlin. Not something he had ever wanted to experience.

He should visit the bishop. There was no benefit to waiting. Locking the door, he hurried to the elderly man's haus. His mood darkened as gray as the clouds looming in the sky. He rapped on the door.

Bishop Weaver peered over his spectacles. "Mark, wilkom. What brings you to my haus this morning?"

Clutching his hat, he traced the brim with his fingers. "I've got some disturbing news."

The man frowned. "Have a seat."

Mark recounted his story. "He stole from our members." He waited for the bishop to speak. This had been harder than he'd thought. He liked and respected Bishop Weaver. To disappoint the man and the community repelled him. He watched the clock tick for a moment. Why didn't the man say something?

"You shouldn't have talked to Abel, but you didn't invite him into your haus. He barged in. You redeemed yourself with me when you asked him to repent of his sin and return to our fold. You've promised you won't have anything to do with him if he returns. If Abel kummes back and I discover you haven't honored your promise to send him away immediately, I will ask the members to shun you. Understand?"

Mark blew out a sigh of relief. "Danki. I'm grateful for your mercy." He told him about Mr. Blauch's reason for withdrawing his blessing. "What can I do? I love Grace and her parents."

"I'll not interfere where Mr. Blauch and Grace are concerned. He has a right to protect his dochder and to do what he believes is in her best interest."

"I understand but, rest assured, these men are not aware of my association with Grace or her parents. They have no reason to go after them."

"They could be watching you. They may have observed you and Grace together. They could use her to extort money from you."

A cold chill prickled through him. "I'd take a beating or a bullet for her."

"Since the men have left, I'll not consult the deacons about contacting the sheriff. I'd rather not involve the Englischers if we don't need to. If these men return, give them what they ask for. I don't want you hurt. Then kumme to me. I'll have to ask the deacons about involving the law then."

"Again, I'm sorry for all this."

"Like I said, I trust you will be true to your word. Otherwise, you will not find me so understanding." He softened. "Be safe, Mark."

Mark blew out a breath. At least he was in good standing with the bishop. One step at a time was all he could handle. He'd trust God to lead him. Hopefully, God's plan included Grace in his life.

Chapter Twelve

Grace buried her face in her pillow and wept Thursday morning. She could never love another man as much as she loved Mark. Why couldn't her daed soften his heart and put himself in Mark's shoes? If her daed had lost a relative or close friend to the outside world, she'd never been told the story. If he had, maybe he would be more sympathetic toward Mark's predicament.

She got up and washed her face. Eyes puffy and red, she dressed and dragged her feet to the kitchen. Mamm was flipping pancakes in the iron skillet.

"Good morning. If those are for me, I can't put anything in my stomach, but danki for them."

Mamm slid the pancakes on a plate. "Your daed told me he found Mark's bruder at his haus. I am sad this has happened, but I must support your daed."

"Mark and I love each other. I wish you would talk to Daed for me. Please?"

Mamm put the skillet aside and circled her arms around Grace. "I did. He's not budging. Give him time. If God's will is for you to marry Mark, he'll soften your daed's heart."

"It pains me Mark is going through this turmoil and I'm not there to help him through it. A man and a woman in love should be there for each other through thick and thin. He has no family. We were his family."

"Mark's a strong man. He'll be fine. God never leaves us, and He's a prayer away. He'll take care of Mark and you no matter."

Pushing her chair back with her legs, she grabbed the quilt she had stitched for him, her midwifery bag, and bid Mamm farewell.

Driving to town, she pushed back the tears stinging her eyes. She had to talk to Mark. Daed wouldn't like it, but she didn't agree with his reasoning right now. Hopefully, he wouldn't find out.

She handed her horse's reins to the liveryman and gently pushed past the men and women entering and exiting the shops along the boardwalk. The familiar banging of the blacksmith's hammer on a horseshoe and the clip-clop of horses' hooves pounding the dirt road frayed her nerves unlike most days when she wilkomed the noise. An Englischer dressed in a belted, flowered cotton dress with her hair in ringlets smiled at Grace. Grace cowered and ducked, rather than offering a kind smile. She had no desire to uplift her sad mood.

Peeking in Mark's window, her breath caught. Devastation hit her. She may never call him husband. She bowed her head and bit her lip. She had to ask how he was doing. Pushing the door open, her eyes pooled with tears.

Eyes red and his face pale, his frown turned into a smile. "Dear Grace."

"I'm so broken without you." She put the quilt on the counter.

He turned his sign to CLOSED, locked the door, gently pulled her in the back room, and held her tight. "I'm so sorry about all this."

Hugging him, she pressed her head against his chest and inhaled the cedar scent on his shirt. This is where she wanted to stay. It was where she belonged. She believed it in her heart. "Mark, I forgave you the moment you told me about it. It's not your fault."

What happened to forgiveness? Her daed's hasty decision to punish her and Mark by withdrawing his blessing from them deeply disappointed her. The bishop spoke about forgiveness often. "Have you talked to the bishop?"

He gently released her but held her hands. "Jah, and he isn't going to ask the members to shun me for talking to Abel, since I asked him to repent and return to our fold. And because I agreed to turn my bruder away should he kumme to my doorstep again."

"Did you tell him about the men searching for Abel?"

"Jah, but he doesn't hold me responsible for them coming to me at the shop. There was nothing I could've done to prevent it. Since it's our way to keep Englischers out of Amish business, he doesn't want to alert the sheriff unless they kumme back. I agree."

"Will he tell the deacons at this time?"

"No. He will keep it to himself unless the men return. He trusts me to keep him informed. The men are gone. There's nothing more to do at this time. His understanding and discretion mean a lot to me."

Relief washed over her, glad the bishop had been sympathetic to Mark's situation. "What good news." She stared at her feet. "I better go to the store. Sarah will be worried about me. I shouldn't risk Daed finding me here, but I had to speak to you."

"I'll wait for your daed to reconsider his decision as long as it takes. We probably shouldn't speak until he changes his mind about us. I don't want to upset him any further. Remember, I love you, and I'm praying for God to intervene. I'll approach your daed again after giving him more time."

Her lips quivered. "I agree we shouldn't converse until this problem is solved, but I want you to remember how much I love you, too. I have a gift for you on the counter."

They walked to the front of the store. She lifted the quilt, passed it to him, and patted the pocket. "I wrote a letter to you and tucked it inside." She blew him a kiss.

Putting a hand to his heart, he waved.

She exited through the connecting door to the dry goods shop. The memory of his arms around her and his scent lingered. Right or wrong, visiting him had been worth the risk.

Minutes later, Sarah whooshed in and caught her kapp in midair. "Sorry I'm late. I haven't gotten over the excitement of you getting married. We'll have to discuss the food. I want to make your favorite chicken and vegetable pie." She threw her bag on the chair and whirled around on her heel. "Grace, why are you frowning? Your eyes are bloodshot, and the color has left your cheeks. What's wrong?" She reached for her hands and held them.

The joy in Sarah's face and the excitement in her voice brought forth the memory of her own happiness before that fateful day when her life came crashing down. Her euphoria in Mark's arms this morning had fled. In Sarah's arms, she could let the floodgates to her emotions open.

Her best friend would understand. She cried and fell in Sarah's arms.

Sarah held her. "You're scaring me. What has happened? Please, Grace, say something."

Taking a deep breath, she raised her head and wiped her eyes with the corner of her apron. "Daed withdrew his permission for Mark and me to marry."

"What? Why? We need to have a serious conversation. I'm locking the door and turning the sign over. We'll open later this morning." Sarah reached for Grace's hand and pulled her into the storeroom where they couldn't be seen from the front window.

"Abel, Mark's bruder, who left him in Lancaster to live in the outside world, showed up at his haus. Mark told me thugs are searching for Abel to collect money he owes them. The men came to Mark's shop questioning and threatening him if he didn't tell them where they could find Abel. Daed went to visit Mark and found him with his bruder. He got angry because Mark allowed the bruder he is supposed to shun in his haus and withdrew his blessing for us to wed." Her lips quivered. "Daed mustn't discover Mark told me about Abel. It would make things worse."

Guiding her to a chair, Sarah held an arm around Grace's waist. "I'll tell Levi, but I won't tell anyone else. I'm sure Levi will understand and want to support Mark." She beamed. "Levi and your daed have a good relationship. Maybe he can speak to him on Mark's behalf."

"It would be worth a try."

She wiped tears from Grace's cheeks. "Where is Abel now?"

"He left. Mark isn't aware of his whereabouts."

"What can I do?"

"Listen to my woes and pray for me." The love of her

life was lost to her. She'd rather remain a spinster if she couldn't marry Mark. Her heart heavy in her chest, she sighed. "I don't know what to do with myself. It's as if someone dear to me has died. In the blink of an eye, my bright future with Mark vanished."

Sarah pulled a chair across from Grace and leaned in. "God performs miracles all the time. Don't give up."

"Daed is a good man, but he's stubborn. It will take a miracle for him to change his mind."

Sarah embraced her in a warm hug. "No matter what happens, God has a plan for your life. He'll not forsake you. I'm here for you for whatever you need. I pray you and Mark will be together."

"Danki, Sarah. Your encouragement means a lot." Pouring her heart out to her best friend had given her some relief. Sarah's arms had provided a safe haven many times during their friendship after Becca left, but she couldn't remember needing Sarah more than she had this morning.

Rain pelting the roof woke Grace on Sunday morning. She lay in bed and reached for the wooden doll Mark had given her. She treasured it even more now. Another week had dragged on. She'd tossed and turned each night since the awful day she'd learned she'd no longer be marrying Mark. Walking around in a fog at work and doing chores at home, she couldn't remember the last time she'd smiled.

Sarah had baked Grace butter cookies and tried to lift her spirits, but to no avail. The pain hadn't diminished. She doubted it ever would. For fear Daed would visit the shop, she stayed away from Mark, but she pictured him in her mind often. She had memorized the sparkle in his eyes, his gentle touch, and his declaration of love.

She understood Daed thought he had her best interests at heart, but nothing could erase the utter sadness looming over her. Why wouldn't he listen to what Mark had to say? Maybe she'd discuss her dilemma with Daed again today.

She wrapped her hair in a bun, pulled on a dark blue dress, and then pinned a white kapp on her head. Entering the kitchen, Daed sat at the table sipping coffee. She joined him. Should she risk asking him about this? It could make things worse. She had to try. "My heart is heavy, Daed. I love Mark. I want what you and Mamm have together. I believe I could have a good marriage with Mark. Is there any way you can find it in your heart to change your mind? Please."

Frowning, he pushed back his chair.

Wincing, she squinted at the scraping sound and froze.

He bowed his head, shoved his hands in his pockets, and went outside.

Tears streamed onto her cheeks. She wiped her damp face with the corner of her apron. The two men who meant the most to her in life were at odds, and she was powerless to bring them together. She hoped God would intercede.

A few minutes later, she sat quiet in the buggy beside Mamm. To lay eyes on Mark would be good but sad.

Close to her ear, Mamm leaned in. "It pains me to see you like this. Have faith. Pray to God for guidance."

Mamm was a prayer warrior. She accepted God's will for each of her prayer requests, and Grace couldn't remember a time when she'd complained if things hadn't gone her way. Grace pinched her lips. Why had God brought Mark into her life if He hadn't intended for them to marry? She viewed the daisies covering several acres of land along either side of the rutted dirt road. A deep pang of regret shot through her. Sarah had been right. Whatever her future held, God would do what was best for her. As she had heard so many times before, it was easier said than done.

Climbing out of the wagon, she searched for Mark. No sign of him. Inside, she sat and stretched her neck. Sitting next to Noah and the other men, Mark gazed into her eyes. Her heart raced. She returned his smile, bowed her head, and turned around before Daed caught sight of her.

An unfamiliar woman and kinner sat in front of her. "Mamm, who is the family sitting in front of us?"

Frowning, Mamm shook her head. "The widow's name is Madeline Plank. The kinner are her dochders. They moved here from Lancaster, Pennsylvania, and moved into her bruder, Peter Miller's, haus. Peter moved to their haus in Lancaster, and he gave them his here. Word is her husband died from a heart attack five days after they arrived. I can't imagine what a shock it must've been for them."

"Why didn't we go to the funeral?"

"She wanted a private ceremony since she had met so few people, having been in town such a short time. I dropped food off to them. It slipped my mind to mention them to you."

"How are they getting along?"

"She is working at the Berlin General Store, but it's evident she's having a hard time. I noticed before they sat that the dochders' dresses are faded and stitched where they must've torn. But they are clean and present a neat appearance. She's a pleasant and kind woman. Her dochders are lovely."

The bishop raised his hand. "If you'll give me your full attention, I'll begin the service."

Grace listened to Bishop Weaver's message on forgiveness. She glanced at her daed. He stared straight ahead, his lips pinched, his arms crossed. No encouragement her Daed would apply the bishop's message to his attitude toward Mark.

The service ended, and she helped set the table then sat and chatted with Sarah about the store. Mark played hide-and-seek with Jonah. They exchanged endearing glimpses on several occasions, and she wanted to run to him and tell him they should get married anyway. It was no use. She wouldn't go against God or her daed. He made no effort to approach her. It was another reason she loved him. He wouldn't do anything to jeopardize her relationship with her parents or God.

Levi joined them. "Grace, I pulled your daed aside and spoke to him about Mark. He won't listen to reason on this matter. I'm sorry. Sarah and I are praying for both of you."

"Danki. I appreciate your thoughtfulness, and I'm sure Mark does too. I'm praying for a miracle."

Sarah came through the door of the shop Monday morning, cheeks pink and cheery. "Grace, I'm pregnant. I stopped by the doctor's office this morning. I suspected it when I'd gained weight. I'm so excited!"

Hands to her cheeks, Grace rushed to her friend. "This is thrilling! Levi must be overjoyed."

Sarah yawned. "We are thrilled, but I've been overly tired. The doctor wants me off my feet as much as possible. Levi went with me to the doctor. He insists we hire someone to take my place. I'm tired all the time and my back and legs ache. I would guess I'm around three and a half to four months."

"I'm not aware of anyone seeking a job. Let's ask around. I can handle the shop for a while by myself. The extra work will keep my mind occupied." She shook off her sadness. "I'm elated for you and Levi. I wonder if you'll have a maedel or a boy."

"Levi and I would like to have a maedel first, but we'll be thrilled to have a boy. I hope our child has his curly red hair and deep brown eyes."

Grace chuckled. "Maybe you'll have twins or triplets."

Gasping, Sarah put a hand to her chest. "You, my mamm, and yours would have to move in!"

They laughed. It warmed Grace's heart to laugh. She'd missed being happy. A pang of guilt nagged at her. She'd sulked about her unhappiness and not paid attention to her friend. She would make a conscious effort to change her attitude. "I'll help you with whatever you need."

"My parents are thrilled. Mamm is probably cooking enough for an army as we speak. She'll kumme to my haus every day to cook, clean, and make sure I don't overdo anything. Levi loves her, but this may be too much family time for him."

Sarah patted her stomach. "Enough chatter about this little one. The black circles under your eyes tell me you're not getting a good night's sleep. I'm so sorry you're going through this sad time in your life. Have you spoken to Mark?"

"No. We agreed to honor Daed's request. I'm confident he'll approach Daed again and try to reason with him, but it can't be soon enough for me. I miss him something terrible."

Sarah covered Grace's hand. "Practicing patience isn't

easy for either of us, but you must try and enjoy your life in the meantime. Sulking won't benefit you."

"Let's drop this subject. I'm ecstatic for you. You have boosted my mood. You should go home and get off your feet."

"Mamm's doting on me, and so is Levi. I like the attention."

Grace turned Sarah toward the door. "Tell your mamm I said hello. Go home and relax." She watched Sarah until her friend was out of sight. Staring at the connecting door, she crossed the room. Putting her hand on the doorknob, she withdrew it.

Mark's shop had been dark when she arrived this morning. Had he kumme in? It would've been a joy to share Sarah's announcement with him. Not long ago, she'd thought she'd be having kinner with Mark shortly after they were married.

The shop door swung open and jerked her out of her thoughts. She recognized Madeline Plank's dochder from church. Grace noticed her hazel eyes, brown hair, and slender frame. She was beautiful.

"How may I help you? Are you shopping for anything in particular?"

The young woman she guessed to be about seventeen wrung her hands and stared at her with a worried face. "I'm Anna Plank. I'm in need of a job. Do you have anything available?"

Putting a hand to her chest, Grace gasped. "Yes. My partner and friend, Sarah Helmuth, is with child and needs to stay off her feet. I need someone to take her place until she decides if she wants to return and bring her boppli to work with her. I had planned to put a notice in the post office and General Store." Grace was certain God had seen their need and sent Anna.

Anna's pleading eyes held hers. "My daed died right after we moved here. I have two younger schweschders and Mamm's wages at the bakery aren't enough to provide for our needs."

Grace liked the young woman on sight. To help someone right now would be the best medicine to lift her mood. Why not give Anna a chance? Circling the counter, Grace clasped Anna's hands. "You're hired. We open at eight and close at five. I can pay you five dollars a week." It was twenty-five cents more than she should pay her, but she couldn't resist offering Anna more money. Her faded gray dress and white apron had been stitched in places where torn, but they were clean. Up close, her frame appeared too thin. This family must be struggling to fend for themselves. "When would you like to begin work?"

"May I stay and work today? I stitch quilts. I'm familiar with most of the patterns you have displayed."

"I'd love to have you stay and work today." Grace explained the purpose of the pocket on the keepsake pocket quilts.

Two Englisch women walked in dressed in calico dresses and big hats with ribbons. Their black boots shined, and their pretty hair was pinned in curls. The older woman approached them. "Can you show us your wedding quilts?"

The younger woman pointed to a keepsake pocket quilt. "Tell me about this quilt."

Grace leaned in to Anna. "You help her, and I'll assist the other."

She watched Anna out of the corner of her eye while her customers awed over a yellow and white keepsake pocket quilt with a heart stitched in the center. "Grandmother would love this quilt. Let's get it for her."

"Let's wait until you've had a chance to view other quilts." The older woman strolled away from the younger one and perused the shop's other textiles.

The younger woman held out the blue wedding quilt. "Mother, I like this pattern. Meet Anna. She showed me the fine stitching around the edges. It's lovely. I'd like to give it to Alfred for a wedding gift. He can cover his legs when he reads in the winter by the fire."

The mamm joined her dochder and fingered the corner. "We'll buy them both." She slid a finger in the pocket. "What do you put in here?"

"You write a letter to the person who will receive the quilt. They can pull the letter out and read it anytime and think of you."

"I'll write a love letter to Alfred and tuck it inside. You and I can write letters to Grandmother and stash them in the heart quilt for her. She would be touched."

The mamm cast an affectionate, endearing glance at her dochder. "The letters are a lovely idea. Let's pay for the quilts."

Grace crossed the room to the counter and grasped the cashbox and accepted the Mamm's money. She recorded the sales in her journal. The wedding quilt stung her heart to touch it. She had one similar to give to Mark on their wedding day.

The two women thanked them, carried their quilts, and pulled the door shut behind them.

Anna put her hands to her cheeks. "The keepsake pocket quilt is a wonderful idea. I'm going to stitch a quilt for Mamm as soon as I can afford to buy the supplies."

She dug in a box and held up a fistful of fabric pieces

in assorted colors. "You can have this material for your quilt."

Anna separated the swatches. "Danki. I really appreciate it."

"You're wilkom. Before another customer kummes in, let me show you the supply room." Grace pointed to the shelves. "This is where we keep extra stock. We have women in town who stitch quilts for us and bring them in on a weekly basis." She gestured to the cot. "I'm a midwife. Most of the Amish women in our community are aware I work here, and from time to time have shown up in need of my services."

"I'd be happy to help you. I'm not squeamish about blood."

"If I need assistance, it's good to know you're willing, but usually we have customers and I'll need you in front to wait on them. I will ask you to heat pots of water on the stove for me if you're not busy." She cupped her ear. "Someone came in. We should return to the front."

An Englisch woman approached them. She grimaced at Grace's birthmark then directed her question to Anna. "I'm interested in a bed covering for my mother. Maybe a plain white quilt would do. Do you have any?"

Anna grabbed one from the shelf. "How does this one suit you?"

Her new helper was going to work out fine. She'd taken the rude woman off her hands.

Grace selected a quilt from the back and hung it on the wall to replace the Jacob's ladder–patterned quilt purchased earlier. The harsh rap and deliberate click of the customer's boots set her teeth on edge.

Anna explained the purpose of a keepsake pocket quilt. She ran her hand along a puffy white material. "If this eyelet one doesn't suit you, we have more."

The woman's smile bloomed. "This is exactly what I had in mind. Thank you. How much is it?"

Anna unpinned the price note and handed it to the woman.

"I'll buy it." The woman followed Anna, carrying the quilt to the counter.

Grace opened the cashbox. The woman wouldn't look at her. She pressed the exact number of coins in Anna's hand and bid them farewell.

Frowning, Anna raised her eyebrows. "The woman was rude to you."

"I'm used to it, at least most of the time. Danki for waiting on her. I'm pleased with how you handle customers. Do you have any questions?"

"No, I'm comfortable waiting on customers and collecting payment. I like working here. Danki for hiring me."

The rest of the day, Grace studied Anna assisting customers. The attractive woman had a clear and pleasant voice and sold quilts and aprons as if she'd worked there for a long time. The young woman couldn't be more perfect for the job. Sarah would be pleased she'd found such a capable Amish woman to take her place.

Grace put a hand to her head. Pain throbbed. Opening her bag, she searched for aspirin powder. She'd have to buy some.

Anna approached her. "You look tired, and your eyes are weary. Are you all right?"

"I have a headache. Do you mind staying here while I go to the apothecary for some aspirin powder?"

Shaking her head, she rested her hand on Grace's arm. "No, you stay. I'll go. I'd like to pick up a small pan from the General Store." Anna hoisted a plain blue bag over her shoulder. "I won't be long."

Grace bid her farewell and put a new patchwork

keepsake quilt on empty hooks in place of the one Anna sold earlier.

The door opened and banged against the wall. Mark and Noah entered carrying Dusty. Blood dripped from the dog's body.

Mark. Gasping, Grace rushed to them. "What happened to Dusty?"

"He's got a large cut on his side. He roams the woods in the early morning when I let him out to do his business. This morning he didn't kumme back around his usual time. I found him like this. There was no one around. I got the bleeding to stop for a time, but he struggled to get up and it started again. I haven't been able to stop it. I fear he needs stitches."

"Follow me to the back room and lower Dusty on the cot." She turned to Noah. "My bag is under the counter. Will you get it for me?"

Noah left but returned in moments, handing her the bag. "Can you tell how he hurt himself?"

Grace bent and gently wiped Dusty's wound and examined him. "It looks as if he's cut himself on wire or a sharp branch." She threw open her bag and selected her stethoscope, bandages, saline solution, thread, and a needle. She grasped clean rags from a small stand.

Mark glanced at Noah. "Will you look in front of my shop? If there are customers, please go and wait on them. The cashbox and journal are under the counter."

"Grace, do you have a rag I can wipe my hands on?"

She indicated the stack beside her. "Grab a cloth from there."

Mark wiped his hands, dug his fingers in his pocket, and pulled out his keys. "Here's the key to the box. I'll be over in a few minutes. Danki."

"Don't worry. I'll be fine. Take care of Dusty." Noah rushed out of the room.

Mark looked at her with worried eyes. "It's so good to finally see you, but I shouldn't be here. I'm sorry to bring him to you. What if your daed kummes in?"

"Let's not worry about it. Chances are he won't. Even so, I'm glad you're here. We should still help each other in time of need. He would want me to care for Dusty, given the circumstances." She was glad Dusty was such a good dog and didn't give her any trouble while she cleaned the wound, stitched it, and applied a bandage. "He'll be sore for a couple of days, but he'll be fine." She met Mark's gaze.

He clasped her hand. "I miss you. I pray each night for God to change your daed's mind about us. I'm so sorry about this, Grace."

She wiped a tear from her cheek. The hurt in his face gripped her heart. He hadn't done anything wrong. Abel had pushed his way into Mark's life and thought only of himself. Not having siblings, she couldn't imagine what it must be like for Mark to grow up sharing a close relationship with Abel only to have him leave then return and cause such heartbreak. "You are a good man. We have to have faith this will work out."

Anna peeked inside. "I'm sorry. I didn't mean to interrupt."

Jerking his hand back, Mark stared at Dusty, hoping Anna hadn't witnessed his gesture.

Grace stepped back from Mark. "Kumme in. Meet Mark King. He owns the store next to ours. He brought his dog, Dusty, in for treatment. Mark found him injured. Mark, Anna Plank."

Putting a hand to her open mouth, she stepped in and studied the dog. "It's nice to meet you, Mr. King."

"Call me Mark. It's a pleasure to meet you. I'm sure we'll run into each other now and then."

"Your dog is beautiful. And please, call me Anna." She turned to Grace. "Will Dusty be all right? Do you need any help?"

"No, Dusty will be fine. His wounds should heal in time."

Anna handed Grace the aspirin powder pack. "I got you three packets."

"I appreciate you getting them for me. If you don't mind, will you go to the front and see if anyone has kumme in?"

"I'd be glad to."

"Danki." Waiting until her new friend was out of sight, she met Mark's eyes. "My life changed for the better when I met you. I've never been happier. Abel ruined everything for us. I pray God will intervene and we can plan our future together."

A door slammed, and they both jumped. "It sounds like several customers have entered. I should help Anna."

"Where's Sarah?"

"She's going to have a boppli! I'm so happy for her and Levi. The doctor ordered her home to rest for an indefinite period of time."

"Levi must be thrilled! I'm happy for them."

"I need someone to take her place at the shop. I noticed Anna in church Sunday, and I asked Mamm about her family. She, her mamm, and her schweschders moved here from Lancaster. Her mamm is a widow.

"Anna came in and asked for a job this morning, and I asked her to start right away. I'm blessed to have her here. She's a hard worker and a sweet woman." Grace gestured for him to follow her to the front and almost bumped into her new helper. "Anna, I thought I heard voices."

"Two women came in looking for the bakery. They are visiting and not familiar with town."

A woman entered, and Anna left to help her customer.

Grace couldn't stand the thought of him leaving. She gestured Mark to the back room again. "When will I see you?"

"I'm not sure. We can't afford for your daed to find us together. I want to give him time to settle down about finding Abel at my haus. Then I'll ask him to reconsider his decision about us." He caressed her cheek. "You're on my mind constantly. I would do anything to regain your daed's trust in me."

"His mind's made up for now, but I'm not giving up hope."

"I agree." He beheld her. "Standing here with you is difficult. Danki for my letter. I've read it over and over again. It's comforting." He gazed into her eyes. "Oh, Grace, I love you."

"I love you, too. I always will."

Dusty barked and moaned.

Grace examined the bandage. "His pain should diminish over the next couple of days as the wound heals, but watch to make sure he doesn't tear his stitches. You can snip them out in about seven days. If the wound doesn't look healthier each day, we'll need to meet again."

Mark tenderly scooped his faithful dog in his arms.

Dusty whimpered.

He petted the animal. "It's all right, boy."

Mark would be walking out the door any minute. Her heart ached to watch him leave and not know what the future held for them. Days ago, she'd been planning a wedding. "I miss you terribly."

He gently caressed her cheek. "I miss the soft sound of your voice and those brown eyes looking at me like you are now. In time, I hope we'll be setting a wedding date. I should go. Your daed could walk in unexpected any minute."

Grace followed him to the connecting door. She opened the door and he went inside. Shutting the door behind him, she wiped a tear from her eye and walked in Anna's direction.

Anna's customer had paid for aprons and left. Anna joined Grace, readjusting supplies on the shelves from customers fingering them. "Is Mark your friend?"

She paused for a moment. "We love each other, but unfortunate circumstances are keeping us apart."

"I'm sorry. I didn't mean to pry."

"You're not. The situation is complicated. We would like to get married, but my daed is upset about something that happened and won't give his blessing."

"I can't imagine what you must be going through. I'll pray for you and Mark."

"Danki. We need God's intervention. My daed's feet are planted firmly in the ground on this matter."

Anna gently squeezed her hand and went to greet the customer coming in the shop. Having Anna here would be good for her. The young woman's compassion and kindness had helped comfort her. She looked forward to learning more about Anna and her family.

Grace went to the back room and gathered the soiled sheets from the cot where she'd treated Dusty. Sad because the sweet dog had been injured, she hoped he'd heal without complications.

In spite of the circumstances surrounding why Mark had shown up, she'd been thrilled he brought Dusty to her. Closing her eyes for a moment, she heaved a big sigh, imagining Mark's familiar cedar scent. Touching her hand, she relived the brush of his fingers. She stepped outside to pump water in a basin and stared at the sky. "Why, God? Why has this happened? Please make a way for us to marry."

A noise alerted her. Heat rose to her face. Oh no, she shouldn't be so careless. Had anyone heard her? She glanced to the left and right, behind the shops next to hers. No one was in sight.

The workday ended, and Grace bid Anna farewell, visited the livery, and steered her horse home. Daed stood outside the barn. "I'll help you secure your horse and then I'd like you to kumme inside. I have an idea I'd like to share with you. Mamm will join us."

Would he tell her good or bad news? Her stomach churned. Mamm or Daed might be sick. She'd taken for granted they'd always be with her. "Are you or Mamm seriously ill?"

"No, we're fine." He took her horse's reins. "You go inside. I'll join you and Mamm in a few minutes."

"I'll wait for you." She sat on the porch step until he was finished and then followed him inside the haus with trepidation.

Mamm sat at the table. "Have a seat. I've put fresh lemonade on the table for us."

Her mamm avoided her gaze and stared at her glass. Not a good sign of what was to kumme. *Oh no, had he found out Mark came to the shop today?* She opened her mouth to explain and then thought better of it.

"As the bishop announced in church a while ago, Esau Erb's fraa passed. He earns a good living as a farmer, adheres to the Amish law, and has a quiet and kind demeanor. I'd like to approach him about an arranged marriage with you."

Grace gasped and grabbed her throat. Heat surged from her head to her toes. *Marry another man?* She couldn't possibly share her life with anyone but Mark. She stifled the urge to scream at her daed. Not something she'd ever let enter her mind before, but she couldn't imagine doing what he was asking of her. "I love Mark King, and he loves me. You've asked men to marry me before, and they have taken one look at my birthmark and declined. I want to marry for love like you and Mamm." Tears pooled in her eyes. "Please, Daed, don't add to my sorrow."

"I understand you're upset about Mark, but you'll get over him in time. I want you to enjoy being a fraa and have kinner. The light has gone out from you. I want to help you."

Grace gripped her apron. Her palms dampened. Esau Erb probably was a decent man, but he wasn't the husband for her. No man would do but Mark. Esau Erb had a permanent slight bend and his weathered ruddy skin made him appear older than forty-five. His fraa had been a frail and kind woman unable to have kinner. The doctors hadn't diagnosed why she died three months ago. Grace empathized with the widower, and she hoped he'd find happiness with another Amish woman, but it wouldn't be with her.

She had to remain calm and convince her daed this was a terrible idea. She wiped her damp eyes and swallowed hard. "I am sympathetic to Mr. Erb's situation, but please don't ask me to wed him. I would be miserable. I'd rather be a spinster. I have the shop and my midwifery skills to keep me busy. Please respect my decision, Daed. I'm begging you."

Grace swallowed hard. Mamm squeezed Daed's hand. The gesture Mamm used to calm Daed eased Grace's mind a bit. She hoped it worked.

Daed patted Mamm's arm and bowed his head for a few moments then looked at Grace. "I'll honor your wishes.

I thought this might help, but I realize it may be too soon for you to consider another man. I don't want to add to your unhappiness. Your mamm and I love you, Grace."

She loved her daed, but his stubbornness about Mark had put a strain on their close relationship. It suffocated her like the humid air on a hot day. She missed the ease of their conversations. "Daed and Mamm, I love you, too."

Her daed stood and pushed back his chair. "I must get to work." He kissed Grace then Mamm's forehead and strolled outside.

Mamm dragged her chair closer to Grace's. "I'm sorry, my sweet dochder. I wish there was something I could do to lift your mood."

"My heart skips a beat each time I encounter Mark. I'd rather be alone the rest of my life than marry anyone but him."

"I'm praying for you. It's all I know to do right now."

A pain pierced Grace's chest as tears formed in her eyes. "I am praying too, and so is Mark."

Chapter Thirteen

Mark fluffed his furry friend's favorite blanket next to him on the floor and then lifted Dusty and set him on it later in the evening. He gently petted the animal. "I worry about you. I wish you'd be more careful out in the woods."

Dusty had cut himself a time or two on jagged branches. Grace had smiled happily at the sight of him entering her store. Talking to her and touching her again was both exciting and painful. Their brief and guarded time together ignited the love he had for her. Her daed's disapproval of him loomed like a thunder cloud.

The windows open, he listened to the crickets and frogs. The night appeared peaceful, but his heart lay heavy. Alone wasn't how he wanted to spend the rest of his life. Grace was the fraa for him. He settled back in his favorite chair and wondered how long he should wait before approaching Mr. Blauch again.

Mark sipped hot coffee and buttered his bread Tuesday morning. The door creaked open.

Noah entered. "Good morning." He bent to pet Dusty.

"You look better, boy. You gave us quite a scare. I'm pleased you're mending."

"Have a seat." Mark got up, opened the cupboard, and passed his friend a plate and cup of steaming hot coffee. "Danki for helping me with my furry friend and for working in the shop."

"I didn't mind managing the store for you, but I prefer working outside and getting my hands dirty." He considered the dog. "I've grown attached to Dusty. He keeps me company during the day. If anything happened to him, I'd really miss him."

"Jah, me too." Mark sipped his coffee. "You're here earlier than usual."

"I'm worried about you. You've not been yourself. Is anything wrong?"

Mark told Noah about his bruder and Mr. Blauch's unfortunate encounter. "I'm sorry to mention my bruder to you since I am to shun him, but I thought you should know in case he might kumme here again. If he does, send him away. Having Mr. Blauch withdraw his blessing for me to marry Grace is the worst thing I've experienced in my life, and I've had my share of sadness. Grace and I are praying God will work a miracle for us."

"I won't mention your bruder to anyone, but I'm glad you told me. I'm sorry you're suffering. I'll pray for you both." Noah sipped his coffee and stroked the oak table. "I've considered exploring the outside world, but leaving my mamm, you, and my friends behind for good scares me. Mamm is taking in enough work, and the neighbors are helping us on a regular basis, so she'd be well taken care of if I left, but I'm torn."

"The outside world brought no good to my bruder's life. The world enticed him to take his mind off God and follow his selfish desires of money and material things.

His greed has brought trouble to his life. Here is where you belong. Follow God and the Amish law. Build a happy life in Berlin."

Noah's worried face bothered Mark. "I'm sorry to bring this up. I shouldn't burden you. I won't make any decisions before talking to you first. I doubt I will ever leave." He stood and pushed his chair back. "Danki, Mark. If there's anything I can do for you or Grace, please don't hesitate to ask."

"Danki, please pray for all of us. Put leaving Berlin out of your mind. God has a plan for your life. Pray for guidance."

"I respect you, Mark. Danki for talking reasonably with me about this. I'll consider your advice." Noah nodded then shut the door behind him.

Mark pondered Noah's intentions as he dipped his dishes in the washbasin and stacked them in the sink. It astonished him Noah contemplated leaving Berlin. Hopefully, Noah had listened to his story about Abel and it would dissuade him. The young man had diligently taken care of his mamm. They had a close relationship. Hopefully, he wouldn't excommunicate himself from her. At least for now, he'd discouraged him from leaving the Amish life.

He viewed the wooden Seth Thomas clock on the mantel then looked at Dusty. "I must get dressed and go to work, boy. It's getting late."

Crossing the room, he pulled his clothes out of his clothespress and got dressed. On his way out the door, he grabbed three boiled eggs and an apple and dropped them, with care not to break the egg shells, in a clean flour sack.

He frowned and groaned. Would he be alone the rest

of his life? No, he had to have faith and trust God. He yearned to chat and eat with Grace at lunch. He missed each little thing about her. The screen door slammed behind him as he walked outside and waved to Noah.

"I'll keep my eye on Dusty."

"Danki. Please, Noah, kumme to me if you consider leaving this Amish life again. It will change your life and not for the better. I care about you. I don't want you to do anything you'll regret."

"I will, but I'm afraid your bruder has tarnished your attitude toward the good the outside world might offer. I wouldn't make the same mistakes as Abel."

"I've learned the hard way our Amish laws are meant to protect us from the outside world."

"I'm not going anywhere right now."

Mark chuckled. "Good."

Mark bid Noah farewell and guided his horse toward the familiar dirt road to town. Even though Noah had assured him he wouldn't get into trouble if he left the Amish community, Mark worried his friend would be lured into the evils of the outside world. Hopefully, Noah would stay and Mark could put his mind to rest about this matter. He wished he could talk to Grace about Noah. They would be in agreement, and it would lessen his burden to discuss it with her.

Leaving the livery, he crossed the boardwalk and glanced at her shop window. She and Anna stretched out a pinwheel quilt for a customer to view. He caught her eye. He thought his heart would burst as he met her gaze. The customer leaned into Grace. She was reluctant but broke their moment.

He unlocked his door and entered his shop. He paused and gazed out the window. Should he step outside and check the street for signs of the villains? No, they were long gone like Abel and had probably given up on him having enough money to satisfy them or keep them in town. Lifting a broom, he brushed the dirt he'd carried in on his boots.

The door whooshed open, and he froze. *Oh no, what are they doing back here again?* He should've listened to his instincts earlier. He stared at their guns and gripped the broom handle tight. "Leave now."

"Mister Amish man is actin' strong and tough. Why, my hands mighta trembled a bit." Buck laughed. "What do ya make of Mister Amish man's attitude, Skinner?"

Skinner snarled and crossed the room. He fisted his hand, lashed into Mark's midsection, and knocked him to the floor. "Mister Amish man needs remindin' we mean business. Nobody talks to me thataway." Placing his boot on Mark's back, he dug his heel into Mark's spine. "Got the picture?"

Mark's stomach clenched. He lay still, barely breathing. His heart thudded. Sweat beaded on his forehead and lips. He'd taken home his earnings. He'd left only a few coins in the cashbox. Not enough to satisfy these men. It would add to their anger. This could be his last day on earth.

Pain shot through his side as Skinner's pointed boot kicked him. "Answer me, you fool."

"Jah, I got it." Mark flexed his hands and gritted his teeth. His side throbbed in sharp pain. "I have little money." He could barely gasp out the words.

Buck marched over, grabbed Mark's hair, and jerked his head back. "Git up!" He let go of Mark's hair, swung him around, and slapped him hard across the face. "We caught sight of Abel in the saloon a couple days ago but lost him. He must've come to you. Where is he?"

Mark struggled to stand, swallowed the blood in his

mouth, and ignored the burning pain where Buck had hold of his hair again. In one quick movement, the man could snap his neck and kill him. Clenching his fists, Mark wanted to punch and kick the men to a bloody pulp. The anger rose like a small flame fanning to a full-blown fire in his stomach. But he must turn the other cheek. It was what he'd been taught to do. Even if it cost him his life, he was done disobeying the Amish law. "I have no idea."

Buck jerked his head back farther.

Skinner lunged forward, swung, and punched Mark in the stomach.

Mark swallowed the scream in his throat. He had to endure their humiliation and pain for Grace's and Anna's sakes. Nothing must alert them to check on him. He jerked forward then fell to the floor on his knees as bile rose and burnt his throat. He touched his burning scalp where hair had been yanked out. Crimson blood covered his fingers.

Buck stepped beside Skinner and pulled Mark upright and pushed him toward the counter. "Show me your cash-box. Give us what you've got. Hand over the money in your pockets, too."

Skinner pulled his pistol out of his holster and peered out the window. "I turned the sign to 'closed,' but it's busy on the boardwalk and street. We best be gettin' on. He ain't gonna give up his brother. The man let us beat him and didn't lift a hand to defend himself. These Amish men are cowards." He spit tobacco on the wooden floor. Without warning, he swung his arm across the toy shelf, and wooden figures flew across the room.

Mark swiped the blood from his brow, held his stomach, and stumbled behind the counter. He fell on his knees and every bone in his body raged with pain. He wasn't sure how long he'd stay alert. *The middle door.*

Grace or Anna might kumme through it at any minute.
This was the only time he was glad he and Grace had
agreed not to speak or visit each other in case her daed
came in unannounced. He pushed the pain out of his
mind and used his hands to push himself up and lean on
the counter. Throwing open the box, he shoved it at Buck
then emptied his pockets. "It's all I've got."

Buck's eyes bulged and he reached across the counter
and dragged Mark's body over it.

The room spun. Mark's entire body pulsated in pain.
He blinked several times and rubbed his neck to remain
alert. He had to stay focused for Grace.

"You rotten lowlife. I'm sick of you not givin' us what
we want. Maybe when your brother hears we done killed
you, he'll figure we mean business and pay up." Buck
pulled his gun and held it to Mark's chest.

Mark's breath caught. His arms flew up in defense.
"Please! No!"

Abel kicked in the door and aimed his rifle. "Put the
gun down."

Mark gasped. *Abel?* What were Abel and the sheriff
doing here?

The sheriff pointed his shotgun at Skinner. "You! Put
your gun on the ground nice and slow like. Then kick it
across the floor to me. One wrong move and I'll shoot.
Got it?"

Skinner grunted. He bent, set his gun on the floor, and
kicked it, sending it to the lawman.

The sheriff put his foot on the pistol and didn't move.

Buck raised his gun.

Mark yelled, "Abel, watch out!"

Abel shot Buck in the leg.

"Ackkkkk!" Buck howled in pain. His gun fell to the
floor as he grabbed his leg. Abel snatched it, shoved

the man's face against the rough boards, and then rolled him over onto his back. He slammed the heel of his boot on Buck's chest, the rifle pointed squarely at his nose. "You move an inch, and I'll shoot you again, you good-for-nothin' scoundrel."

Mark gasped. Abel was still an excellent shot. Puzzled, he couldn't imagine why his bruder was here.

The sheriff pushed Skinner to the ground, rolled him over, and handcuffed him.

A deputy barged in. "Sheriff, are you all right? I returned to the office from checking on the widows and Mr. Blauch and his daughter rushed in and told us she heard a violent commotion in here. Who are these men?" He grabbed Buck's cuffed hands and the back of his pants. He tilted his head to Abel. "I've got him."

The sheriff roughly pulled the villain to his feet. "They're robbers and up to no good. They belong in jail. As you can see, your prisoner's been shot. He's too dangerous to take to the doctor's office. We'll have the doctor come to the jail and fix him up." He shoved his prisoner to the door. "Abel, thank you for your help." He nodded to Mark. "You need to have the doctor take a look at you. They worked you over pretty bad."

Gasping and relieved, Mark said, "Danki for your assistance, Sheriff. I'll be fine."

Abel narrowed his eyes at Buck and Skinner. "I hope you both rot in jail."

Buck snarled. "I ever git my hands on you, you're a dead man."

Skinner spat at Abel. "Watch your back. If I do get out, I'm comin' for ya too." He struggled to get free.

The sheriff threw him to the ground and held a pistol to his head. "You try anything else and you'll be the dead man. Do you understand me?"

"Ya, I got it."

Pulling his prisoner up, the sheriff headed for the door. "I'll notify sheriffs in other communities I have you two in custody. I suspect you've done enough damage in other locations, besides this town, to put you away for a long time." He and the deputy nodded to everyone and escorted the criminals out of the store.

Abel pulled a chair and led Mark to it. "Sit and catch your breath. I'm so sorry about everything. I had to come back and try and fix things for you here. The Amish man at your door the day I left your haus stared right at me red-faced and frowning. I worried he'd tell the members you allowed me into your haus and shun you. I also had to do something about Buck and Skinner."

Before Mark could say a word, Grace, Mr. Blauch, and Bishop Weaver entered.

"The sheriff told us to kumme in." Grace dashed to Mark, stopping a few feet out of his reach but close enough he caught sight of the shimmering wet tears on her cheeks. "Awful thudding and scraping noises coming from your store caught my attention. I got scared and ran outside. When I peeked in the window, I was terrified the two men inside were going to kill you. I hurried to fetch the sheriff and bumped into Bishop Weaver and Daed and Abel on the way. I told them you were in trouble and I had to alert the sheriff, and the bishop agreed and they accompanied me. Several minutes ago, the deputy returned to his office. Daed and I alerted him the sheriff might need help."

The aches couldn't overshadow his desperate need to reach out and embrace her. He didn't know which was worse, the physical pain or the torment of not being allowed to hold her.

His attention swung to Mr. Blauch. The man had a pleasant demeanor about him. Something must have happened, but what? He had so many questions. "Grace, you saved my life getting help. Another few minutes and the men may have killed me."

Her words repeated in his mind. Why were his bruder, Bishop Weaver, and Mr. Blauch together? He wanted to ask his bruder questions. He glanced at the bishop. "May I have permission to speak to my bruder? If not, I understand."

The bishop raised his eyes over his spectacles and peered at him. "In this case, I'll make an exception."

"I'm sorry, Abel. I'm thankful you saved my life today, but you are the reason my life was at risk. I've lost the love of my life because of you." He avoided eye contact with Mr. Blauch. "Her daed won't forgive me for talking to you the first time. If you care about me at all, stay away unless you're ready to ask God and the members for forgiveness and return to the Amish life."

Abel shuffled his feet. "I have spoken to Mr. Blauch and Bishop Weaver on your behalf. I'll let Mr. Blauch explain our conversation."

Mark stood and groaned. "You're making things worse." He gripped his throbbing head and sat.

"It's all right. Listen to Mr. Blauch."

Mr. Blauch dragged a chair and sat across from Mark. "Abel explained his actions and your innocence the day I found him at your haus. The bishop brought him to me. Abel told me you had not invited him in. He said you begged him to turn his life and did nothing else."

Raking a hand through his hair, Mr. Blauch heaved a big sigh. "I'm sorry. I judged you harshly and didn't give you a chance to explain the day I found Abel with you. I misunderstood. I blamed you for his transgressions and bringing these men into our community, when you were innocent of wrongdoing."

Grace moved closer but didn't touch him. Having her near eased the stabbing aches in his side and back. His forehead thumped, and the back of his head burned. He'd never experienced such agony, but Grace next to him and her daed apologizing was the best medicine for taking his mind away from it.

"Your apology means a lot to me. Will you reconsider letting Grace and me marry?"

"Jah, you and Grace have my blessing." He drew in a breath. "I hope you will forgive me." He stood. "I'm relieved you're all right, son. You didn't deserve any of this. If there's anything I can do while you recuperate, let me know. After all, I'm practically your daed."

Tears pooled in Mark's eyes. "I'm so thankful to you and, of course, I forgive you." He grabbed the counter and attempted to get up, but his knees buckled.

Mr. Blauch caught him and lowered him back to the chair. "Don't stand. Please sit and gather your strength. As far as I'm concerned, this is over. We don't need to speak of it again. You and Grace can plan your wedding."

Bishop Weaver hadn't said a word. He knelt and rested a hand on Mark's knee. "After you've had time to heal, we'll schedule dates for marital instruction and a wedding." He winked. "You and Grace can still have November fifteenth."

She beamed. "Danki. I was hoping we could reserve the same date." She bounced on her toes and met Mark's eyes. "I'm so joyful I could climb the highest mountain without taking a breath."

Mark wiped his eyes. "Me too. This terrible day has turned wonderful fast. A day I'll remember for very different reasons. The day God worked a miracle in our lives."

The bishop said, "I agree."

Abel leaned close to Mark. "I had to come back and speak on your behalf. I never meant to bring any harm to you. I've been selfish. Please forgive me. I love you, bruder."

Mark wiped a tear. "I forgive you, and I love you, too."

Bishop Weaver faced Abel. "Son, won't you consider asking God and the members for forgiveness and return to our fold?"

Shaking his head, Abel stuffed his hands in his pockets. "I have been courting a woman in Louisville, Kentucky. She believes in God, attends church, and she loves me. After I left, I had time to think and pray. My first stop was here to make things right, and my next stop is to ask her to marry me." He dug in his pockets, pulled out a handful of coins, and passed them to the bishop. "I'm sorry for stealing from the members. This should be more than enough to cover their losses. I stole things from Levi, Mark, and one other haus."

Mark rubbed the ache in his neck. "Bishop, the other haus Abel is referring to is Samuel's. Mrs. Paulson told Grace and Sarah about the robbery shortly after it happened. Please give Samuel and Levi my share."

The bishop stared at the money. "I'll hand this money to Samuel and Levi."

Grace wrinkled her nose at Abel. "What will you do for work?"

"Her daed owns two hardware stores. She's begged me to work for him. He's offered to take me under his wing. I've managed to hide my drinking and money troubles from her. It's time I change before I mess up the one good thing in my life. She attends church services in town. I'll go with her." He whispered in Mark's ear, "The scarf you found is for her. She's a wonderful woman."

Mark stretched out his hand, but Abel bent and gently hugged him. "Mark, I hope you and Grace are happy. Take care."

His bruder wiped his damp eyes.

"Be safe, Abel."

Abel paused. "Grace, take care of him. He's a wise and honest man. He'll be a good husband." He bid the men farewell and crossed the room. Glancing over his shoulder, he grinned at Mark then shut the door behind him.

Mark swallowed around the lump in his throat and wiped tears from his eyes as he watched Abel walk out the door and out of his life. The knowledge his bruder was safe and had changed his life for the better made it easier.

Mr. Blauch pulled the door open. "I'm going to ask the doctor to return with me and take a look at you, Mark. His examining you here is better than taking you to his office. I'm sure it's painful for you to move any more than necessary."

"I'll stay with Bishop Weaver and Mark until you return." Grace had a radiant glow.

Mark's heart soared once again to have her for his future fraa. God had worked a miracle in their lives. In a day, God had saved his life, given him peace about Abel, and blessed him with the best gift of all, Grace.

Bishop Weaver darted his eyes to Abel then Grace. "Abel's chosen his life. We must never speak of him again. Understood?"

Grace and Mark nodded.

Mr. Blauch and a man carrying a medical bag entered. Mark recognized him as Dr. Rogers. He passed the doctor's office each day going to the livery. He approached Mark. "Mr. King, I'm Dr. Rogers. I understand from Mr. Blauch you've been beaten. Tell me where you hurt." He winced. "Your scalp is bleeding." He examined the wound.

Mark pointed to his side. "Please call me Mark. Danki for coming. I can move my arms and legs. I don't suspect anything is broken. I am sore. They punched and kicked me several times. I suspect I have a patch of hair missing."

Mr. Blauch gave his dochder a curt nod. "Grace, you should step outside while Mark is examined. Bishop Weaver, I'll wait and then escort him home. Noah works for him. Either he or I will stay if he'd like us to. I'm sure Grace and her mamm will bring him food."

"I'll go to my shop. I'm sure Anna is wondering what has happened. I left her alone to take care of the store. After I talk to Anna, I'll head home."

Bishop Weaver followed her. "If anyone needs anything, please let me know. I'll be on my way. Take care."

Mark, Dr. Rogers, and Mr. Blauch bid the bishop and Grace farewell.

Pulling up a chair, Grace's daed sat.

Mark moaned as the doctor pressed harder on his side. Glancing at the door of the dry goods shop, Mark sighed. He must talk to Grace about their future soon. A conversation he would enjoy. The sound of Dr. Rogers's voice jerked him out of his thoughts.

Dr. Rogers unclasped his medical bag and pulled out a stethoscope then listened to Mark's heart. Mark's lips parted, and he grimaced in pain as Dr. Rogers instructed him to move his arms and legs. He pressed on different parts of his body and examined him closely.

"Son, you're a lucky man. You don't have any broken bones. Your bruised ribs and body will ache for a week or so but improve with time." He dug in his bag, pulled out several packets of aspirin powder, and pressed them in

Mark's palm. "Take a teaspoon of this with water every four hours. The medication will help lessen the pain."

"Danki, Doctor."

The doctor put his stethoscope back in his bag and pulled out a roll of muslin fabric. "I'll apply liniment to this and wrap it around your middle. It will ease the pain. I'll leave the jar of liniment with you and you can reapply it as needed. It's up to you how long you wear the binding."

Dr. Rogers applied liniment to the muslin and wrapped Mark's midsection. "I hope this helps you." He put the jar on the counter, pulled out a clean rag, wiped his hands, and threw it in his bag and closed it. He unscrewed another lid. "I'm applying salve to your wounded head. The bleeding has ceased. I'll put a bandage on it. You can take it off tomorrow. The affected area is small."

"Danki, Dr. Rogers. How much do I owe you?"

Patting Mark's shoulder, Dr. Rogers grinned. "Mr. Blauch asked me about my fee and paid it before we came here. Thank him." He shook Mark's hand. "If you need anything, please don't hesitate to ask. Take care."

"I appreciate your kindness." Mark waited until the doctor left and then said to Mr. Blauch, "I must pay you back for my medical care."

Mr. Blauch shoved his hands in his pockets and dipped his chin. "No, please let me do this for you. I'm sorry this happened. I shouldn't have acted in haste in my decision to judge you. I admit my wrong. I hope you'll forgive me. I've never witnessed Grace suffer like she has since I withdrew my blessing for the two of you to marry. I'm sure this wasn't easy on you, either."

Mark trembled through the pain in his legs. This man had spoken the words he'd wanted to hear for so long. The woman he loved and adored would stand with him in front of their friends and family to exchange vows in a marriage ceremony. He would be Grace's husband soon. God had answered his prayers. "I forgive you. I'm so relieved and thankful you've changed your mind. Grace means the world to me. I was miserable without her. You have made me a very happy man. We don't have to talk about the past. I'm interested in discussing the future."

Grinning and heaving a big sigh, Mr. Blauch crossed his arms. "Son, it's time I take you home. I'll get your wagon from the livery and tie it to the back of my wagon. Your animal will be fine following along behind."

"I appreciate your help."

Mark waited until the door closed before letting the tears fall down his cheeks. He swiped his face with his sleeve and closed his eyes. "Danki, Heavenly Father, for all You've done today. Amen."

Mr. Blauch stepped inside and stretched out his arm. "Ready to go, son?"

Mark gripped the man's arm and took slow steps to the door. As he climbed into the wagon, stabbing pains shot through him. Wincing, he bit his tongue to stifle the moans wanting to escape. Settled on the bench, he pictured his bed, anxious to slide into it. A few days ago, he wouldn't have imagined Grace's daed would be taking such good care of him.

Mr. Blauch grabbed onto the bench and hoisted himself into the wagon. He guided the horse to Mark's. "Do you need me to help Noah while you recover?"

"Danki, but no, Noah has everything under control." The wagon wheels hitting ruts in the dirt road sent more pain radiating throughout Mark's battered limbs. He found the trip home pleasant most days, but today each turn of the wagon wheel set his teeth on edge in agony.

"If you change your mind, I'm available." Mr. Blauch tucked his chin to his chest. "I'm looking forward to having you in our family and learning more about you. It will be good to have a son."

"I miss my daed. I'll appreciate having you in my life."

Mr. Blauch's words lessened the pain a little. Mark would not only gain a fraa but a mamm and daed. Parents he respected. Images of him and Grace sharing meals and family holidays with Mr. and Mrs. Blauch filled his mind. It was a comfort to have two people in addition to Grace to rely on in adversity as well as good times. It felt good to have them back in his life, even if it had been only for one day.

Mr. Blauch's openness meant a lot. Men didn't usually speak from the heart, but Grace's daed had done his best to express his gratitude and right his wrongs. This man had accepted him as a son, not just as Grace's husband. A position he had hoped to hold in the Blauch family. Jah, God had done more for him than he asked or expected.

"I suspect Mrs. Blauch will tell me how happy she is you and I have reconciled. She supports me in my decisions, no matter what, but she did plead your case first."

Mark was touched she'd spoken on his behalf to her husband. He looked forward to talking to her soon. "She's a woman who shines with God's love. I'm pleased to soon have her for my mamm."

Mr. Blauch rested a hand on Mark's shoulder. "I'm glad you left off the in-law part. If you hadn't, I would've asked you to."

Grace's daed had gone a step beyond his wildest expectations, offering such a caring gesture. It touched him. Mark swallowed at a poignant memory. "She reminds me of my mamm, and you remind me of my daed."

Pulling in front of Mark's haus, Grace's daed secured

the horses, jumped down, and helped ease Mark off the bench.

Sweat beaded on Mark's forehead, as he leaned heavy into his future daed's arms. Taking slow steps, he thought he'd never get to his bedroom.

Dusty struggled to his feet and barked a greeting. His tongue hung out of his mouth and his tail wagged.

Mark stroked Dusty's silky coat. "Hi, boy. How's my faithful companion?"

Lowering himself to the edge of the bed, Mark yawned. "Danki for your help. I'll be fine."

Dusty whined and licked his hand. He settled close to his master's feet.

Mr. Blauch bent and gently carried the dog onto the bed. He rubbed the dog's ear. "There you go."

Dusty lay close to his master.

Mark stroked his new friend's fur. "I'm a bit ragged, boy, but we'll get well together."

Noah clamored into the room and rushed to Mark's side. "Mr. Blauch, Mark, what happened?"

"Thugs roughed me up, but the sheriff and my bruder arrived in time to rescue me danki to Grace." Mark paused and drew in a shallow breath. "The sheriff arrested the criminals, and we now have no more trouble. I asked my bruder to stay with me, but he insists on returning to Louisville, Kentucky, and has left for good. He was the one staying in the barn." Talking hurt but he wanted Noah to learn the full story from him. "After today, we mustn't mention my bruder again."

"I understand." Noah winced. "Are you badly hurt?"

"The pain doesn't hurt near as bad since I discovered my bruder spoke to Mr. Blauch and the bishop before he came to the store, and Mr. Blauch gave his blessing once again for Grace and me to marry."

"I'm thrilled for you." He faced Mr. Blauch. "You won't be sorry. Mark's an honorable and respectable man. You'll be blessed to have him for a son-in-law."

"I agree, Noah. Before I leave, is there anything either of you need?"

"If you don't mind, I could use a glass of water. I'd like to take the medicine the doctor gave me before going to sleep."

"I'll fetch your water." Noah glanced over his shoulder at Mr. Blauch. "I'll stay here tonight in the other bedroom in case Mark needs anything. He might be sore tomorrow. I'll make eggs and toast for breakfast."

"Excellent idea, Noah." Mr. Blauch patted Noah's back and nodded to Mark. "You get some rest, son." He crossed the room. "Take care, Noah." He moved as if to leave then stopped. "Mark, I'll take care of your horse and wagon before I go."

"Danki." He watched Mr. Blauch leave.

Mark shifted to get comfortable and moaned. "Noah, I appreciate you staying here tonight."

"Do you want anything to eat?"

"No, I'm too tired to lift a fork to my mouth."

"It will take me a minute to fetch your water, and then I'll leave you to rest." Noah stepped out of the room.

Staring at the ceiling, an idea popped into Mark's head.

Chapter Fourteen

Grace found Mamm in front of the fire stitching Daed's pants. She rushed to her. "Mamm! You're never going to believe what happened today! I stood in our store and then jumped when loud thudding and scraping noises came from Mark's shop. The commotion sounded violent and scared me."

Dropping the pants in her lap, Mamm put a hand to her throat. "What did you do?"

"Afraid to open the connecting door to our shops, I asked Anna to take care of our customers while I went to peek in the window of Mark's shop. I then rushed to tell the sheriff men were attacking Mark. On my way, I ran into Daed, Bishop Weaver, and an Englischer. The Englischer was Abel, Mark's bruder. They accompanied me to the sheriff's office."

Mamm's mouth hung open. "Jah, he came here to meet with your daed. We can talk about their conversation in a minute. What happened to Mark? Is he all right?"

"The sheriff and Mark's bruder burst into Mark's store to apprehend the criminals. The sheriff had asked Abel to kumme with him since his deputy wasn't there at the time. When he said yes, the sheriff tossed him a gun. In minutes, they had rescued Mark. After taking the criminals out of the store, the sheriff let the bishop, Daed, and me in. My heart broke at the sight of blood running out of Mark's swollen mouth and the way he doubled over in pain, holding his side. He'd been beaten."

"He should be examined by a doctor."

"Daed fetched the doctor, and he came to Mark's shop. Thankfully, he doesn't have any broken bones. The doctor gave him medication to make him more comfortable."

"Where's Mark now?"

"Daed delivered him home. Noah should still be there working. They will take good care of him."

Mamm cocked her head. "Don't you have other news?"

Grace bounced on her toes. "I've saved the best news for last. Daed has given Mark and me permission to marry! Oh, Mamm, isn't it wonderful! God intervened and answered my prayer. The bishop said we can have November fifteenth for our wedding date."

Mamm grinned. "We will have to get busy! This will be perfect timing." She hugged Grace. "Mark's bruder and the bishop came to our haus to speak to your daed. After listening to Mark's bruder, your daed couldn't get out of here fast enough to apologize to Mark. It pained him you were sad and upset to not marry Mark. He looked like the weight of the world had been lifted from his shoulders when he left here to speak to Mark and then you. He couldn't wait to ask the two of you to forgive him and offer his blessing for the two of you to wed."

Grace folded her hands against her chest. "I'm so happy Daed changed his mind. Now we can put the sad event behind us. I'm ready to plan my future with Mark."

"I'm thrilled for you both. God is so gracious. We can get our fabric back out and stitch you a new dress. Mark will need a new shirt and pants." She pressed a hand to her chest. "We are going to have so much fun." Mamm caressed Grace's cheek. "My dochder is getting married. I'll be sad when you leave this haus but happy you've found your true love."

"I won't be far. We'll be together often." While leaving home would be sad in some ways, Grace was thrilled to wed Mark, share his haus, and make a new life with him. The time had kumme for her to leave and start her own family. Her parents would be near, and she'd cook meals for them and give Mamm a rest from always preparing food for the family. She would soon clean, cook, and wash clothes in her own home and have private and intimate conversations with Mark. She would love being his fraa.

Mamm pressed a hand to her chest. "It would've been nice if Mark's bruder had asked God and the church for forgiveness for his transgressions and returned to the Amish life."

"It would have meant a great deal to Mark to have his bruder as a part of his life, but the man has refused to stay. His bruder claims he won't get into any more trouble. He has met a woman in Kentucky he plans to marry, and he has an opportunity to work for her daed. At least Mark can rest easier knowing his bruder is safe."

Mamm frowned. "There's nothing Mark can do but pray for him." She put her needle and thread in the sewing box. "I'm sure this wedding will cheer him. In church, he can't take his eyes off of you. I worried your daed would catch him staring. I didn't want him more irritated."

Grace giggled. Mamm hadn't said a word. Her mamm had watched her and Mark exchange looks and hadn't scolded her. Being the prayer warrior her mamm had always been, Grace was sure she'd prayed for God to intervene on their behalf too. "I love him so much. In spite of the dangerous men hurting Mark, it's been a wonderful day. One I'll not forget."

"Did you speak with Anna after all the commotion ended?"

"Yes. I went back to the shop and explained everything. She said the gunshots and banging around scared her but she stayed put to wait on customers. She said two couples stayed a long time in the store after I left. The men didn't want to leave her alone. It was kind of them. She is mature beyond her years and has been a big help to me. She's become a fast friend. Sweet and considerate, she's thrilled for me and wants to help with the wedding plans."

Knock. Knock. Startled, they paused. Grace shivered at the insistent loud rapping. Heart pounding, she rushed with Mamm to the door.

Levi stood as pale as chalk, with a white knuckle grip on his hat. "Kumme quick. Something's wrong with Sarah."

Grace grabbed her medical bag. A sick sense of worry caught in her throat. "What is it?"

Levi kept pace alongside her, walking to his buggy. "I'll tell you on the way."

Mamm stood at the door. "Tell Sarah I'm praying for her." She stepped outside. "I'll have your daed fetch you in an hour or two."

Glancing over her shoulder, Grace said, "Danki, Mamm." She scrambled into the waiting buggy. She stowed her bag between herself and Levi. "Tell me what happened."

"She had gone to the bedroom to fold clothes and cried out for me. I left the kitchen and ran to her. I found her doubled over, clutching her stomach. The blood on the floor shocked me, and I almost dropped the glass in my hand. Grace, I'm worried."

Grace froze but willed herself to stay calm. Levi was terrified. It wouldn't benefit anyone if she fell apart. Riveting fear shot from her head to her toes. "I am too, but we have to stay calm for Sarah." She stared at her lap and fidgeted with the corner of her apron. "How much blood was on her and the floor?" Grace hoped he'd say droplets and not a puddle. She closed her eyes for a moment in anticipation of his answer.

Levi blanched. Grace understood his hesitation. This personal conversation would be difficult to talk about with another woman. Her being Sarah's best friend didn't change this. "Not a lot."

She breathed easier and relaxed a little. There wasn't a puddle of blood on the floor. *This is encouraging news.* "What did you do next?"

"I carried her to our bed."

Grace's heart ached for him.

He urged the horses in a faster trot. "Could she lose the boppli? How serious is this?"

Grace carefully thought about what to say. She had no idea what she would discover when they arrived. "I'm not sure until I examine her." Her friend's haus came into view. "Why don't you go into town and fetch the doctor. It may be nothing, but I'd like to have his opinion."

Levi nodded. He halted the horses.

She jumped to the ground, ran, and opened the door. She drew in a deep breath and uttered a quick prayer then headed for the bedroom. "Sarah, it's me, Grace."

Sarah stretched out her arms. Beads of sweat covered her forehead and upper lip. Her cheeks glowed deep pink.

"I'm so glad you're here. I'm scared something is wrong. I doubled over in excruciating pain and then blood trickled down my legs and onto the floor."

Grace poured water from the white pitcher on the corner table into the matching bowl and dampened a cloth she retrieved from the cabinet below. Dabbing Sarah's face, she forced a grin and spoke in a calm tone. "Relax and take a deep breath. I want you to stay as calm as possible for me. It's important for your boppli. Levi is fetching the doctor."

Sarah reached for Grace's arm and held it in a tight grip. "Can't you examine me and tell me something . . . anything?"

Gently dropping the cloth in the bowl, Grace covered her friend's hand. "Yes, I will, but it won't hurt to have Dr. Rogers's advice." She untied her bag and pulled out what she needed. She swallowed hard then peeled back the covers. A rush of relief swept through her. A few spots of blood wet the sheets, not the puddle she'd feared might have formed since Levi had kumme to fetch her.

Grace inserted the tips of the stethoscope in her ears and listened to Sarah's heart. Her friend's heart rate was normal. Tenderly, she pressed Sarah's stomach. It would be too early to hear the infant's heartbeat. "You and the boppli seem all right. I would be more concerned if there had been more blood. Droplets like you've had are not uncommon, although I tell expectant mamms to take it easy when this happens and rest. Propping your feet up helps." She grabbed a chair pillow and put it under Sarah's feet and then pulled the sheet over her friend.

Sarah gave a heavy sigh as she rose to a sitting position. "Danki, Grace. Before you arrived, I was sick with worry."

Wincing, Grace patted her friend's arm. "At this point, I believe your boppli is probably fine."

Levi and Dr. Rogers strode into the room.

Hoping the doctor agreed with her assessment, she stepped back and watched him. "Dr. Rogers, I checked her and everything seems normal, but I wanted your opinion."

"It's a pleasure to see you again, Grace. I don't mind coming with Levi to check Sarah at all."

Levi kissed Sarah's forehead. "Are you all right?"

"I haven't had any pain since you left. Grace checked me, and the bleeding has stopped. I'm much better."

Levi removed his hat and twisted the brim. "Grace, Dr. Rogers, danki for kumming. I'll be in the kitchen if you need anything."

The doctor opened his medical bag. "Sarah, I asked you to take it easy. Have you been overexerting yourself?"

"No, I haven't done any heavy lifting."

"All right, I understand. This is normal for some women expecting a baby. It may be nothing."

He examined Sarah. "You assessed the situation well, Grace." He turned to Sarah. "I believe your boppli is fine. Stay in bed as much as possible for the next two weeks. If you don't have any more pain or bleeding, then you can do a little more on your feet with caution."

Sarah and Grace thanked and bid him farewell.

Levi came in. "Dr. Rogers told me you have to take it easy. He said you and our boppli are all right."

Sarah dropped her head back on the pillow. "Yes, he and Grace have relieved my mind."

Levi sat on the edge of the bed. "I'll ask your mamm to kumme and stay with us."

"Excellent idea about fetching Mamm. I'm sure you'll be glad. You love her cooking."

Grace stood at the foot of the bed. "Everybody loves your mamm's cooking. She and my mamm have a knack for making the best dish, no matter what it is."

Sarah patted the edge of the bed. "Do you have a few minutes to stay and chat? I've missed you."

Levi stood. "I'll leave you alone to visit."

"No, Levi, stay." She shot her arms up. "Mark and I are getting married!"

Sarah pressed a hand to her heart. "I'm so thrilled for you, Grace!"

Levi sighed. "I'm delighted you two can finally be together. Sarah and I have been praying for you both. What changed your daed's mind about Mark?"

Grace told the story to Sarah and Levi.

Levi exclaimed, "Is Mark hurt?"

"They roughed him up, but they didn't break any bones. He's bruised and sore. The sheriff arrested the men and they're in jail. It tore my heart in two to find Mark bleeding and in such pain."

"I'm relieved Mark and your daed have mended their relationship." Sarah hugged herself. "I'm so joyful I'll be attending your wedding!"

Levi stood. "Give Mark our best wishes. I'll be busy here since Sarah must rest, but tell him to visit when he is better."

"I'm sure he'll look forward to seeing you."

Sarah leaned forward. "When is the date?"

"The bishop let us keep November fifteenth. We'll have to set up our premarital instruction meetings before then."

"I'm sure the bishop can work it out."

"While Grace is here with you, I'll head to your mamm's haus. I'll tell her what's happened and ask her to kumme back with me." Levi walked over to Grace. "Is this all right with you?"

"Yes, go ahead. If Daed arrives to pick me up, I'm sure he won't mind waiting."

Sarah blew him a kiss. "Danki, sweetheart. It will give Grace and me more time to discuss her wedding."

Levi blushed and waved good-bye.

Sarah gripped Grace's hand after Levi left. "Do you have any questions about your wedding night?"

What would her first intimate experience with Mark be like? Sarah had told her what to expect in general, but she was still apprehensive about it. She wasn't sure what to do to please him. "No, I have an idea of what will happen based on what you told me after you and Levi got married. I'm nervous, but I trust Mark." She shrugged her shoulders. "I'll let him take the lead and go from there." She squinted. "Is there anything else you need to tell me?"

Gently squeezing her hand, Sarah leaned closer to her. "You have nothing to worry about. It will be a special act of love you'll enjoy. Do what kummes natural."

"It's sweet of you to want to put me at ease. I treasure our friendship. Danki for your encouragement."

"What may I do for the wedding?"

"You must take care of your boppli, which means you obey Dr. Rogers's orders."

Sarah tapped her chin. "I'll kumme up with something to do for you while I'm twiddling my thumbs in this bed."

Her friend had trouble keeping still. Grace worried her mood would plummet. "You can work on the project you had in mind, as long as you can do it in bed."

"I promise to behave." She gently squeezed Grace's fingers. "I'm so happy for you. This is really going to happen. God worked a miracle in your life. I fretted your daed would stand firm in his decision."

"I had faith God would intercede. Everything worked out. Mark didn't get the outcome he would've liked with his bruder, but at least he can rest knowing he's safe and the criminals are behind bars. We can finally get married and plan our future. You and Levi are having a boppli. There is so much for all of us to look forward to in the coming months."

"Anna must've been frightened hearing the scuffle next door, when you left to fetch the sheriff."

"She is brave to have stayed and managed the shop during this ordeal. I'm thankful the connecting door to our shops remained locked."

"You both were brave."

"It all happened so fast. I told her what happened afterward. She's kind, smart, and good company. I like her. She genuinely likes working at the store. I believe God sent her to us. She wants to help with the wedding."

"I'd like to sit and chat with her." Sarah tapped her chin. "I have an idea in mind for a gift for you. Would you ask Anna to bring me white and light blue cotton fabric from the store? It would give us a chance to visit."

"I'm sure she'd love to. How many yards of material would you need?"

"Eight total would be good." Sarah clapped her hands. "We have so much planning to do. Please let me help you stitch your dress or Mark's shirt and pants."

"No. I want you to rest."

"Staying off my feet is hard. I hope I'm able to kumme to the wedding."

"You and your boppli's health are most important to me. If you have to miss the wedding, it will be sad but worth it for both of us. This boppli will be a joy to all of us."

"Can you believe it? I'll be a mamm soon."

Sarah rubbed her stomach. "My tummy is sticking out a little. I love it! Thanks to you and Dr. Rogers, I can relax and not worry. Levi and I are discussing names. Do you have any suggestions?"

Grace thought for a moment. "Hmmm . . . I like Elizabeth, Katie, and Lily for a maedel. Nathaniel has always been a favorite of mine, but I also like Jeremiah and Isaiah for boy names."

"I like Lily for a maedel and Jeremiah for a boy. I'll suggest those to Levi. I'm no good at kumming up with names. Danki."

Horses neighed.

Grace peeked out the window. "Levi and your mamm are pulling up out front, and Daed is coming down the lane. I must be going." She rolled her shoulders. "Since your mamm lives two streets away from you, it will be easy for her to go back and forth and check on your daed. You behave and let your mamm wait on you. I'll be over soon." She hugged her friend then strode to the door and opened it. "Hello, Miriam!"

Mrs. Miriam Mast hugged Grace then stepped back and gazed at her with worried eyes. "Grace, is Sarah all right? Should I be worried?"

Grace loved Miriam. The kind and compassionate woman was like a second mamm to her. She didn't want her upset. "No, Sarah's fine. It's not unusual to experience a little bleeding in the first three months of pregnancy. She should take it easy as a precaution, though."

Pressing a hand to her chest, Miriam's breath whooshed out. "I'm so thrilled about this boppli. I've already stitched white sheets and knitted three sets of booties."

"This should be an exciting year for both Sarah and me." Grace bounced on her toes. "I'm getting married to Mark King!"

Miriam's cheeks dimpled. "I'm so thrilled for you, Grace. I want to help. Tell me what to do."

Sharing her announcement made the anticipation of marrying Mark even more thrilling. "I'm sure Mamm will speak to you about the after-wedding meal. I wouldn't mind having some of your special chicken and dumplings."

"Say no more. You'll have them, and I'll make your favorite apple tarts."

"Danki." Grace kissed Miriam's cheek. "Please keep the news to yourself until the bishop announces it." She grinned. "I'll say good-bye to Levi and be on my way."

Miriam walked into the haus.

Grace approached Levi standing and talking to her daed, sitting in the wagon. "Sarah's resting and she'll be in capable hands with you and her mamm." She put a hand on her daed's arm. "We should head home. Mamm must be wondering what happened to Sarah."

Her daed held the reins. "Jah, you're right. Take good care of Sarah, Levi. If you need anything, ask."

"Danki." Levi waited and watched them prepare to leave.

Grace climbed in the wagon. "How's Mark?"

"He'll be all right. Noah's staying with him tonight."

The thought of the beating he'd taken at the hands of those outlaws quelled her.

She put a hand on his arm. "Danki for your blessing to allow Mark and me to marry."

"Grace, please forgive me. I'm sorry for putting you and Mark through a sad and difficult time. I want nothing more than for you and Mark to enjoy a happy life together."

"I forgive you, Daed." She hugged his arm. "I'm over the moon joyful today. Part of my joy is greater because of your acceptance of Mark into our family."

"Don't worry. We can put this ordeal behind us. I

couldn't ask for a better son than Mark. He remained strong through a tough situation. He's proven he's a good man."

"From our first meeting, he's been helpful to Sarah and me, and then to our community at large."

"I love you, Grace. It's important to me you're happy. I'm glad everything is working out in your favor. You have a bright future ahead."

Minutes later, Daed pulled back on the reins and halted the horse. She loved her daed. They had always worked out their misunderstandings. They had mended this difficult fence in their relationship. She could relax and enjoy their conversations again.

"You go in and tell your mamm about Sarah. I'll be in soon. I'll take care of the horse and wagon."

Grace jumped out. "I'd be glad to help you."

"No. Your mamm will be sick with worry about Sarah. Put her mind at ease."

She skipped up the porch steps and pushed through the door. Entering the kitchen, she drew in a deep breath of fresh baked bread and stew. "Mamm, Sarah is all right. Dr. Rogers came to examine her. She is to stay in bed as much as possible for the next two weeks."

"I couldn't stop fretting about her and watching the clock, hoping you'd return soon with good news. Will Levi fetch her mamm to help out?"

"He brought Miriam to their haus before I left. I got to tell her our wedding date. She's thrilled."

She dipped stew into serving bowls. "Where's your daed?"

"He's stowing the wagon."

Mamm kissed her cheek. "I'm pleased the two of you will be on happier terms. I'm certain he and Mark will form a close relationship as time goes on. He'll be thrilled when you have kinner. So will I."

"It will be a joy to watch him entertain my kinner. He's a good daed, and I suspect he'll be an even better grossdaadi. No doubt I'll have a hard time separating you from my kinner."

They chuckled.

Life was about to get even more exciting.

Chapter Fifteen

Mark opened his eyes and eased himself into a sitting position Wednesday morning. Examining the bruises on his arms, he raised his shirt and found more of the same deep purple bruising around the binding on his ribs. The criminals' faces and their fists punching him tormented his mind. He hoped the bad part of that day would soon become a distant memory. Shaking his head, he scooted to the edge of the bed.

Dusty looked up and thumped his tail on the floor.

Easing off the bed, Mark scratched Dusty behind his ears. "Good morning, boy. Are you feeling better?"

Noah peeked in. "Were you able to sleep? I'd like to fix you breakfast. Are you hungry? Do eggs and toast sound good?"

"I'm starving. Will you join me?"

"I'll keep you company for a short time, and then I should do chores." Noah glanced out the window. "Bishop Weaver is coming up the lane. I'll greet him and bring him inside."

"Danki, it will give me time to throw some water on my face." Mark hobbled over to the bowl of water on a small stand, washed, and wiped his face then stepped to the sitting room. "I appreciate your help yesterday, Bishop Weaver."

"I came to check on you. How are you feeling?"

"I'm moving slow, but I'll be fine. Kumme to the kitchen table. Noah offered to fix breakfast. Have you eaten?"

"No breakfast for me, danki. My stomach is full from too much coffee and food this morning at the Berlin Restaurant. I have a busy day ahead. I can't stay long."

"You and Mark take your time and visit, Bishop. I'll prepare food for Mark and me."

"Danki, Noah. Bishop Weaver and I will stay in the sitting room. These chairs are more comfortable." He gestured to the settee. "Please have a seat." Mark waited until Noah left the room, and then he eased his body slowly onto his favorite chair. "I'd like to schedule marital counseling meetings with you for Grace and me."

The bishop's cheeks dimpled. "I suspected you'd be in a hurry to put a plan in motion to wed Grace. It's the other reason I came here today. You and Grace may kumme to my haus for marital instruction on Tuesdays and Thursdays for the next several weeks. Will five thirty fit into your schedules? We'll see how much time we have for each session to determine how many more we need."

"I'll tell Grace. Five thirty will give us both enough time to lock up our shops and walk to your haus. Is there anything I need to prepare?"

"No, I'll go over biblical principles, finances, and other topics for putting you on the right path to a successful marriage." He rose. "I'm glad everything worked out for you and Grace. I look forward to officiating the wedding."

Mark bid the bishop farewell and moved to the kitchen for his breakfast. He stepped outside and breathed the fresh air heading for the workshop. He wouldn't rest until he told Grace their counseling dates were set.

Saturday afternoon, Mark crossed the yard, crunching the brown leaves beneath his boots. He reveled in the slightly cool breeze on his way to find Noah. He found his friend in the garden. "Would you help me with something?"

"Sure, I'd be glad to." Noah followed Mark.

"I've built a cradle for Sarah and Levi. You've probably noticed it in the workshop. I need help lifting it into my wagon."

"I peeked at it the other day and thought you were selling it in the store. They will appreciate the beautiful piece." He studied Mark. "You're moving a little better than you were this morning."

"I swallowed some aspirin powder and drank water, and the medicine has helped ease the aches and pains." He uncovered an oak cradle. "Do you have time to go with me to take this to them? I'd like to deliver the cradle today."

Noah slid the bag off his shoulder and dropped it onto an old weathered trunk. He sniffed in the scent of the fragrant wood. "I never tire of the cedar scent. You outdid yourself on this piece. This cradle is the prettiest one I've laid eyes on. I admire your talent."

"You're kind. If you want to learn to work with wood, I'll be glad to teach you."

"I'll take you up on your offer. In the winter, it would give me something to do."

"If you like constructing the things I sell in my store and do a good job, I'll buy your pieces from you. You can use the wood in my workshop. Construct a stool first and follow the pattern of the one already made in the barn."

"I'm eager to get started. After the harvest and wedding, I'll have time."

Noah and Mark carried the cradle into the wagon, climbed down, and covered it with an old blanket.

Mark groaned, leaned against the wagon, and held his side.

Noah said, "I should've asked a neighbor to help load this. It's too soon after your ordeal for you to lift it."

"I'll be fine, but when we take it out, let's have Levi help you." Mark straightened and wiped his forehead with his sleeve. A wave of nausea passed.

"I'll hitch up the horse, and we'll go there now."

"Before we go to Levi and Sarah's haus, let's go into town. I'd like to speak to Grace about something and show her the cradle."

"She'll love it."

Mark stepped outside, washed his hands at the pump, and then joined Noah in the barn. He wiped his hands on his pant legs to dry them then climbed in the wagon.

Noah led the horse outside, hitched it to his wagon, and drove down the lane.

Mark listened to Noah prattle on about helping harvest the fields, his mamm's selections for canning vegetables, and furniture he was anxious to learn how to construct. He'd liked working alongside Noah in the barn, garden, and fields. Even better, he'd love teaching him how to build things out of wood.

His friend stopped in front of the store. Together, they walked inside the shop.

Grace and Anna stood at the counter sorting through quilts. Grace darted to them. "Mark, you look much better." She waved Noah over. "Kumme here, it's good to see you." She gestured to Anna. "Mark, you met Anna when you brought Dusty in for treatment."

"Jah, it's nice to see you again."

"How are you and Dusty feeling?"

"Dusty and I are on the mend. Danki for your concern."

Grace gestured to Noah. "Anna, Noah Schwartz works for Mark doing farming and chores."

Noah removed his hat and bowed his head a little. "It's a pleasure to meet you."

Anna blushed. "It's nice to meet you."

Mark pulled Grace aside. "The bishop visited me. Our counseling dates are set for Tuesdays and Thursdays at five thirty."

Grace beamed. "I'm so happy! Everything is going smoothly."

"The days and time work out perfectly."

He glimpsed at Noah and Anna, thankful they were chatting and not paying attention to him and Grace. Relieved no customers were coming through the door as well, he grazed her hand.

"I want to hold you in my arms."

Her cheeks pinked. "It won't be long and we'll be together each day."

"You can count on it."

"I wish it was tomorrow."

"I'm ticking the days off until I can carry you over the threshold to *our* haus."

She blanched. "I like hearing you say 'our haus.'"

Grace peered over at Noah and Anna. "They aren't having any trouble finding things to talk about. Look at those cheery faces. Wouldn't it be wonderful if they were interested in each other?"

Mark chuckled. "I remember the first time I met you.

I was smitten at the sight of you. Noah looks enamored with her already."

The attraction the couple portrayed on their shy faces warmed his heart. He hoped Noah would decide to stay in Berlin. Maybe falling in love with an Amish woman would entice him to stay. He was reminded, once again, of the first time he met Grace. The overwhelming connection he had with her, he couldn't quite explain it at the time. The same one he experienced over and over again each time he saw her.

"You made an excellent impression on me during our first meeting, Mr. King." She blushed. "It didn't take me long to fall in love with you."

"You had my heart early on, Grace Blauch. No doubt about it."

Noah's laugh interrupted them.

Mark viewed the couple. They were both beaming and seemed unaware of anyone around them.

Grace smiled. "Anna and I drove to Sarah's. They chatted for a bit, and we delivered fabric Sarah requested. They enjoyed each other's company. Sarah liked her. She and Levi are so excited for us."

A customer entered. "Oh sorry, I'm in the wrong place. I'm looking for the post office." She ducked out before any of them could answer.

"I have a present for Sarah and Levi. I wanted to show it to you first. Noah and I have it in the wagon. We're taking it to them after we leave here."

Grace stepped to the door. "Anna, can you watch the store for a minute?"

She nodded then returned her attention to Noah.

Mark and Grace stepped outside. He slowly climbed in the wagon. He winced and uncovered the cradle.

She stepped to the bench, sat, and turned around to view him and the piece. "Oh, Mark! Be careful."

"It's getting better." He motioned to the gift for Sarah and Levi. "Do you like it?"

She perused the piece. "This is an exquisite cradle! I love it!"

"Someday, I'll make a cradle for our kinner."

"What a wonderful thought." She stroked the side of it.

Mark covered the cradle again. "May I tell Sarah and Levi we've got our counseling dates set?"

"Yes, please tell them. Noah reminds me of you. You both take initiative and help. It's one of the many traits I love about you."

"He's become a good friend to me, as Anna has to you. Wouldn't it be something if they had a budding romance?"

"Yes, I'd like watching their attraction grow."

"We're accumulating a nice group of close friends. I'm really happy I chose to settle down in Berlin."

She gazed at him. "I'm thankful your haus in Berlin will soon be my address."

He gripped the side and stepped out of the wagon and reached for her hand. "Me too."

She jumped down. "We're fortunate Levi and Sarah are our age. It will be convenient to live close to them."

"You can change and decorate the haus anyway you'd like. I'm looking forward to your special touches."

"I'm eager to organize the cupboards and arrange the furniture. Most of all, I'm yearning to get into our own routine. My parents like to drink hot chocolate by the fire at night. Mamm knits and Daed reads his Holy Bible. They discuss their day. They have a rule never to go to bed angry. I'm not sure if they follow it all the time, but it's a good practice."

Mark covered the cradle. "Let's follow this same rule in our marriage."

"I can be stubborn. If we have an argument late in the day, it might be difficult to resolve before we go to bed. We might need to further discuss it the next day."

He shrugged his shoulders. "We'll resolve our issues faster if we're tired and anxious to get some rest." He winked.

She raised her eyebrows. "Good point. When I told her Mamm and Daed's rule, Sarah suggested they practice it. She said the rule has worked quite well for them. Let's try it."

Noah came out of the shop. "I'm sorry to interrupt, but the shop is getting busy with customers. Anna asked me to fetch you."

"It's our busiest time of the day. I should go back inside. Danki, Noah." She bid Mark farewell.

Mark waited until she left and climbed on the bench seat.

Noah untied the horse and got in. He jiggled the reins. "Anna and I couldn't help but notice you and Grace seem excited about something."

"Bishop Weaver gave us our dates for our counseling. I wanted to tell her first before anyone else."

"Congratulations! I'd love to help with anything you need."

"I appreciate it. I can't think of anything at the minute." He paused. "How did you like Anna?"

Noah blushed. "She's very sweet."

He'd been right. Noah had found Anna attractive, and she seemed interested in him. "Grace told me Anna is a hard worker and kind to customers, and they have become good friends."

"I have trouble talking to young women my age, but

I found conversation easy with Anna. I want to spend more time with her and learn more about her. I find her intriguing."

"I understand what you mean, Noah. Grace had the same effect on me when we met."

Noah grinned. "Your countenance changes around Grace. You beam like a full moon lighting the sky on a dark night." He halted the horse in front of the Helmuths' haus. "Whoa, boy."

Levi stepped to the wagon and greeted them. "What a nice surprise." He wiped sweat from his neck with a handkerchief.

"I hope this isn't a bad time to stop by." Mark took his time stepping out of the wagon.

"No, kumme in. You're not as pale, but you're moving a little slow. Are you getting better? Congratulations on your wedding date. I'm sorry for the difficult time you've been through."

"I've put the unpleasantness behind me. I'm impatient and have pushed myself with chores, but I can't sit still. I stayed out of the shop today, but I'll open it tomorrow."

Mark watched as Noah threw back the cover and exposed the cradle. "Do you like it, Levi?"

"This is such a beautiful cradle! Sarah will be so pleased." He climbed in the wagon and stroked the edge then rocked it back and forth. "Mark, you've outdone yourself. It's perfect in every way." Levi and Noah carried it inside.

Mark led the way and held the door open for them. He gestured to Sarah. "I brought you a present."

Sarah was dressed and had her legs outstretched on the settee with a quilt covering her. She put her hands to her open mouth in surprise. "Mark, Noah, kumme in and sit."

She cocked her head to study what they were carrying inside. "A cradle! Oh Mark, danki!"

Noah and Levi set it on the floor in front of her. She leaned over and stroked the wood. "It's exquisite." A tear trickled down her cheek. "This means so much to us, Mark. Danki."

"I wanted you to have something special for your new addition to your family."

"Hopefully, we'll have more kinner and put it to good use. I love it. It's perfect."

Noah nodded. "Mark does very good work, but this is one of my favorite pieces. He's going to teach me how to construct items for his shop after the harvest and his wedding."

Levi slapped Noah's shoulder. "The more knowledge and skill you have to earn money, the better. You're blessed to have such a talented craftsman as Mark for guidance."

"I agree."

Mark's face heated. "I could use a hand in making furniture for the store. Business has increased, and I have a difficult time keeping up with the demand. We'll both benefit from this."

"The cradle is our first piece of boppli furniture. It's hard to believe we'll be placing a newborn in it before long."

"I'm impatient. I can't wait to be a daed and hold the little one in my arms. I've always wanted kinner. I hope I'm as good a daed as mine was to me." He looked lovingly at Sarah. "Sarah will be an excellent mamm. She takes wonderful care of me."

Mark studied the couple. The bishop had been right. Their marriage was a good example for him and Grace to follow. The way they gazed into each other's eyes, lifted each other up with kind words, and teased each other lovingly. He had no doubt his friends would be wonderful parents. "I'm relieved you and Sarah will have kinner before Grace and me, then you can educate us."

Sarah smoothed the quilt on her legs. "I'm a little scared to raise kinner, but it's thrilling, too." She gave Mark a mischievous grin. "The love of your life and Anna were here earlier. They dropped off some fabric for me. Anna's a delightful young woman. I'm happy she's working for us."

"Grace told me. Noah and I went to the shop before we came here to show her the cradle. She loved it. Noah and Anna got better acquainted."

Noah's cheeks pinked. "She's a delightful maedel."

"Delightful?" Sarah cocked her head. "What else do you have to say about her?"

"Uh-oh, I apologize, Noah. I opened up a can of worms. Sarah's going to want details." Mark chuckled.

Noah pursed his lips. "You're not sorry. You and Levi are enjoying watching me squirm."

Levi and Mark laughed.

Levi winked at Sarah. "Go easy on him."

"Seriously, Noah, are you going to pursue your interest in her?"

"I'm sure Anna and I will have more conversations, but that's all I have to say on the matter."

"If you like Anna, you may not want to wait too long to tell her you're interested in her. No doubt many available Amish men will approach her soon."

Mark stifled the chuckle in his throat. Sarah had been direct the first time she'd introduced him to Grace. She loved to play matchmaker, and Noah and Anna would be her next project. She wanted everyone to find happiness like she had with Levi. He found it endearing.

Noah cleared his throat and shifted in his chair. "Enough talk about me. Mark has big news."

Sarah crossed her arms. "Tell us! What is it?"

He liked being the one to deliver this information to Levi and Sarah, thankful Grace gave him the privilege. Saying it out loud heightened his joy even more. "Our marital counseling dates are set! All our plans with the bishop are in place."

"The two of you must be ecstatic!"

"She would've told you, but when she found out I was coming here, she said I should tell you."

Sarah grinned. "I'm glad the counseling didn't interrupt having the wedding date you wanted. I stitched a kapp for Grace a day after the first time you asked her daed for her hand in marriage. I had a feeling things would work out. It's tucked away in my clothespress for safekeeping." She pressed a hand to her heart. "This makes my day! The cradle did too! We're going to have a marked year to remember!"

Chapter Sixteen

Grace woke on November fifteenth. Her wedding day! The weeks had passed by quickly. The harvest meal in October had been delicious and an enjoyable celebration, but today would burn in her memory forever. Her wedding day had finally arrived. She lay in bed and hugged herself. She would become Mrs. King today. The bishop had announced their wedding date in a Sunday service, and weeks later, their meetings with Bishop Weaver were over. They'd met six times to discuss how to manage their finances and how to settle their differences.

The bishop encouraged them to compromise when a disagreement arose. He told them what God's Holy Word has to say about raising kinner. He instructed them to continue honoring God in all they did. She and Mark had gotten even better acquainted with the bishop and appreciated his compassion for them and his guidance.

God had blessed her. Through scriptures, God hadn't promised life would be easy and, at times, it had been difficult, especially concerning her birthmark and almost losing Mark, but she'd always found comfort reading her Bible.

God had given her Mark, more than she'd ever hoped or dreamed for in a husband. She was thankful to not have an arranged marriage but to have the opportunity to fall in love first. Her parents' relationship had grown with Mark, and her friends had accepted him without question. Mark had earned his good reputation in their tight-knit community.

As she glanced around her room, her lip quivered. She'd created too many memories to count in this haus. It wouldn't be the same ever again. She would miss Mamm clanging pans in the kitchen and Daed's boots thudding on the floorboards as he crossed a room. Mamm and Daed couldn't be quiet if they tried. Her family had a routine for daily living. She would miss it and her parents, but life was about to take on a whole new meaning. One she was eager to begin.

Mamm peeked inside her door. She was carrying a wrapped package. "Are you up? This is your big day." She stepped in and sat on the edge of the bed. She stroked her dochder's cheek. A tear trickled onto her apron. "I'm so happy for you, but sad, too. I'll miss you."

Grace covered her hand. "I was reminiscing about my life here with you and Daed. I've been blessed God gave me you and Daed. You've provided me with love, understanding, and advice. The example of your marriage has set the tone for mine. I'm thankful I'm only a short distance away. I'll need recipes and advice, and we will have to keep up on all the gossip!"

She and her mamm laughed.

Grace lifted her mamm's hand and kissed her fingers. "We'll get together often."

"I am relieved you're staying here in Berlin, unlike some couples who move to another community. I'd be heartbroken." She beamed. "I have no doubt God had it in His plan all along for you and Mark to marry. I'm always here if you need me for anything." She passed her the gift.

"Danki, Mamm." Grace untied the twine and pulled back the white cloth. She lifted out a stack of white sheets and pillow cases. Underneath the bundle lay a delicate white gown. She unfolded the garment and held it up. "Oh, Mamm, this is beautiful, and the sheets will kumme in handy. I appreciate all the time it took for you to stitch these presents. I will treasure them."

"I wanted you to have something special for your wedding night. Do you have any questions?"

"No, I trust Mark."

"Trust is all you need."

Mamm took the gifts from Grace. "You must climb out of this bed and get ready for your big day. I have your dress hanging on my door."

"Your chicken and noodles have scented the haus. They will be delicious."

"Our friends are making enough food to feed two villages. I'll leave you to get washed up."

Grace got out of bed, rinsed her face and hands, and fixed her hair in a tight bun. She had packed her clothes, boots, brush, comb, toothbrush, and hairpins and placed them in a bag last night. It had been strange. The idea she wouldn't stay here ever again as a single woman. At the same time, she was ecstatic to marry Mark and share a haus with him. It would be a whole new adventure and lifetime commitment she was certain about taking on.

She put on an older dress and strolled to the kitchen.

Daed sat drinking his coffee and had his Bible open. He patted the seat next to him. "Kumme sit with me." He pulled out a wrapped gift and slid it across the table. "Open it."

"Danki, Daed!" Grace peeled back the dishtowel and found a small, plain cedar box about the size of her hand. A tear escaped her eyes. She opened the lid and peered inside. "Daed! This is so sweet of you. I'll think of you each time I use it."

"Since you were little, I bought you hard candy each time I went to town to run errands. You made the pieces last instead of devouring it all at once. You place this box in your new haus, and each time I go to town, I'll bring you back candy to fill it." He patted her shoulder. "You'll always be my little maedel." His eyes wet with tears, he whispered, "I love you, Grace."

Grace hugged him tight and listened to the beat of his heart. He held her, and then she raised her face to him. "This means so much to me. I like carrying on our tradition."

"You've been a blessing to your mamm and me. You have a soft and forgiving heart. I treasure your forgiveness after the way I treated you and Mark regarding the incident with his bruder. Again, I'm sorry, Grace. It was wrong."

Putting a finger to his lips, she shook her head. "God intervened. It's all right. You did what you thought was best for me. We don't ever need to discuss it again. I love you, Daed."

"I'm having a difficult time letting you go. I'll miss having you here. It will be quite an adjustment for your mamm and me."

"You can visit us anytime. We'll be close."

"This is a bittersweet day for me, but I'm looking forward to having a son. Thankfully, he's exactly the kind of man I'd choose for you. I have no doubt he'll take care of you."

Mamm hurried into the kitchen, leaned over her iron pot on the woodstove, and stirred her simmering chicken and dumplings. "We're getting a late start. We must get ready and be on our way."

Grace poured herself a cup of coffee, drank a couple sips, and then set it on the counter. Too jittery to drink anymore or eat anything, excitement filled her whole being. She'd be Mrs. Mark King in a few hours. "I'll get my dress on. I've already pinned my hair."

Mamm finished loading her baskets with containers of food. "Oh, this is so exciting!"

Grace walked to her Mamm's room, removed her dress from the door, and closed it. Holding the material to her nose, she inhaled the fresh cotton scent. She removed her outer clothing then shrugged into her plain blue wedding dress with a short cape. This dress mimicked her others, but the material was crisp and new. She felt prettier in it. She put on her new kapp Sarah stitched for her and tied it in a tidy bow underneath her chin. Stepping to her room, she searched for her present for Mark, found it, and hugged it to her chest and grabbed her other bag. She carried both outside and climbed in the wagon, throwing her bag in the back and stuffing the wrapped quilt under the bench. "I'm ready."

Daed jiggled the reins and the horse trotted down the lane. "I hope you have a wonderful day, Grace." He cleared his throat and stared straight ahead. His voice quivered. "Don't be a stranger."

"I'll be over often." She gently patted his arm.

Mamm held Grace's hand. The sun shined bright in the

cloudless sky. The slightly cool crisp air, but warmer than normal weather, was comfortable with her shawl. God had provided the perfect weather for her wedding day.

On the way, her parents discussed the abundant harvest this fall and how it would be a good start for her and Mark. They chatted about the bountiful harvest meal they had in October. Mamm circled an arm around Grace's waist. "I'll help you with the winter canning."

"We'll help each other."

Halting the horse, Daed handed the reins to the volunteer stable hand and helped Grace and her mamm out of the wagon. Tables and wooden benches stood in rows. Earlier in the week, Daed had asked his friends to bring their tables and arrange them for the wedding meal. Mamm had coordinated with the women in the community as to what food to bring. Grace admired the many baskets waiting for emptying after the service. It touched her heart her friends had gone to so much trouble to celebrate her special day.

Minutes later, Grace walked alongside her parents and watched her friends file in the barn.

Her heart quickened. Mark approached them in his new crisp white shirt and black pants. He exchanged a warm greeting with her parents and then pulled her gently aside. "Are you ready to become Mrs. King?"

She blushed. "I truly am. I cannot wait!"

Her parents walked in front of them.

She followed them alongside Mark.

Sarah and Levi joined them. Sarah leaned close to Grace's ear. "I'm so glad the doctor said I can get out and about more. I wouldn't want to miss your special day!"

"I'm pleased you're here, but you take it easy. You're precious to me."

"I will. I couldn't be happier for you, Grace."

Levi gently slapped Mark on the back. "Are you nervous?"

"No, I'm ready to move on with our lives."

Grace pressed a hand to her stomach to quell the dancing butterflies. She didn't want to stutter or hesitate while reciting her vows. It was her worst fear. *Talk slow and deliberate. Concentrate.* She walked alongside Mark and the Helmuths and her parents inside the barn. A sea of black filled the benches. Big smiles crossed their faces. She wanted to remember each moment of this day.

Sitting next to Mark, she glimpsed at her parents and the Helmuths. Her favorite people were right next to her and her husband-to-be. The only one missing was Becca. She pressed her heart. Becca would want her to enjoy her day and not be sad about their parting. Pushing the pang of sadness away, she joined her family and friends in song.

The bishop prayed, led them in several more songs, delivered his message, and led them in the Lord's Prayer.

He motioned to Grace and Mark. "Please join me at the front."

Grace's lip quivered.

Mark's eyes sparkled with tears.

The bishop gestured to Mark. "Do you, Mark King, take Grace Blauch to be your lawful fraa?"

Mark spoke in a strong baritone voice. "I do."

The bishop asked Grace if she agreed to take Mark has her lawful husband. "I do."

"Mark, please repeat after me. I, Mark King, take Grace Blauch for my wedded fraa to have and to hold, for better or for worse, for richer, for poorer, in sickness and in health, to love and to cherish; from this day forward until death do us part."

When it was Grace's turn, she swallowed. She wanted to speak loud enough for her friends and family to understand her, to understand that without a doubt she loved this man. She loved him beyond measure.

"I, Grace Blauch, take thee, Mark King, for my wedded husband to have and to hold, for better or for worse, for richer, for poorer, in sickness and in health, to love and to cherish; from this day forward until death do us part."

The significance of their vows meant so much to her. She'd have been disappointed if she fumbled over the words, but she needn't worry anymore. She'd said them perfectly, just the way she wanted Mark to remember for years to kumme. She was certain even their friends in the back could hear the love in her strong voice.

The bishop wished them well, prayed for the food, and dismissed them for the after-wedding meal.

Mark whispered in her ear. "You look so pretty today, Mrs. King. I'm so happy I may burst!"

"Oh, Mark, I like the sound of 'Mrs. Grace King.' You've made me the happiest maedel in the world!"

Levi and Sarah wished them well. She was glad Sarah had shown no further signs of trouble with her pregnancy.

Noah and Anna expressed their best wishes. Friends gathered round and congratulated them. Mamm and Daed hugged them with tears in their eyes.

Mamm whispered in her ear, "You are beautiful, Grace. I'm so thrilled for you."

Mrs. Zook wished Grace and Mark well and asked Mamm where she wanted the meat dishes placed on the table.

Mamm joined the crowd of waiting women and instructed them on the placement of the food.

Women unloaded their baskets and arranged their dishes on the tables, according to her wishes.

Daed, Mark, and Levi helped carry more benches to the tables.

Sarah pulled Grace to a corner away from the crowd and handed her a gift. "Grace, you have a radiant glow about you. I'm so thrilled for you and Mark. He's so in love with you, and you with him. The way you look at each other is endearing." She passed her the gift. "I wanted us to have a private moment before you sat to eat and open your gifts."

"You're so sweet!" Grace peeled back the cotton wrap. "You're so clever. I like the tablecloth you wrapped the present in, and the material is my favorite light blue color. It matches my wedding dress. Danki!" She unfolded a white stitched wedding ring quilt. "Oh, Sarah! This is so pretty. I really like it!"

Patting the pocket, Sarah wiped a tear with her other hand. "Read this."

Removing the note, Grace whispered, *"Dearest Grace, You love and forgive others unconditionally. You shine with God's love in how you treat everyone. You look for the best in people. I've learned to follow your example. I couldn't ask for a better friend. I love you with all my heart and wish for you much happiness in your married life to Mark. I'm always here if you need me. I love you. Sarah."*

Grace blinked back tears. She gently squeezed Sarah's hand. "I love you, too, dear friend. Danki. I'll treasure this letter forever."

Grinning, Sarah clasped her hand. "This will add a whole new aspect to our friendship. Married, we'll have even more in common and to share. Look at all this food! Let's eat. I'm hungry!" She pulled Grace to the table with Mark and Levi.

Under the table, Mark squeezed her hand now and then during the wedding meal.

Mamm asked Daed, Levi, and Noah to pull benches in a circle, and Grace unwrapped their presents.

She unwrapped each gift. The women oohed and ahhed, while the men chatted amongst themselves. She held up each present and thanked the giver. The aprons, sheets, coverlets, wooden bowls, washbasins, utensils, and pots and pans would all be put to good use.

The crowd dwindled. Mamm and her friends cleared the dishes, and her daed, Mark, Levi, and Noah returned the borrowed benches to the barn. The four men laughed and talked. Mark fit right in with her friends and family. This bode well for their future.

Grace helped the men load the wagon with the wedding gifts and her personal belongings and medical bag. She transferred her gift to Mark with extra care, hiding it under several of the others, out of his view. She bubbled with excitement. In a few minutes, they'd be home, and she could give it him.

Sarah sat and watched them. "Levi, don't drop the glass bowl!"

"Don't worry, I've got it."

Grace chuckled. Levi had more patience than any man she had met.

Mamm had finished clearing the tables and joined them. "There isn't room for a thimble in this wagon. It is full to the brim. You'll enjoy using everything you received. I liked them all."

Sarah and Mamm commented about the presents.

Grace eavesdropped on Levi and Mark's conversation over Sarah's shoulder.

Levi handed Mark a package. "Sarah stitched a keepsake wedding ring quilt for you and Grace, but I wanted to give you something from me. You're like a bruder to me, Mark. I'm always available if you need anything."

He accepted the wooden box, lifted the lid, and pulled out a pocketknife. "I feel the same way, Levi. Knowing my past, you'll understand how much this means to me." He flipped the knife from side to side in his palm. "This is really going to kumme in handy. The handle on mine is loose. I'll throw it away and think of you whenever I use this one. Danki."

Levi slapped Mark's back. "Congratulations!"

"I appreciate it."

Grace dabbed her eyes with her fingertips. Levi's thoughtfulness overwhelmed her. She blinked back tears and hoped Mamm and Sarah wouldn't notice.

They were absorbed in their discussion to her relief.

Mark approached and held out his arm to her. "Are you ready to go home, Mrs. King?"

Looping her arm through his, she grinned. "Why yes, I am, Mr. King."

They bid the Helmuths and her parents farewell and walked to their wagon. Mark drove them home.

She snuggled close to his muscular arm and warmth. "We are so blessed, Mr. King!"

"Jah, we have a lifetime of blessings to look forward to."

She squeezed his arm. "I noticed Anna and Noah sat together at the wedding meal and found our spot under the oak tree."

"Good. I hope Noah doesn't break her heart. Even if he stays in Berlin, he has a free spirit. He may wait longer than most men before he's ready to consider marriage. He's content spending time alone."

"I'll pray for them."

Mark stopped the horse in front of the haus. "I'll bring

the gifts in a little later. They will be fine in the wagon for a little while. I have something else in mind." He grasped her hand.

Heart fluttering, she jumped down.

He picked her up in his arms and carried her over the threshold.

She squealed with delight, "I'm Mr. King's fraa!"

He kissed her full on the lips before setting her onto her feet.

Holding her close, he nuzzled her neck then smothered her with soft kisses.

She giggled, and then they flopped on the settee. "I don't want this day to end."

"I agree. I can finally call you my fraa."

"I'll be back in a minute." She scurried to the wagon, found her gift, and came inside. "This is for you."

He unwrapped the present and removed the letter sticking out of the pocket on the folded dark blue patchwork quilt. He whispered, *"Mark, I love you with all my heart. Your acceptance of my birthmark from the first day we met and thereafter meant more to me than I can fully express in words. From that day forward, I've felt beautiful in your eyes. A gift you gave me. I love your kind smile, big brown eyes, protective arms, gentle ways, and trust in God. I love you. Forever yours, Grace."*

He set the note aside and pulled her into his arms, kissing her softly on the mouth. "I'm going to stow my note in my drawer and pull it out and read it now and then. I'll make a point to read it on this same day each year." His lips curved in a mischievous grin. "I will also read it aloud when we have a disagreement!" He kissed her nose. "I'm teasing."

She chuckled. "I know."

Reaching for her hand, he tilted his head toward the

door. "Kumme with me. I have a surprise for you in the barn."

The gleam in his eye told her she'd like whatever he had in mind to show her.

He opened the door and led her inside. Uncovering a cedar hope chest, he stepped back. "This is for you, Mrs. King."

Her hand flew to her open mouth. "Oh, Mark! It's beautiful! I love it!" She beheld it then stroked the top. "Your finish on this piece is as smooth as silk. And oh, how I like the cedar scent. I'll treasure it always."

He winked. "Open the lid."

She opened the rounded top and squealed with delight. "It's the Jacob's ladder quilt you bought from the shop when we first met!"

"Do you remember what you told me when I bought this quilt?"

She blushed. She eyed the note peeking out of the keepsake pocket. "I explained the purpose of the keepsake pocket on the quilt and suggested you write a letter to someone special and give it to them."

"I chose you for my special someone. The note inside the pocket is for you."

"Mark, you have surprised me beyond measure today. Becoming your fraa was more than I ever hoped or dreamed. I love this special hope chest and quilt." She tugged the paper out and unfolded it. *"My dearest Grace, you've made me the happiest man alive marrying me today. I'm looking forward to spending a lifetime with you. I love everything about you. Most of all, your sweet and forgiving heart and perseverance to discover the best in me and in each person you meet. I'm fortunate and blessed to call you my fraa. Love always, Mark."* She blinked back the tears pooling in her eyes. "I'll treasure this note and read it each year on our anniversary when you read mine."

He wiped a tear trickling down her birthmark. "The strong attraction I had for you the first time we met is still unexplainable. You are the prettiest woman I have ever laid eyes on. I missed your laugh and pleasing voice whenever we've been apart." He held her tight. "I will do my best to love, protect, and honor you all the days of my life, my precious Grace."

Grace inhaled Mark's woodsy scent, happy she'd get to smell it each day, and pressed her cheek against his chest. She closed her eyes. *Dearest Heavenly Father, danki for the best day of my life!*

Pennsylvania Dutch/German
Glossary

Ausbund	Amish song hymnal
boppli	baby
bruder	brother
daed	dad
dochder	daughter
Englischer	non-Amish male or female
fraa	wife
grandmudder	grandmother
haus	house
jah	yes
kapp	covering for Amish woman's hair
kinner	children
kumme	come
maedel	girl
mamm	mother, mom
Ordnung	Amish laws
schweschder	sister

Please turn the page
for an exciting sneak peek of
Molly Jebber's next
Keepsake Pocket Quilt Amish romance,

TWO SUITORS FOR ANNA,

coming from Kensington Publishing in February 2017!

1903, Berlin, Ohio

It was Monday morning and Anna flipped the Grace and Sarah Dry Goods Shop sign to open. Glancing out the window, she saw an Englischer buying a newspaper. A boppli was running away from his mamm. The blacksmith had a line of customers outside his door. The streets of Berlin bustled with men and women entering and leaving the shops, restaurants, post office, and livery.

She squinted and held her nose inches from the window. Noah crossed the boardwalk dodging the horse-drawn wagons and buggies, and cars. He was headed in her direction. She loved his sandy blond hair, sky blue eyes, and tall thin frame. Restless and carefree, Noah loved change. During their two year friendship, he'd rearranged his chore schedule often, experimented growing different kinds of herbs, and built all kinds of things out of wood. Interesting and a delight most of the time, she enjoyed these changes but his latest obsession put her nerves on edge.

All he talked about was traveling to different Amish communities over the next several years to experience living in other locations. She'd avoided answering hoping he'd forget the silly notion. He'd hinted at marrying her, but he hadn't proposed. She and her family and friends had assumed they'd wed someday. The last two months, she wasn't sure God wanted them to wed. She and Noah no longer wanted the same path for their lives. She wasn't sure what to say if he did ask her to leave and marry him. He'd been quieter than usual before and after the church service yesterday.

Noah sauntered in and set his sewing box on the counter. "Good morning. It's only the sixth of July, and already, the sun is blazing hot. I like this time of year. All the plants and flowers are in full bloom. They're pretty, just like you." He touched her nose then grinned.

"You're sweet." She studied him. His big blue eyes were hard to resist. "What are you carrying?"

"I finished handcrafting a sewing box out of maple, and I wanted to show it to you before I delivered it to Mark's shop next door."

She peeked inside and gasped. "I like the way you varied the sections in the lift out box. You did a wonderful job. It's beautiful." She grinned. "Mark will be pleased."

"I can't take all the credit. Mark's been a good teacher and friend. Taking care of his livestock and farm is fun rather than work. I wish he had more time to spend with me in the workshop. He's got great ideas for constructing different household products. I've changed some of his designs like adding more sections to this sewing box." He patted the lid. "I'm excited he's offered to sell my products in his store. I'll need the money for *our* future soon." He winked.

She wasn't surprised he wasn't satisfied to construct his creations the way Mark showed him. He liked doing things his way. Anna opened her mouth to respond to his comment about his plans for the money, but shut it. An attractive Amish man strolled in the shop. He looked familiar. He was several inches shorter than Noah. Powerful muscles bulged in his sleeves. She guessed him a couple of years older than Noah. "May I help you?"

He removed his hat and gave her a sheepish grin. "Jah, I'm here to purchase much needed kitchen towels."

"I'm Anna Plank, and this is Noah Schwartz. I'll be glad to show you what we have in stock."

"I'm Daniel Bontrager. I relocated here from Lancaster, Pennsylvania." He shook Noah's hand.

Anna snapped her fingers and smiled. "I recognize you from the church I attended in Lancaster. It's been three years since I've lived there."

Daniel raised his eyebrow. "Jah, now I remember you. Our families were acquainted, but didn't really know each other well. We missed a lot of social gatherings. Our farm and our roof repair business kept Daed and me busy. Mamm managed the haus and altered clothes for a few Englisch families in town for extra money."

"I understand. The Amish community was much larger there. It's easier to get acquainted with other Amish families in Berlin, since it's smaller. You'll like this community."

Noah crossed his arms. "Are you any relation to Jonathan and Adele Bontrager?"

"Jah, he was my bruder."

Anna frowned. "Adele was a sweet woman. I miss her. I was shocked when she and the boppli died in childbirth, and then when Jonathan died from a tragic heart attack a few months later. You have my deepest sympathy."

"Danki for your kind words."

Noah cleared his throat and put a hand on Daniel's shoulder. "I'm sorry this happened to you. What made you choose to leave Lancaster and move here?"

He acknowledged Noah's concern with a nod. "My parents have passed. They were shot in a robbery while shopping in the general store almost two years ago. The robber had killed them along with the owner. The sheriff had been walking to the shop when he heard the gunfire. He'd rushed in and killed the man."

Anna heaved a big breath. "Were you in town when it happened?"

"My brother and I were working at home. The sheriff and the bishop came together and told us the dreadful news on the tenth of November in 1899. Two years later, Jonathan and Adele married and moved to Berlin." He shuffled his feet. "Jonathan wrote how much he loved this town. I'm ready for a fresh start. My Lancaster neighbors don't mean any harm, but they still gossip about the robbery. I had to get away." He gave a resigned shrug. "I sold everything, and am ready to start a new life here."

He must feel so alone. Curious to learn more details about the robbery, she didn't want to upset him and it would be rude. "I understand."

Noah stretched out his hand. "I'm sorry you suffered the loss of your parents in such a horrific way, and then your bruder and his family too."

Daniel cleared his throat. "It was hard at the time to accept, but I'm doing all right and friends have been good to me. Mr. Zook was a close friend of Jonathan's, and he arranged everything for my bruder's funeral and cared for the farm and animals until I arrived. I'm happy with what I've experienced in Berlin thus far."

Noah shook Daniel's hand. "Mr. Zook's a fine man. It's been a pleasure meeting you, Daniel. My mamm and I live on the last farm on South Street. Stop and visit anytime. I'm happy to help with whatever you need. Don't hesitate to ask."

"Danki, Noah." He strolled over to a stack of towels on a shelf.

Anna tilted her head and followed Noah to the door. "Would you like to kumme to supper this evening?" She'd ask him later why he was so quiet yesterday.

"Of course, I'd never turn down your mamm's cooking." He winked. "After supper, I'd like to talk to you about our future." He left through the connecting door to Mark's shop.

She paused for a moment and watched Noah leave. What would he say about their future? She loved him, but she had questions. She sighed and glanced at Daniel. She didn't have time to think about tonight. She should help Daniel. Walking to him, she pointed to the top towel. "We have a wide variety of towels."

Leah rushed in minutes later and threw her bag under the counter. "Good morning."

"Leah, please meet Daniel Bontrager. He's moved into his bruder, Jonathan Bontrager's home. You probably don't remember him, but he attended our church in Lancaster."

Smiling, Leah stood next to Anna. "I'm Anna's schweschder. I apologize. I don't remember you."

He tilted his head. "I'm not offended. There were a lot of members in the church. It's hard to get to know everyone. I'm pleased to make your acquaintance. Your schweschder has been kind and was about to show me towels for my kitchen." He scanned the walls surrounding him. "I like this shop. You have an interesting arrangement of patterned quilts on the walls."

"Anna, you should show him our keepsake pocket quilts."

He walked over to a star patterned dark brown and white quilt. He patted the pocket. "What do you put in here?"

Anna removed the quilt from the hooks, draped it over her arm, and untied the ribbon holding the pocket closed. "You write a letter to the person receiving the quilt and tuck it inside. The quilt and letter become keepsakes."

"I like the idea. I could use a quilt. I'll buy this one."

Leah joined them. "I'll wrap it for you, while Anna shows you our selection of dry goods."

Anna pulled two different sized white cloths off the oak shelf. "Touch the thickness of each one."

He fingered the material. "These will last me a long time. I'll take three of the thicker cloths."

A drop of water dripped onto her sleeve. She blinked a few times and touched the wet spot. Pointing to the ceiling, she sighed. "We have a leak in the roof. Yesterday, I had to put a bucket under it to catch the water. I'm thankful for the hot sun today."

He peered up at the moisture on the ceiling. "I'd be glad to fix it for you. The cost will be minimal."

She smiled wide. "That would be wonderful. I'll ask Grace King, my employer, for permission. She has to approve maintenance costs."

"I'll stop in on Friday to take a look at the damage and give you an estimate. Please assure Mrs. King I'll give her a fair price. If she agrees to me doing the work, I'll schedule a time with you for next week."

Anna nodded, unpinned the price notes, and pulled her cashbox from under the counter.

He pressed the correct change in her hand. "I'll probably be back to buy more dry goods. I haven't finished going through everything yet."

Leah passed her the paper and twine. "Kumme back anytime. These are my favorite towels. They keep their shape and absorb the water much better than the rest of the ones we sell."

He smiled but kept his eyes on Anna.

Her cheeks pinked. She wrapped his purchase and handed him the package. "Have a pleasant day, Mr. Bontrager. Enjoy Berlin."

"I'll talk to you Friday, Miss Plank."

"Call me Anna."

"Only if you call me Daniel."

"Agreed."

Daniel tipped his hat and put his hand on the doorknob. "Danki for your help."

Leah closed the sales journal and stowed it under the counter. She chuckled. "Noah better hurry and ask you to marry him. He's got competition. Daniel Bontrager couldn't pry his striking dark brown eyes away from you."

Anna sucked in her bottom lip. Daniel had matured and was more attractive than she remembered from three years ago. The Amish community in Lancaster met in a large barn, and it was full to the brim with members every other Sunday. No wonder their families hadn't gotten better acquainted. Noah seemed to like Daniel, but then Noah befriended others easily. It was another reason she'd fallen in love with him. She had noticed Daniel staring at her, but she wouldn't admit this to Leah. "You missed Noah earlier."

"Did he meet Daniel?"

"Yes, they got along well." She hung another quilt in place of the one Daniel bought. "Noah's coming to supper tonight. He wants to talk about *our* future."

Leah's eyes rounded, and she put a hand to her mouth. "So Noah's finally going to discuss your future. This could be the night Noah proposes to you! A night you'll never forget."

More from Bestselling Author
JANET DAILEY

Calder Storm	0-8217-7543-X	$7.99US/$10.99CAN
Close to You	1-4201-1714-9	$5.99US/$6.99CAN
Crazy in Love	1-4201-0303-2	$4.99US/$5.99CAN
Dance With Me	1-4201-2213-4	$5.99US/$6.99CAN
Everything	1-4201-2214-2	$5.99US/$6.99CAN
Forever	1-4201-2215-0	$5.99US/$6.99CAN
Green Calder Grass	0-8217-7222-8	$7.99US/$10.99CAN
Heiress	1-4201-0002-5	$6.99US/$7.99CAN
Lone Calder Star	0-8217-7542-1	$7.99US/$10.99CAN
Lover Man	1-4201-0666-X	$4.99US/$5.99CAN
Masquerade	1-4201-0005-X	$6.99US/$8.99CAN
Mistletoe and Molly	1-4201-0041-6	$6.99US/$9.99CAN
Rivals	1-4201-0003-3	$6.99US/$7.99CAN
Santa in a Stetson	1-4201-0664-3	$6.99US/$9.99CAN
Santa in Montana	1-4201-1474-3	$7.99US/$9.99CAN
Searching for Santa	1-4201-0306-7	$6.99US/$9.99CAN
Something More	0-8217-7544-8	$7.99US/$9.99CAN
Stealing Kisses	1-4201-0304-0	$4.99US/$5.99CAN
Tangled Vines	1-4201-0004-1	$6.99US/$8.99CAN
Texas Kiss	1-4201-0665-1	$4.99US/$5.99CAN
That Loving Feeling	1-4201-1713-0	$5.99US/$6.99CAN
To Santa With Love	1-4201-2073-5	$6.99US/$7.99CAN
When You Kiss Me	1-4201-0667-8	$4.99US/$5.99CAN
Yes, I Do	1-4201-0305-9	$4.99US/$5.99CAN

Available Wherever Books Are Sold!

Check out our website at www.kensingtonbooks.com.